PIT

A NOVEL BY

MICHAEL P. NAUGHTON

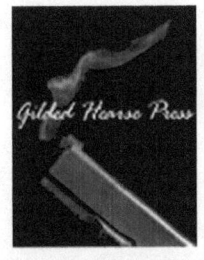

Gilded Hearse Press

Los Angeles

First Printing

"Pit"
Edited by Donna Novak

ISBN-13: 978-0-9778669-3-9
ISBN-10: 0-9778669-3-9

Library of Congress Catalogue in Publication Data
LCCN: 2022951292
9 8 7 6 5 4 3 2

Gilded Hearse Press
Los Angeles, CA

www.GildedHearse.com
www.MichaelPNaughton.com

Printed in the United States

For Zuko and my wife, Donna, and the special everlasting love and bond the 3 of us will forever share.

PIT

PROLOGUE

January 1, 2019, 4:33 a.m.
Downtown Los Angeles, California

THE CAGED BLACK DOG'S NAME WAS KALI. Her canine breed was a Pakistani Bully Kutta (PBK) rooted in the Mastiff family.

Also nicknamed "Beast from the East."

Kali, the mythological Hindu goddess of destruction.

Kali, "She Who is Black"" or "She Who is Death."

The Arab man who trained and sold her for dogfighting would have no interest concerning this historical or mythological fact. He just thought it was cool to satirically misspell Cali, short for California, with a K like the Krenshaw mafia gangsters who spelled their gang with a K instead of a C.

Her powerful breed was popular in Pakistan and India, could take down a bear and was often used for bear-baiting.

Not today.

Today Kali would destroy a human life.

Kali was supposed to fetch ten grand from the buyer only known as 'Killer.' The Arab man was told to collect the cash, no questions asked, in exchange for this purebred

PBK animal or beast. He would never see the cash or the cold light of day.

Kali had traveled a long distance through the night from San Bernardino in the back of an SUV. Cramped and confined in a cage, her massive head staring into the darkness. No sleep from hunger. Deliberately starved in preparation for the kill. Her characteristic short and smooth fur hung on her emaciated body like an ill-fitted overcoat. Her massive head and 140-pound body barely fit in the cage. This made Kali stir-crazy and claustrophobic. She would run for her life when she was unlocked from this hell and torture, like a bull released from the pen in a bullfight. She had not tasted canine flesh since her last fight three days ago and was still in a great deal of pain, unable to lick her wounds or turn her head around where her hindquarters hurt most.

She could hear the monotone drone of the driver's deep voice talking non-stop over the blaring music.

There was nothing but darkness and movement in the vehicle and the rolling of the highway.

The black SUV veered off the I-10 West past downtown heading for Highway 1, also commonly known as Pacific Coast Highway. Kali felt the sensation of the twisting and turning of the vehicle, accelerating and decelerating.

The driver reached across his seat and grabbed a torn scrap of paper with an address scrawled on it. It appeared to be ripped from an invoice book of some sort. He clicked on the overhead dome light to illuminate the location where he knew he was going. He crumpled the scrap of paper in his fist, tossed it on the floorboard, and continued his vertiginous highway journey through the city of Los Angeles. His massive fist tugged and reached into his glove compartment and pulled out a prescription bottle underneath a semiautomatic. His GPS enabled Radar on his dashboard alerted him. He eased up on the accelerator, cut his speed to 55, and noticed an LAPD highway patrol car cruising for tickets.

The black SUV with tinted windows switched lanes, careful to stay behind the traffic cop.

He downed two painkillers with a swig of his Monster Energy drink and watched the highway patrol car with its flashing lights pulling over a Mexican landscaper in his beat-up Toyota in front of him.

He mock saluted the traffic cop as he cruised by.

The traffic cop never even noticed him.

PART ONE:

CANINE

HOMICIDE

1

January 1, 2019, 5:35 a.m.
Zuma Beach, California

SHEILA EVANS NEVER LOOKED BACK on her life when she ran, but today would be different.

Today, all the life she had ever known would flash before her eyes.

She stretched, warming up her cold muscles along the shoreline of Westward Beach located near Zuma Beach in Malibu.

It was New Year's Day. Chilly temperatures and passing holidays chased the tourists away, including the locals.

Vacant for once. Secluded for now.

"Idlers washed off in a winter ecstasy..." as California poet Robinson Jeffers once wrote.

It was 52 degrees. The thick marine layer would eventually burn off, along with Sheila's 160 calories during her routine morning jog. The full blazing sun would not puncture the sky for another hour. She checked the time on her iPod; it was now 5:35 am. She scrolled its tracking wheel and selected some generic, aerobic Techno-mix. The music pulsated in her ears.

Blood vessels dilated. Her muscles filled with oxygen. By 5:50 her warm-up was complete. Her pace picked up now.

Her lips were still stiff and sore from yesterday's Re-stylane injections. The cool air was soothing as it passed between them. *Don't look back. Life is gaining on you. Don't let it,* she told herself. She still turned heads wherever she went and was used to gawkers and paparazzi. She was once a star, after all, and her career was making a comeback. Hollywood loved comebacks.

There was one now. A fan perhaps. Staring down on her from the bluff.

She first sensed the dark figure while she stretched. A large man that seemed harmless, maybe a resident of the Malibu community enjoying the peace of a new year. He stood behind a black SUV, or truck, parked along the ledge wearing aviator shades and a Hoodie. She could not tell from the distance and did not have her contact lenses in, but thought the back hatch appeared to be open. Maybe a surfer getting his board out of his vehicle.

Stay focused, she told herself, shifting her mind to the winding shoreline, sprinting now and picking up the pace again. The waves of the ocean were calming. Her heart rate accelerating and reaching its target rate.

She did not know what made her look back over her shoulder a second time, maybe instinct. Maybe to check on her gawker who had now disappeared from the ledge. Maybe it was that she sensed another pair of eyes on her. That's when she first noticed the massive, black animal as it rounded the corner of the rocks directly beneath the SUV and the dark figure. Her initial thought was that it belonged to the gawker.

Any dog made her smile, and she did smile at first until she realized it was charging behind her.

Unfriendly. Unleashed. Vicious.

Her smile faded to quiver as she attempted to mouth the panicked words, "Hey," to the owner or driver above.

Nothing came out, just a short burst of air like a toy without a squeaker or as if being struck with laryngitis.

The charging dog was too big to be unattended. It was a Rott or Presa or Pit, she could not tell. Adrenaline shot through her body along with a quick jolt of heat. The beast was going to attack her. She was prey. Why couldn't she scream? Her brain was racing along with the beast, gaining in stature as it charged closer like a bull with its colossal skull. Now, no more than 17 yards away.

Don't look back. Run faster.

She caught a final glimpse of the mysterious man who reappeared on the ledge of the highway, his back turned to her and the ocean, as he got something out of his hatch.

There was a lifeguard tower up ahead, but she would never make it. Too far. Instead, Sheila made a split-second decision to make a run for the rocks. She made a sharp left turn away from the water. No other choice. The only choice. The sand felt like wet cement. Her heart was pounding in her eardrums.

The beast was several feet behind her.

Outrunning her.

A bloodcurdling scream finally released itself from Sheila's tight throat as the animal clamped down on her torso. The impact was like a car crash. She could hear and feel her bones snap. The pain was instant and excruciating, shooting through every nerve in her body. Her face slammed into the sand. The jaws of the beast swallowed her petite frame. Sheila could feel the warm rush of her blood with the violent thrashing. She pounded her flailing fists into the sand, then clawing, scratching and reaching behind her, feeling the stickiness of fur and blood.

God, please make it stop!

Somebody, anybody, please help me!

Dizzy and nauseous, she kept fading in and out like a strobe light.

The beast was ripping her apart.

I'm going to die, was all she could think, but she did not stop fighting. She was too young to die.

The beast was dragging her back in the direction of the water.

Thrashing.

Tugging.

She could see her own blood splatter on the beach like paint.

She could feel the wet sand in her fists and underneath her nails, and she tasted sand as she clawed for the rocks, as if dropping from a ledge.

Sheila could see the sea foam and peaceful waves mixed with her blood before she released her grip, quit struggling, and let go of life.

2

AT ELEVEN MINUTES TO SUNRISE actor Mel Gibson's maid found herself surrounded at gunpoint. She was not acting. She was not on a movie set. She was, however, the latest victim of "celebrity swatting," and she was scared out of her mind and confused when she opened the door to a SWAT team.

Celebrity swatting was a high-profile crime prank where the perpetrator would call 911 and claim that the celebrity was in grave danger. Life-threatening danger. Usually involving guns, bombs, and hostages. The suspects are typically hard to trace because they mask their pranks through tech-savvy means and contacts through multiple computer servers. The LAPD stopped publicizing them to combat the nonsense. The famously swatted included: Tom Cruise, Simon Cowell, Justin Bieber, Clint Eastwood, the Kardashians, and various other Hollywood types whom had been on the receiving end of these dangerous pranks.

Mel was filming in Europe when the Police Captain finally reached the movie star on the phone. The Captain apologized profusely about the false alarm and interrupting the superstar while filming. He expected F Bombs to be going off on the other end of the phone. The Captain was anticipating the crazy Martin Riggs rant – the character Mel played in *Lethal Weapon* – and said so to every nearby SWAT team member, police officer, firefighter, and FBI agent on his property standing nearby waiting to witness the altercation. Instead, Mel was polite, gracious and thanked them for looking after his place while he was gone and was thankful that no one was hurt. The Captain felt embarrassed when he hung up and caught sight of his peers standing around, staring at him, smirking. He cleared his throat, yelled at them for standing around, and ordered everyone to pack up and leave the property immediately. A total waste of departmental resources and time. The prankster prick, anonymous now, whoever it was, might be laughing in the safety of his own home, but the Captain made a promise to himself that he would not need Mel Gibson's help when he caught the evil, little bastard who was responsible.

7 A.M. PST - West Los Angeles

Detective Leo "Lee" Van Cleef was immaculately dressed and on his first cup of brew in the comfort of his kitchen in West Los Angeles. The window blinds were slightly parted and emitted enough street light and dawn to illuminate his tall physique and the steam still rising from his coffee cup. Christmas lights were still hanging from the awning above the outside providing some additional light.

The Los Angeles local weather channel with the latest buxom, mini-skirted Meteorologist played on his television in the next room. The sound was off. Van Cleef was more interested in the situation outside. He stood motionless to the side of the window, parting the blinds, spying, peering at a man walking his black Labrador in front of his house.

A flash of the kitchen light startled him, along with his wife and their four-year-old Doberman pincher entering the room.

"Kill the light," Van Cleef said. His voice had a deep, morning raspiness as he looked over his shoulder at his wife, Claudia.

"What?" Claudia said as she groped for the coffee pot.

"The light. Kill it. Turn it off. Turn it off," Van Cleef said. He pointed at the Tiffany light overhead.

Claudia Van Cleef snapped the kitchen light off. She was not sure whether to duck for cover or join her husband at the window. She decided to move away from the window but also figured it was not a life-threatening situation because her husband had his coffee cup in his hand instead of his .38.

"Don't stand in front of the window," He said. "Step aside—"

"I'm not in the window… What the hell is going on? Is it another graffiti tagger?"

"No, nothing like… It's— I'm watching Serpico out there."

"Serpico?"

"The guy I told you about. Scrappy dude out there with his black Lab… Y'know the guy I told you about? The guy I think that's leaving the horse manure on our front lawn every day."

Claudia squinted past the blinds and observed the short, Italian or Iranian bearded man with a fishing hat and poncho resembling Al Pacino's character in *Serpico* from the classic 70s film. It registered with Claudia now, but took a moment. Her husband had ranted about him recently and was his latest obsession. She moved away from the window.

"Well, I think it's the blonde chick with the Taco Bell Chihuahua if you ask me," Claudia said. "Oh, and don't forget we have my work party tonight."

"It's not the blonde chick with the Chihuahua mix and I didn't ask you. Don't start in on her… The crap on our lawn is bigger than her dog. What time is the party and where is it at?"

"9 p.m. at Spago in Beverly Hills. We can't be late. Leonardo might show up."

Van Cleef only heard half of what his wife had said and could care less what celebrity 'might' be there.

"Y'know, the problem I have with assholes like this?" Van Cleef said, keeping his eyes on 'Serpico.' "He starts a bad trend— It takes one irresponsible person like this moron and then everyone stops picking up their dog poop and nobody gives a shit anymore— it's part of the deal… you own a dog, you pick up their shit. It's that simple— I'm willing to bet that this joker doesn't even own a home in this neighborhood. Never seen him before and it just started happening. It's got to be him."

"Honey, you're gonna give yourself a migraine," Claudia said. "Can I turn the light on now?"

"No, leave it off— Everyone else picks up their shit but this guy… thinks he's special or something – And I've seen the girl with the Chihuahua pick up after her dog."

"Well, I haven't, at least not since they started charging for plastic bags at the grocery store. She used to pick up after it, not lately — and I wouldn't go sayin' anything to Scorpio unless—"

"Serpico—"

"Serpico, whatever— you're exaggerating again about the dog feces and you're crabby this morning. Did you have your second cup of coffee yet?"

The last thing Van Cleef wanted to get into was a rift with his wife over a trivial matter. He decided to tune her out and carried on the conversation with himself, repeating, "It's got to be him."

His Doberman nudged her nose under his crotch and started whimpering and fussing, blowing Van Cleef's cover by barking at the Lab and Serpico out on their front lawn.

"Go on Bacall... Scat... Dammit." He walked backward over her Doberman's body like a football player doing reverse tire runs, spilling his coffee on the floor. He said to Claudia, "Honey, please... Can you let her out the back? I gotta get going downtown..."

Van Cleef's cell phone rang. It was his supervisor, Lieutenant Mike Carruthers from the Homicide Special Section of LAPD. Van Cleef ceased his mystery shitter stakeout and moved away from the window and into the front room.

"Van Cleef, we're going to need you down in Malibu," Lieutenant Carruthers said.

"I was just about to head downtown. I've got a deposition this—"

"I got you out of it. We got a possible homicide down in Zuma— mauling. The responding officer is waiting for you to take over."

"Did you just say mauling?" Van Cleef asked.

"That's what it looks like," Lieutenant Carruthers said. "I'll patch you through to the responding officer at the scene in a moment."

"Who is the victim?"

"We think some model or reality TV star. High profile. That's all we know so far."

"Are the Malibu detectives there yet."

"Not yet," Lieutenant Carruthers said. "They're wrapping up a celebrity swat at Mel Gibson's estate— that's off the record, of course."

Van Cleef superficially glanced at the television set in the next room, the sexy Meteorologist sauntering back and forth, emphasizing Live Doppler and colder temperatures for the week. Van Cleef turned the volume up slightly with the remote, noting the current temperature. He turned his attention back outside to his front lawn. Serpico and his black Lab had vanished.

"Traffic on PCH is gonna be a bitch by—" Van Cleef said, as he checked his watch and mumbled to himself, "I suppose I could take Sunset Boulevard over and that'll save me some time."

"I'm patching you through to officer Charlie Watts at the crime scene," Lieutenant Carruthers said before transferring the call.

Before Van Cleef could say, "Sure, go ahead," there was a brief silence and then a different voice on the other end, the voice distraught and shaky with a slightly higher pitch from the rush of adrenaline. It was officer Watts.

"This is Detective Van Cleef," he said. He turned off the television as he listened, slipped on his suit jacket, and grabbed his keys. He could hear the ocean mixed with a cacophony of upset voices in the background.

"What makes you think it's a homicide?" Van Cleef asked.

"Well sir," Officer Watts said. "There is no sign of the dog. The woman was mauled to death... like a Grizzly attack— it's pretty gruesome, blood everywhere on the beach and I was told that you're investigating—"

"Wait a minute, back up," Van Cleef said. "What makes you think it's a dog and not a shark attack?"

"Well, sir," Officer Watts said. "Last time I checked, sharks don't have paws and she doesn't appear to be in swimwear."

Van Cleef hung up with Officer Watts, skipping breakfast. He exited out the side door to his car and opened the gate to his driveway. He noticed a brazen, homeless scavenger picking through his blue recyclable container at the end of his driveway. Los Angeles residents have their three-color trash can system: Blue for recyclables. Green for gardeners, and brown for garbage. The scavenger was a Mexican male with a grimy Dodger's cap twisted on his head. His shopping cart was loaded like a mule, saddle bagged with white and brown Hefty bags bulging with plastic pilfered from Van Cleef's neighborhood that this homeless stranger collected throughout the morning. This indicated that it was indeed a Tuesday morning. Van Cleef could always count on recyclable scavengers in his neighborhood on Tuesdays. He wondered how much money a loaded, stolen shopping cart overflowing with plastic could net a person and was it really worth it? Wouldn't it be more productive to pick through the Classifieds instead of trash and find a real job? The mule-cart of plastic was blocking the end of his driveway. He honked his horn as he backed up, watching in his rearview mirror as the scavenger extracted himself from the blue recyclable bin. He smiled at Van Cleef with his rotting teeth. Van Cleef noticed his discarded Arrowhead bottles in his grimy mitts.

He took one last glance at Serpico and his black Lab a few houses down the street, who was now watching the homeless person digging through Van Cleef's trash. Van Cleef thought about how much he needed a vacation away from L.A. All the other detectives in Homicide Special commuted long distances leaving their gruesome work behind, but Van Cleef was an anomaly. He lived in West Los Angeles because his wife worked at one of the major motion picture studios, and he lost the coin toss for staying local. So, they both got to work with celebrities, but the only difference was his were often dead or suspects.

He hit the gas in his black Dodge Challenger and made his way out to Malibu.

First call-out of the day for the New Year.

3

VAN CLEEF PARKED ALONG Cliffside Drive. It was too late. The Zuma Beach crime scene was already a media circus. The looky-loos, including TMZ, were tipped off that a Malibu actress was eaten alive by a shark or something. A shark attack would be good ratings for them. Van Cleef's partner, Jose Espinoza, from HSS was waiting for him.

Van Cleef put on his Ray-Bans. It was showtime. He ducked under the yellow tape and introduced himself to Officer Watts as the detective he spoke with on the phone. Van Cleef signed the crime scene logbook, entered his badge number, date, and time in at 8:13 am. He noticed three other signatures and dropped his pen. He looked down from the bluff-top and saw a heavy-set man in a tan sheriff's uniform lumbering away from the corpse. He figured that had to be Malibu Chief, Richard Mohan, from the Lost Hills Station. The two talking "suits," the shorter white one with a buzz cut and the other a husky black detective who were conferring with each other and standing over the black tarp, were Detectives Alston and Overstreet whom he had worked with before on the Mitrice Richardson investigation. The Malibu divisional detectives' shoes shined even at a distance and had not been caked with sand yet from walking the beach.

That was a good and bad sign. Bad that they were not wearing protective booties over their shoes and good that they might not have tainted evidence by traipsing through it. Their shoeprints would have to be entered into exclusionary evidence to eliminate their additional foot traffic at the crime scene. Van Cleef would catch them on their way out.

Van Cleef's partner, Espinoza, approached and they took the stairway from the east side down to the shoreline. The corpse of Sheila Evans was waiting for them below.

Van Cleef paused for a moment and took a deep breath when they reached the bottom of the stairs.

He stopped dead in his tracks. He could feel all the eyes at his back.

He acknowledged and nodded to the other detectives as he kneeled, then pulled back the tarp.

"My God," Van Cleef said. He swallowed, taking a deeper breath, examining the badly disfigured body. 'Mauled' was putting it mildly. It looked like she was put through a meat grinder. She was nearly nude with only shreds of bloodied fabric hanging from her body.

He noticed her throat was torn apart from her head, and he also noticed remarkable defense wounds and bite marks on her hands, wrists, and forearms. Her sweatsuit, or what was left of it, was shredded; bloodied and soiled pieces of fabric lay scattered nearby. He noticed a frayed, white earbud cord, probably from an iPod, hanging from her right ear. The iPod was nowhere near the body.

He felt unbalanced as he stood and then proceeded to walk a typical spiral pattern around the body following the paw prints towards the cliff. Overstreet and Alston were on his heels waiting for Van Cleef to speak.

"Who discovered her body?" Van Cleef asked.

"Officer Watts," Overstreet said. "He just started his shift. Highway patrol."

"No sign of an animal anywhere?" Van Cleef asked, surveying the scene.

"Nowhere," Alston said.

"So, we have some wild animal or possible dog on the loose that mauled a jogger like a Grizzly and then just vanishes into thin air?"

Chief Mohan appeared out of nowhere and said, "No dog was capable of doing that." He stood over the body chewing his gum, arms folded. If there was any truth to the idea that people resemble their dogs, Mohan had to own a Mastiff. He was built like one too. Saggy, weather-beaten skin and a drooping face.

"You guess it was a pack of wild coyotes, Chief?" Van Cleef asked in a skeptical tone as he stood up. He was a good foot taller than Mohan.

"Could be," Mohan said. "It's typical for them to come down this far to the shore once they run out of groceries. They have been known to attack people. However, these look more like a mountain lion, or maybe cougar prints. Besides we don't allow dogs on this beach."

Since when do people in L.A. follow rules? Van Cleef thought to himself. He shifted his glance to Overstreet and asked, "Crime lab and medical examiner on their way?"

Overstreet looked at Chief Mohan, taking a cue on whether to respond to Van Cleef or not.

Mohan nodded in approval as if to say, *"Answer the man's question."*

"Stuck in traffic," Overstreet said. "We had some commotion with a celebrity swatter this morning, so they're going to be delayed in traffic and all for obvious reasons."

Overstreet answered in a cool tone of voice. Van Cleef sensed instant attitude from Overstreet, the black detective. He was used to it from divisional detectives that were competitive. He did not care, instead, he crouched down and took a closer look at the paw print impressions and said, "Don't let anyone near these prints. Captain, I need an impression kit ASAP, and watch where you step. I want this area tented too." Van Cleef shouted out to everyone within the crime scene barrier, "Listen up! Watch where you step. I want everyone walking this beach to walk it like you're walking on Kung Fu rice paper, understand?"

"I think Overstreet and Alston can handle this," Chief Mohan said.

"Carruthers doesn't, that's why he called us," Van Cleef said. "It's my crime scene now. Besides your detectives might have already contaminated it." He pointed at Chief Mohan's shoes, minus the protective booties he should have been wearing.

Chief Mohan followed Van Cleef's gaze down to his uncovered shoes and stopped chewing his gum and said, "Oh, I see. I get it. Bring in the HSS hotshots to talk to the media."

"No, that's what I want you to do. The media are the last people I want to talk to, personally. In fact, you wanna help out? Get your guys to get the media out of here."

"Now what exactly do you want us to tell them?" Chief Mohan asked.

"Nothing," Van Cleef said. "Just move them along. Especially TMZ."

Captain Mohan was used to giving orders, not taking them. He glanced at Detective Overstreet with a cynical look in his eyes. Van Cleef maintained eye contact with both, tuning into their hesitation.

"Detective Overstreet," Van Cleef said. "Grab me a pair of gloves, tweezers, and a container in your vehicle." He knew most detectives would have those items. Van Cleef had a toolbox in the trunk of his Dodge Challenger but wanted Overstreet to follow his orders.

Overstreet squinted into the rising sun, hesitated a moment, and then said, "Sure, anything you say, boss."

Van Cleef waited for the pair of disposable tweezers, lost in thought, replaying possible scenarios in his mind.

Overstreet returned fifteen minutes later with a pair of latex gloves and a small vile.

Van Cleef plucked a few short hairs from Sheila Evan's sweatsuit. He lifted his shades and strained his eyesight at the bloody hair strands, twisting the tweezed strands and examining them against the rising sun. They looked like canine fibers to him.

Van Cleef walked away from the body and stood near the outcropping of rocks. He visualized the mauling and recreated the animal charging at the victim in his mind. He crouched down eye-level with the paw prints and noticed transferred bloodstains embedded in the print. He blurted out, "*They were the footprints of a gigantic hound.*"

"Yeah, I can see that, Leo," Espinoza said, in a no-shit sort of way.

"No, not these tracks," Van Cleef said, realizing he had been thinking out loud. "It's a classic line from Sherlock Holmes— We have a positive ID on the victim yet?"

"We're confirming," Espinoza said. "However, we think she was one of America's Top Models."

"Really?" Van Cleef said. "Which season?"

"Don't know, never watched it."

"Didn't figure you did. I guess it doesn't matter much now. Today she's America's top murder."

Van Cleef and Espinoza walked back over to Officer Watts. Espinoza's face looked paler. His eyes were swollen, and he looked sick to his stomach. Van Cleef advised him to get some fresh air elsewhere.

"Any witnesses?" Van Cleef asked, noticing Detective Overstreet walking up.

"Just one," Overstreet said, pointing to a disheveled millennial leaning against his badly dented and beat up 1998 Nissan Altima car with missing hubcaps and a surfboard jutting out of his passenger side window. He was talking on a cell phone and kept pacing, running his fingers through his hair.

"You interview him yet?" Van Cleef asked.

"Yeah, briefly," Overstreet said. "He's a stoned bonehead. Doesn't know anything."

4

THE BONEHEAD'S NAME WAS Tad Keller. He looked like that *Minute to Win It* dude, Guy Fieri. Tad was short for Thaddeus. His tan was deeper than early January in Malibu could explain. There he slouched in his board shorts and Birkenstocks. He wore cheap sunglasses, the kind you buy off a plastic rack in a gas station for ten bucks. The kind with the fluorescent orange temple piece or arm extending over the ear. The kind a construction worker might wear, but Tad didn't look like he lifted anything heavier than a 40 ounce. He kept his shades on when Van Cleef walked up and just stared at the ground. The scent of Patchouli or Sandalwood emanated from his flesh. Van Cleef heard a rumor that pot smokers favored the oil to cover up the smell of marijuana. He pegged Tad as a Malibu pothead, which was of minor concern now.

Van Cleef opened his notebook and introduced himself. He could acclimate to any character when it came to interviewing witnesses and suspects. He used the cool, brotherly street style and leaned against the rear bumper of Tad's beat-out Nissan Altima, his postural echo mirroring Tad's. This would appear casual along with Van Cleef's small talk routine.

"So, you want to give me the lowdown on what happened here, or what you saw?"

"Yeah, like I already told the other detective, dude..." Tad said. "I saw a dark green SUV parked earlier this morning on the side of the road... and that's all I saw."

Tad jerked his thumb over his shoulder at PCH highway and then placed his hands in his pockets.

"But you didn't score a look at the driver?"

"Nah."

"Did you hear anyone screaming? Anyone crying for help?"

"Nah, nothing like that."

"Any animal sounds like a dog or anything unusual like that?"

"Nah. Nothing."

They stood in silence staring across at the distant Catalina Island, which was visible on this clear January morning. Malibu sheriff's helicopters were circling now, occasionally blotting out the sun like passing clouds. Van Cleef could hear the crashing waves below mixed with distant conversations of detectives. It was possible to hear a woman screaming from up here he deduced, unless Sheila Evans did not see the animal coming.

A surprise attack.

It was evident that she was struck from behind, found face down in the sand. The animal instinctively went for her jugular. The sand could have muffled her scream for help, or a crushed larynx prevented her from screaming.

"Do you have an iPod or iPhone?" Van Cleef asked.

"Yeah," Tad said, reaching into his back pocket and showing Van Cleef.

"Were you listening to it at the time that you saw the SUV?"

Tad was unsure. He said, "Um, I don't— I don't, like, remember."

Van Cleef noticed some CDs scattered on his seat. Mostly Gangster Rap. White boy thinking it was hip or something.

"I see Dr. Dre there," Van Cleef said, pointing to one of the scratched-up CDs on the seat. "Is Dre on your iPod too?"

Tad noticed the Chronic CD by Dr. Dre that Van Cleef was referencing. "Oh, ah yeah… stuff like that."

"Cool," Van Cleef said. "Did you make any cell phone calls or were you talking to anyone on the cell around or about the time you saw that SUV?"

Again, Tad's mind was vacant along with his stare.

Van Cleef told him to take his time. Tad thought about it several seconds more and shook his head.

"See any whales?" Van Cleef asked, changing the subject.

"Nah," Tad looked down at his feet. Van Cleef's eyes followed. He noticed Tad was wearing black and yellow Sportia Rock Climbing shoes.

"So, you were going to catch some waves?"

"Yeah, I was gonna do a little surfing."

"They say this is a great place to whale watch. They migrate this time of year."

"That's really, like, not my kinda thing— I mean it's okay if you're a tourist," Tad said, scratching his head and touching the tips of his spiky hair.

Van Cleef smiled and said, "Yeah, I suppose it would be, like, kinda boring. So, you into rock climbing too?"

"What?" Tad asked. His slouching got straighter along with the last question.

"Rock climbing."

Tad noticed Van Cleef looking at his other pair of shoes in the backseat of his car.

"Oh, yeah those— a little. I'm not a professional or anything like that."

"Me neither," Van Cleef lied. "I've done a little myself back in the day." He glanced over his shoulder at the back seat of Tad's Altima and noticed a second, larger pair of rock climbing shoes, Evolv Kaos II brand, the rip-and-stick kind. Van Cleef asked, "Anyone else with you today?"

"Nah, just me."

"So, you were just here to hang out today, is that about right?"

"Yeah, that's about right... just hang out."

"Where do you work, Tad?"

"Oh, ah I work at Paradise Cove, part-time. It's my day off."

"Paradise Cove, the restaurant?" Van Cleef asked, remembering eating there in the past.

"Yeah. The restaurant."

"What kinda work?"

"Server."

"Good tips?"

"Nah, not really... are you kidding? People are tight-wads." Tad frowned when he thought about the paltry sums of money the locals left on the table.

"How are the waves this time of year?"

"Awesome."

Van Cleef looked at the large rock that could have blocked Tad's view of the murder.

"Where was the SUV when you came back?"

"It wasn't there. It was gone."

Van Cleef thought Tad was being truthful. He gave him his card and said, "Thank you, Tad, you've been very helpful."

Van Cleef turned to walk away and then bumped into Detective Overstreet who was carrying a baggy with a black object that resembled a charred cigar.

"Crazy place to go surfing, dude," Overstreet said to Tad.

"Scuze me?" Tad said, looking over the roof of his car. Defensive.

"I said, you'd have to be crazy to surf over there," Overstreet said. "We've had several shark attacks and the riptides are dangerous. Haven't you heard? You read signs? They got 'em posted down there."

Tad had a stupid grin on his face and said, "Sharks don't bother me."

"Yeah, well they will if one of 'em takes a bite outta you," Overstreet said. "You local?"

Tad released a nervous laugh and said, "No, I'm not crazy."

"I didn't say Loco. Clean out your ears, dude."

Van Cleef placed his arm on Detective Overstreet's shoulder and walked him away from Tad. He spoke to him in a hushed tone. "Easy Overstreet—"

"Listen, Van Cleef," Overstreet said. "I don't think your surfer dude knows shit. These kinda guys are a dime-a-dozen out here. I wouldn't waste my time with him if it were me."

Van Cleef took a deep breath of salt air and told himself to relax. Keep a cool head. Be kind to his fellow detective. He asked Overstreet what was in the baggy.

Overstreet raised the plastic baggy to Van Cleef's eye-level with his latex gloves and said, "I found this over by the stairs. Looks like dog feces."

Van Cleef grinned and said, "I don't think you know shit either."

"What?" Overstreet said.

"That isn't dog shit."

Overstreet lifted the baggy to his eye-level and asked, "Well then, what the hell is it?"

"Scat."

"Scat?"

"Yeah. Scat is coyote shit. It looks different, sorta like a burnt stogie."

Van Cleef changed the subject taking note that Overstreet was embarrassed standing with his evidence bag of Coyote scat. Overstreet was confused and wondered if a coyote attacked Sheila Evans.

"While we're on the subject of scat, why don't you see if you can get TMZ to scat… send them on their way."

"I've dealt with them before… They're cool. I was talking with TMZ about the celebrity swat and then we got to talking about Charlie Sheen. Charlie's a resident here. We've been up to his place a couple of times— the cameraman thought he recognized me… says I reminded him of Denzel Washington," Overstreet said, proud of himself with his white teeth gleaming in the sun.

"Do me a favor," Van Cleef said.

"Hey, it's your show," Overstreet said.

"Tell that cameraman and TMZ to go track down another celebrity and move out. Otherwise, don't speak to them. When you're done, start door-knocking, see if anyone is missing their pet Cujo."

Overstreet was unsure of Van Cleef. He walked away in the direction of TMZ. The long haired cameraman with the goatee was waiting for his return with his Panasonic handheld camera, hoping to get the scoop.

Van Cleef stood overlooking one of the tide pools. His thoughtful expression turned to disgust. He crouched down for closer inspection. He glanced up to see Espinoza coming out of the public restroom area, straightening his tie. He did not look well.

"I was wondering where you went," Van Cleef said. "You disappeared on me. I'm concerned about you 'Spinoza… you okay or what? Did you have a little too much to drink on New Year's Eve?"

"No," he said, hovering over a nearby garbage can, queasy and unsteady. He looked like he was ready to hurl, his dark complexion turning lighter by the minute. "No. Nothing like that. I didn't have anything to drink yesterday."

"I know this one is pretty gruesome. Look, I can have—"

"No. No... It's not that... I don't know if it was something I ate... my stomach is grinding, I'm burning up, and my nose just keeps—"

Espinoza did the Dracula sneeze, the kind where you hold your arm over your face and sneeze into your elbow like Dracula holding up his cape. He was a wreck.

Van Cleef stood back from his partner a moment with concern. "Sounds to me like you've got that nasty flu bug that's been going around. Carruthers had it last month. It's a particularly bad strain this year. My wife talked me into a flu shot for the first time in years. I think you'd better take the day off and get some rest. I can have the Malibu detectives finish up here."

"It's okay, it's okay. I don't want those guys taking this one from us."

"Who? Overstreet and Alston?"

"Yeah. Those guys."

"They can't. Carruthers called it. It's our crime scene."

"That Overstreet is an ass. He thought I was a maintenance man."

"Tell me about it. Already picked up on that. Listen, don't worry about him."

Espinoza did not want to tell Van Cleef that he vomited. He never called in sick and rarely got sick, and this was no time to be out. Besides his wife was having another baby and he needed to put in more overtime.

"I heard they're pissed off about some false alarm this morning," Espinoza said as he coughed. "So now they see something big with this—"

"Don't worry, José," Van Cleef said in his soothing, low tone of voice.

"Don't let anyone know I'm sick."

"No problem brother, but just one thing..."

Espinoza raised his eyebrows and suppressed a cough.

"Next time you throw up," Van Cleef said. "Don't do it in the tide pools."

Alston interrupted them, tapping Van Cleef on the back and said, "Her name is Sheila Plotkin. Better known as Sheila Evans, or at least what's left of her."

"Sheila Evans, the actress from all those '80s action flicks?" Van Cleef asked, recalling the sculptured, bronze '80s actress.

Alston nodded and said, "That's her all right."

"Man, she was a major movie star a while back. I read that Quentin Tarantino was going to use her in his next picture. Great actress. She was talented... what a shame. She did put up one helluva fight."

"So, she was never on America's Top Model?" Alston asked, confused.

"We'll let TMZ think she was," Van Cleef winked at Alston, grinning.

Alston smiled, referenced his notes, and continued. "She's a local resident of Malibu. She's married to a Dr. Jordan Plotkin. He's a prominent Beverly Hills plastic surgeon to the stars."

Van Cleef recalled seeing some scars on her skin during his initial examination. He was developing an acute eye these days for the new "nipped and tucked" generation of homicide victims.

5

"HAS HER HUSBAND BEEN NOTIFIED?" Van Cleef asked. "Where is he...? Is he on his way?"

"Yes," Alston confirmed. "He's on his way up from San Diego."

"San Diego?" Van Cleef whistled. "He's a long way from Tipperary, like the song... His office down there?"

"No," Alston said, referencing some notes. "They said he was at a medical convention. At least that's what his answering service told me. They keep paging the doctor and are trying to locate him. Told him it's an emergency."

Van Cleef looked at his watch. It was now 8:50 a.m. It would be another long day on too little sleep. Dinner at Spago with his wife was not going to happen. He decided to put that call off until later in the day. He was starving and should have grabbed something to eat on his way out, he thought. He did not make a habit of skipping meals since that could trigger a migraine. He was in the rare 20% of the population that suffered from ocular migraines where he would get an aura and visual disturbances for about 20 minutes, and then he would feel nauseous and wiped-out for the next couple of days. He had migraines since he was 17 years old and learned to live with them. Stress, diet, poor sleep habits, bright lights, noise, and environmental changes were all suspect as triggers. The city was not conducive to a healthy lifestyle. Being a detective only compounded the stress. He always put it out of his mind and only worried about migraines when he knew he was not taking care of himself. Today was one of those days. He chased the thought of a migraine out of his head.

"Did you go through her cell phone?" Van Cleef asked Alston.

"We didn't find one on or around her."

Van Cleef deduced that it was possible she had it when she was jogging but the impact might have knocked it out of her hand and pitched it into the ocean, or she did not have it on her to begin with because she lived nearby.

"What about an iPod?' he asked.

"Didn't find that either."

That bothered Van Cleef since Sheila had one bloody earbud in her right ear which would indicate that she was listening to an iPod or some other device while she was jogging.

"Let's take a walk," he said.

Van Cleef and Alston followed the paw prints to the end of a large outcropping of rocks where the rocks met the shoreline. They scaled the rocks to the highway.

Van Cleef said, "Did you know this is where they filmed the famous Statue of Liberty scene from the original *Planet of the Apes* movie with Heston… you know the 'damn you all to hell' scene?"

Alston did not know and never saw the original movie.

They reached the top of the cliff where PCH ran north and south.

Van Cleef examined the highway and surroundings. There were no homes nearby on this stretch of PCH and no entrance point or visible trails to indicate the dog had come down the side of the mountain on the other side of the highway.

"The dog most likely ran down the highway," Van Cleef said.

"From someone's home?" Alston asked. "Mad dog on the loose?"

"Dunno."

"Maybe broke loose from a yard or something."

Van Cleef inspected the side of the road carefully, trekking back and forth and then looking down at the crime scene.

No visible tire tracks.

"I want a tire impression kit for this area anyway," Van Cleef said.

He kneeled down, pulled a tissue out from his pocket, and picked up a fragment of what appeared to be wood.

"What is that?" Alston asked.

"Wood from something." Van Cleef said. "I'll want this entered into evidence and this area marked and photographed."

Van Cleef noticed a few matching paw prints near the area where he found the piece of wood. They disappeared by the cliff they had scaled.

"This is where the dog came down from," Van Cleef said, nodding his head.

Another detective wearing gloves interrupted them. He handed Van Cleef a black JanSport fanny pack. Van Cleef thanked him and carefully removed Sheila Plotkin's driver's license. He held the license between his thumb and forefinger, then extended it away from his eyes, and then moved it closer to him. He stared at the gorgeous model photo of the smiling face staring back at him from the DMV photo for several minutes. He was just thinking, holding it up close and then extending his arm out, then holding it at a distance, level with his eyes and blocking the black tarp with Sheila underneath it in the distance on the shore of the Pacific.

Van Cleef reserved his opinion, theories, and first impressions of the crime scene. The dog or animal in question was either on the loose, up in the mountains, or hiding somewhere. He would have to get Animal Control involved to capture it before it killed again.

"Alston?" Van Cleef called out over his shoulder.

"Over here," Alston said, turning around from his conversation with another highway patrol officer and Captain Mohan who had become useless and uncooperative.

"Join Overstreet and start door knocking the residents. See if anybody lost a dog or heard anything. Also, let people know a vicious dog is on the loose and to keep their pets inside and gates locked."

"You got it."

Van Cleef shouted out one more order as Alston walked away.

"Have another officer meet me over at 2214 N. Ramirez Canyon Road," He said. "See if the husband is back from San Diego and we'll make the notification of her death after we interview him."

Officer Watts finished taking notes and pointed to the Crime Lab van that had just pulled up alongside PCH.

Van Cleef took Captain Mohan aside and asked, "You own a dog, Captain?"

Chief Mohan hesitated as if it were a trick question or if his own canine was a suspect. "As a matter of fact I do... why do you ask?"

"Mastiff by any chance?"

Mohan looked stunned with disbelieve and said, "Overstreet or Alston musta said something. Why are you asking?"

"Just a lucky guess," Van Cleef said, grinning.

"You own any dogs?"

"Yes, I do as a matter of fact, a Doberman."

Van Cleef observed the crime lab technicians pull up in their white van, easing into action. Routine for them. It was not like the CSI television show. The lab techs did not have stylish clothing, perfect hair, or approach the crime scene in slow motion like models on a runway to hip techno music, but they did what they do best: photographing, videotaping, and documenting the crime scene and establishing a chain of evidence.

Van Cleef sat in his car on Cliffside Drive for a moment, mentally processing the gore of a vicious animal attack. He lowered his sun visor and pulled down an old photo from behind the compact mirror of his other dog that recently passed away, a German shepherd named Bogart. The photo featured Bogart and Bacall, his Doberman, running on the beach. He noticed the lenses of his Ray-Bans became fogged, which meant his eyes were welling up and he was getting emotional about the recent loss. He shook it off, placed the photo of his German shepherd back in his sun visor, and folded it up. He removed his sunglasses and cleaned the fogged-up lenses.

He reached over into his back seat and grabbed a Los Angeles Times newspaper. The paper was folded in half and worn out.

The headline was dated one month earlier and read:

"RETIRED LAPD HOMICIDE DETECTIVE
MAULED TO DEATH BY HIS
FAMILY PIT BULL..."

6

VAN CLEEF PARKED his Dodge Challenger outside the gates of the Plotkin residence. He noted Malibu sheriff George Higgins was parked and waiting alongside the steep, winding road across from him.

The Plotkin estate was a Victorian-era home with a stone exterior. It reminded Van Cleef of the stony mansions on Lakeshore Drive in Gross Pointe, Michigan, just outside of Detroit's East Side where his parents used to take Sunday drives after church in the summertime. Where all the rich people lived. Where his family would drive and dream of a better life.

Van Cleef and Sheriff Higgins exited their vehicles and walked up the long incline, serpentine dirt road. A large iron gate divided them and the Plotkin estate. Van Cleef took note of the various cars parked in the driveway beyond the gate. Two Jags: one midnight blue, the other lime green, and one black SUV.

Death notices were never easy. Van Cleef told Higgins that he would break the news. Sheriff Higgins was with the

California Highway Patrol (CHP) for 25 years and he was used to the drill. Mainly informing families of highway fatalities. He was relieved that Van Cleef was the bearer of bad news this time.

Two dogs charged out of the front door: One black Lab and the other a cinnamon color Chow. They stood barking at Van Cleef and Higgins from behind the gate. Van Cleef pressed the button on the gate's call box.

A uniformed maid peered out the front door and opened it to call off the dogs.

The gates opened slowly inward. The two dogs hesitated and then obediently ran back to her. She opened a fenced area on the side of the estate and closed the dogs behind the fence.

Van Cleef entered taking note of the sprawling environs: A zen-like lagoon with cascading waterfalls and fountains. A tennis court visible to the right of the estate. Italian Marble. Imported everything. The finest of everything. The kind of estate one would find in a copy of Architectural Digest. The kind of estate Van Cleef or Higgins would never afford. They waited for the maid to return from securing the dogs. At closer inspection, it would appear that Dr. Plotkin might have done some cosmetic surgery on her. A glint of Spanish features now obscured by Botox lips, breasts too large for her petite frame and a perfect little turned-up nose. A telenovela type. She introduced herself as "Monique."

"You are the detective that Mister Plotkin is expecting," she said in an innocent tone.

"Yes."

"Mister Plotkin is waiting for you inside," she said, smiling.

Van Cleef noticed a slight attraction from Monique, despite the grim circumstances. She batted her eyelashes and blushed.

They followed Monique through the front door of the estate and to the foyer. Dr. Plotkin and an older man, who appeared to be more suitable for a round of golf, emerged from a study underneath the wooden circular staircase to join them.

Dr. Plotkin exhibited a handsome and trustworthy face. He was tan with strong Mediterranean features and piercing green eyes framed by designer glasses. Van Cleef glanced up at the expensive chandelier overhead and caught a glimpse of his own tall shadow on the polished marble floor. Dr. Plotkin introduced himself. The older one did not.

"We'll be meeting in my office," Dr. Plotkin said to Monique.

Monique took the cue to leave the men in private. She closed the sliding wooden door between them.

Dr. Plotkin's office was more like a library with a desk. Nothing out of place. Just books, mostly medical references. Dr. Plotkin took a seat behind his desk. He introduced the other man as his attorney, who sat to his left like a witness taking the stand, except this seat was a fine Parisian imported antique. Van Cleef and Higgins took their seats across from them. They both sat on the edge, not getting too comfortable.

Dr. Plotkin's attorney introduced himself as Attorney Gordon Goldstone. Van Cleef passed his business card across to him. Goldstone patted his empty shirt pocket, shrugged, and said, "I'm afraid I'm out of business cards. I'm easy to locate. I'm the only attorney named Gordon Goldstone in Century City who represents the Plotkin family."

"Dr. Plotkin, I'm Detective Leo Van Cleef with the LAPD —"

"Good, then do you mind explaining to me and my attorney what was so urgent that I return home from an important business trip? They said it had to do with my wife, but would not say what... Was there a robbery...? Accident? Where is she? What is going on?"

Dr. Plotkin came into the ring swinging. He was defensive and condescending. Van Cleef was used to this in his dealings with high profile cases, especially with celebrities and wealthy people.

"We'll get to that in a moment," Van Cleef said. "I understand you were at a medical conference, or summit, this morning, is that right?"

"Yes, that is right. I was one of the keynote speakers. They were very upset that I had to cancel— no one is telling me anything, just that it's an emergency—"

"I understand. Does your wife typically attend these speaker conferences with you?"

"No. I mean, sometimes, but not this time because she had her own event that she was running— this evening at the Four Season's Hotel— some animal rights event or fundraiser."

Van Cleef took notes and asked, "Were you going to attend her event tonight?"

"No, the Plastic Surgeon's Conference was a two-day event. I had business meetings lined up. Important meetings. Meetings that you are keeping me from," he said, pushing up his glasses on his nose and checking his phone. Van Cleef wondered, was that Sheila's missing phone?

"I understand. When did you speak to your wife last?"

"Last night, before I went to bed."

"But not this morning?"

Dr. Plokin shifted his glance to Goldstone. Goldstone nodded to him, approving the question.

"No," he said.

"Did you text or e-mail her? Anything like that?"

"No. Detective Van Cleef, my wife and I have been married for thirteen years— Just celebrated our thirteenth anniversary. We do not text or e-mail each other like silly teenagers. We are both extremely busy, professional people. She's a very busy woman."

"Was it her regular routine to jog alone on the beach so early in the morning?"

Dr. Plotkin frowned as he bolted up from his seat. He was feeling uneasy now and said, "Yes, that was part of her routine... I still don't know what—"

"Alone, without the dogs?"

Dr. Plotkin glanced outside his window and did not respond, confused.

Van Cleef clarified and rephrased his question, "Those are your family dogs?"

He pointed outside at the two large dogs rollicking and playing with a tug-toy, their patterns warped through the French doors' window panes. The Lab was in a play-bow stance.

"Ah, yes. Yes, you are referring to Grace and Buster."

Van Cleef suppressed a smile and asked, "Which one is Grace and which one is Buster?" This friendly question seemed to throw Plotkin's concentration out the window. He kept self-consciously fixing his collar and had to think about it for a minute, even though it was a simple question.

"Grace is the Chow and Buster is the Lab, why?" he asked.

"Did your wife typically take them with her on her morning jogs?"

"Always," Dr. Plotkin said, examining his watch.

"Does she typically walk or drive down to the beach?"

"Walk... We live close by," Dr. Plotkin said, bracing himself on the corner of his desk. "I'd like to speak with my wife, detective. Where the hell is she?"

"Did she frequent Westward Beach with your dogs?" Van Cleef asked the question knowing that "No Dogs Are

Allowed" on that beach.

Dr. Plotkin cocked his head and said, "Detective, I don't pay attention to which beach. She has her routine like most normal people."

Dr. Plotkin's cell phone rang. It startled him. He glanced down momentarily, frowned, and suppressed the second ring by letting the incoming call go to voicemail. Van Cleef noticed it was an iPhone. He checked his watch again.

Van Cleef observed beads of sweat forming on Dr. Plotkin's forehead. He said, "Dr. Plotkin, I am with the homicide section of LAPD and I am afraid I have some bad news—"

Dr. Plotkin turned as white as a freshly bleached sheet and collapsed back down in his seat.

"My God, what has happened to her?"

"We don't know. There seems to have been an accident."

Dr. Plotkin raised his voice, shouting at Van Cleef. He was shaking now. He asked,

"Traffic accident? Car? Was she hit by a car?— I warned her about the traffic on PCH and crossing—"

Dr. Plotkin's mind raced to the commotion on PCH prior to coming home and the unusual sound of helicopters overhead.

"No," Van Cleef said. "Animal attack of some sort."

"Animal?"

"That's what it looks like at this time. We don't—"

"Why would anyone want to kill my wife?"

Dr. Plotkin rubbed the side of his cheek; his hands were shaking and unsteady.

Van Cleef found the doctor's choice of words peculiar since he indicated it was an accident.

Sheriff Higgins spoke up and said, "We'll need a positive identification... Would you like us—"

Dr. Plotkin stood up again, almost lurching at Van Cleef. Goldstone extended his palm in front of him in a 'stop' gesture. Dr. Plotkin eased back down in his seat.

"That's all right, Detective Van Cleef," Goldstone said, standing in between the men. "I will drive my client down to the coroner's office."

Van Cleef was used to a variety of reactions when it came to death notices: Anger. Disbelieve. Denial. Hysteria. Dr. Plotkin ran the whole gamut of emotions. He insisted that the detectives had ID'ed the wrong person.

"Dr. Plotkin," Van Cleef said. "I understand this is difficult to accept—"

Dr. Plotkin and Goldstone looked at each other with consternation, then back at Van Cleef and Sheriff Higgins. Dr. Plotkin was unstable and remained seated. Goldstone poured him a drink.

Van Cleef and Higgins started to walk to the door. Van Cleef paused and asked, "By the way, whose SUV is parked in the driveway?"

"His wife's," Goldstone said. "It belonged to his wife."

"Anyone else drive it?"

Dr. Plotkin did not hear Van Cleef's question. His concentration was on Sheila's death. Van Cleef repeated his question. "Did anyone else have access to her SUV, or would anyone else use that vehicle?"

Dr. Plotkin shook his head slowly. His eyes were squeezed tight in a painful expression.

Van Cleef turned to Sheriff Higgins and said, "Interview the neighbors and gather statements from them before we leave. I'll also want the SUV checked out— Let's get a lab tech—"

Gordon Goldstone stood up and challenged Van Cleef. He said, "Detective Van Cliff—"

"Van Cleef."

"Van Cleef," Goldstone said. "This is not a crime scene, and I am afraid you will need a warrant beyond this interview. Is that understood?"

"Fair enough," he said. "We'd also like to ask your maid a few questions, if you don't mind."

Goldstone walked Van Cleef away from Dr. Plotkin and to the front door. He lowered his voice almost to a whisper, looking back over his shoulder at the distraught Dr. Plotkin, "Detective, I think you've asked enough questions. We can arrange an interview with you downtown if you would like. I represent the family and can be present with the maid. Comprendé?"

Van Cleef repeated, "Comprendé." He turned back around and said, "We're going to need the crime lab to take some DNA samples from the dogs."

"Now why in the world would you need that?" Goldstone asked with a slight smirk. "Are they suspects too?"

"I doubt it," Van Cleef said. "But, we'd like to make sure."

Van Cleef stepped outside. He noticed a text from his wife Claudia reminding him of their dinner at Spago with all of her entertainment industry colleagues.

Not tonight, Van Cleef thought. This wouldn't be the first time he skipped out on an 'important' event and was sure word was already reaching Beverly Hills and Hollywood about Dr. Plotkin and his now-deceased wife. He would explain later.

In the meantime, he would grab an unglamorous quick carry out at Burgers & Beer on Heathercliff Road in the proximity of Point Dume and the crime scene and continue his investigation into the night.

7

January 1, 9:45 P.M.
Lancaster, California

70 MILES NORTH OF LOS ANGELES near the Kern County Line, the Lancaster Sheriff's Department, FBI, and a select team of ASPCA (American Society for the Prevention of Cruelty to Animals) investigators waited in the cool air of an otherwise arid desert. All law enforcement units focused their weapons on a foreclosed Victorian farmhouse that seemed antiquated and out of place with the surrounding wasteland.

No lights, motion, or movement detected from inside the house. Not a soul stirred.

The furtive creep of law enforcement outside from the Sheriffs, FBI agents and ASPCA investigators tactically closed in on the farmhouse, ready to raid the house as planned with an executed search warrant in hand. They called this dogfighting raid "Operation Hellhound."

The columned front porch gave the facade of a decrepit Southern Plantation estate from the 1800s.

Frank Nelson, the Senior Director of the ASPCA's Anti-Cruelty Behavioral Group, and Cheyenne Devine, the

Director of Blood Sports, were the last in line.

The lead FBI Agent, Warren Slezick, spoke briefly to his organized entry team of twenty men. He divided them into two teams: one to cover the front, the other to cover the rear of the property. He pressed the button on his ballistic vest and spoke calmly into the activated hands-free mic.

They formed two snake positions: one team crept quietly to the front with a battering ram, the second team assembled around the back of the farmhouse.

The point man stood on the front porch with his team, gripping their submachine guns and semi-automatics.

Waiting.

He pulled back the screen door. It creaked as it widened in the still air. The metal battering ram shattered the rotting wood of the door with minimum force. The first officer tossed a flash-bang grenade into the front room. A flash of light illuminated the empty room. A quick glimpse of heavily draped windows covered with bedraggled blankets that looked like they came from the Salvation Army were visible as the smoke dispersed throughout the room.

The foyer was cleared fast and methodically.

FBI team members systematically shouted "clear" as they entered individual rooms searching for suspects. The living room had swaths of ripped carpet on a badly damaged and chewed up wood-paneled floor.

They took notice of two makeshift, small treadmills in the center of the living room and made their way up the staircase to the second level of the farmhouse. Still no movement from any area of the house and no movement overhead as the SWAT team and FBI ascended the staircase in a single file formation. Every step of the near rotting wood creaked on their way up.

One of the SWAT team members paused for a moment, feeling the sensation of stepping on something on the dimly lit staircase. He looked down. A mound of wooden granules like sand or tiny wooden pellets caked his boot.

"Termites," he whispered over his shoulder, then proceeded upward.

The SWAT team paused at the top of the stairs surrounding the door located directly in front of them.

Another team covered the second door at the end of the hall.

The point man twisted the doorknob slowly. The door was locked and latched above the door handle. He signaled to the other members to take their positions.

In a split second, the door was busted off the hinges by the SWAT team. The room was empty and devoid of furniture. Large swaths of red carpet were left behind and randomly scattered on the floor. They appeared to have scratch lines from dogfighting marked on them.

The two SWAT teams converged in the main bedroom of the residence and completed their sweep in a matter of minutes, concluding that the perpetrators or occupants were long gone.

Frank Nelson and Cheyenne Devine waited impatiently outside until they were given the green light to enter the premises. FBI Agent Warren Slezick emerged from an adjacent room incensed, advising them not to go too heavy on introductions. Just finish their investigation and move on.

They were too late. "The Show" was over.

Slezick spoke to himself, irritated. He paced back and forth like a wildcat. "Waste of fucking time and resources— Months of planning down the drain. I should've gone with my gut on our informant; we shouldn't have listened to him—"

"Not entirely," Nelson said, standing behind Slezick.

"Not entirely what?" Slezick asked in a condescending tone.

"There is evidence of dogfighting here," Cheyenne Devine said, shining a flashlight on what appeared to be dried blood dripped on the rotting floorboards.

"The dogs weren't all we were after," Slezick said. "We had evidence. We wanted the assholes… the ring."

"If you don't mind," Devine said, "we'll begin collecting the DNA samples and run them through the canine CODIS, hopefully get a hit."

"Be my guest," Slezick said, stepping out of their way and checking his watch. "I'll give you a half-hour before we roll out of here and pack it up."

The canine CODIS (Combined DNA Index System) criminal dogfighting DNA database was the first in the nation to track criminals, breeders, and trainers consolidating and sharing the info with law enforcement and authorities. CODIS for criminals dated back to 1990. Four years later in 1994, the DNA Identification Act authorized the FBI to set up the NDIS (National DNA Index System), which became fully functional in 1998 to help streamline any CODIS lab that needed to share and compare DNA samples.

Cheyenne Devine took charge and instructed the criminalist and crime scene investigators to gather the abandoned, rolled up, red carpet and all other trace evidence they collected for further photographing, fingerprinting, and forensic analysis.

One of the officers requested Devine and Nelson follow him outside. He had something they both might be interested in seeing. The three of them proceeded out back to a dilapidated woodshed.

"We found four large pieces of bloodstained pressboard tossed in this shed," the Lancaster Sheriff said.

Nelson watched his partner, Devine, closely inspect the wood and then mentally measure it.

He asked them and another sheriff nearby from the

crime lab to help them reconstruct a box, standing the 3 ft. x 6 ft. pieces of wood and joining them.

"We have a 'pit,' gentleman," Cheyenne Devine announced.

This dogfighting raid had been months in preparation. The farmhouse reeked of urine and fecal matter and smelt worse than any kennel they had been to in recent memory.

Another crime scene investigator from the ASPCA pulled a wooden stand out from the shed.

"What the hell is that?" Another Lancaster Sheriff asked, stepping in to examine the contraption.

"They call it a 'rape stand,'" Frank Nelson said. "It's used for forced breeding."

The sheriff shook his head, chasing the sadistic graphic images out of his mind of what went on in this farmhouse. He exited the backyard.

The backstory on the farmhouse was that it was foreclosed on months ago by the bank. The last owners abandoned it. A Midwestern family from Ohio had left the place a wreck, along with the keys on the kitchen sink, and moved back to Ohio where they came from. The father was a factory worker. Unemployed. The mother was a schoolteacher. Also unemployed. They had a 10-year-old daughter. The only dog association they had was that they caught the Greyhound out of town and returned where they came from.

They were cleared as suspects before the raid and were not involved in any dogfighting or criminal activity. The real and elusive dogfighting ring blew through town, did their business, had "the show" as it was called in dogfighting parlance, and then pulled up stakes and moved on.

The ring had to know the house was vacant, which meant they knew someone in the area or someone in the area knew them. But who?

Frank Nelson stood on the side of the dirt road, thinking, observing the crime lab hauling out evidence in boxes and plastic containers— technicians documenting and logging evidence and the constant flashes and clicks of photographs. His thoughts were interrupted by the familiar sound of an LAPD's Air Support Division (ASD). A Bell 206B3 Jet Ranger helicopter hovered above him illuminating the barren night and uneventful raid.

Frank Nelson waved it on, shielding the blowing dust from his face and eyes.

He walked back over to the back porch of the farmhouse and stopped one of the crime scene investigators who had a small bottle in an evidence baggie.

"Hold up," Nelson said. "Can I have a look at that?"

The crime scene investigator handed Frank the baggie.

Frank took a closer look at the bag's contents, which was an empty bottle of Gorilla Glue. He held the small bottle at eye-level with the friendly little picture of the chimp on it.

"Anything important?" The crime scene investigator asked, curious.

"They weren't binding wood with it, I can tell you that much."

Frank Nelson flashed Devine a look and handed the evidence bag with the Gorilla Glue bottle back to the investigator.

They both knew its purpose.

Another officer emerged from behind and called out in Frank Nelson's direction, "Are you Frank Nelson?"

"That I am," Frank said.

"We got routed a call from a terrified Mexican restaurant owner over on 10th Street… claims he's trapped inside by a vicious pit bull and the dog won't let him out and he wants Policía. He's hysterical and muttered something in Spanish—"

"What else did he say?"

"I don't know," the Lancaster officer said. "I don't speak Spanish."

"What else did he say in English then?"

"Just more mixed English about how he is a 'prisoner' and 'trapped' and oh, he kept repeating, "No me gustan perros..."

"I don't like dogs," Nelson said, translating in Spanish for the officer.

"We have officers headed over there now," the Lancaster officer said.

That was all Frank Nelson needed to hear, which escalated the dog situation to an emergency. He'd have to beat them over to the restaurant fast if he wanted to see the dog alive. He said, "Tell the responding officers under no circumstance to shoot the dog. What's the name of the restaurant again?"

"It's Dinora something on 10th a couple of miles east. Listen, I can't guarantee—"

He tuned out the officer and turned to Cheyenne and asked, "You good here?"

"Sure," she said. "I'll wrap it up and meet you over there when I'm done."

Warren Slezick emerged on the back porch impatiently clockwatching and admonishing Cheyenne Devine that she had 8 minutes left to wrap it up.

Agent Warren Slezick left the back porch and went back inside, avoiding eye contact and conversation embarrassed by the uneventful raid. He stood alone checked out, massaging the back of his neck. He ripped up the search warrant and tossed the pieces on the floor. He snapped out of his depression, stuck his head out the door in the hallway. and yelled at the top of his lungs at everyone to start packing up and to move out and move on.

The dogfighting raid was an abject failure.

His informant lied.

8

January 2, 7 a.m. Los Angeles

ANIMAL RIGHTS ACTIVISTS and reporters crowded the entrance to the Police Administration Building or PAB the morning after the Sheila Evans mauling. The PAB was located at 100 West First Street in Downtown Los Angeles. A press conference was scheduled for 9 a.m. with the Chief of Police and the Mayor of Los Angeles.

Van Cleef observed the mob outside while he waited for the elevator, occasionally catching a glimpse of hand-painted signs both pro and anti-pit bull. People were getting ugly with each other, calling each other names, and the LAPD was trying to hold them back while they guarded the entrance. Van Cleef entered the elevator reviewing a mental checklist in his mind of priorities in his investigation. Aside from the brief half-hour nap in his car in Malibu, he had worked nearly twenty-four hours straight before coming downtown.

Police Captain Thomas Ware III was at the helm of the 500,000 square foot headquarters that housed five sections that had combined robbery and homicide divisions since

1969. The special sections were Robbery, Homicide, Special Assault, Cold Case Homicides, and Special Investigations. Each had a Lieutenant.

Van Cleef entered the 7th floor squad room. At first he thought he got off on the wrong floor and took a double-take. Half the desks were empty and he did not recognize most of the detectives seated at the ones that were occupied. The squad room sergeant was watching the ABC News coverage with other detectives in the video conference room.

Van Cleef walked past them down the hall on his way to Lieutenant Mike Carruthers's office and stood in the doorway with a newspaper tucked under his arm.

"A pack of vicious pit bulls killed Sheila Evans?" Van Cleef said, tossing the L.A. Times Newspaper on Carruthers's desk. Carruthers had a military crew cut and large ears that heard everything in the squad room and on the streets. He pretended not to hear Van Cleef. The department staff and officers nicknamed him "Mach" short for Machiavelli. He did favor being feared over loved.

Lieutenant Carruthers looked at the article superficially. It didn't faze him. He ignored the paper and Van Cleef. He eventually felt Van Cleef's eyes burning a hole in the top of his head. Van Cleef stood, arms folded, demanding an explanation.

"We don't even know that it is a dog that did this, and the media is already pinning it on pits?" Van Cleef said, "Did you see the protesters outside?"

"No," Lieutenant Carruthers said. "They weren't there when I came in. We'll fill them in soon on what we have."

"We don't have anything yet."

"We know that. They don't. They just need to know we're on top of whatever it is they don't know."

Lieutenant Carruthers continued to write up a report. He hesitated a moment, threw his pen on the desk, leaned back and said, "Jesus, Leo... you act like I tipped them off. You know it sells papers, besides how do you know it was not a pack of pit bulls like what happened out in Palmdale a few years ago?"

Van Cleef did not answer Carruthers.

Carruthers liked to see cool hand Leo lose his cool every now and then.

Van Cleef decided to change the subject and asked, "And where the hell is everybody? Where's Espinoza? Who are all those other people in there? Are they here for training?"

Lieutenant Carruthers said, "Out sick with the flu. Espinoza called in. Got it coming out of both ends—"

"Lieutenant please... spare me the gory details. I got an autopsy to attend this morning."

"No worries, I got someone to pick up the slack. I assigned Overstreet to you from Malibu. He's Espinoza 'til Espinoza gets better."

Van Cleef's curiosity turned to disgust. "Longstreet from Malibu?" he asked.

"Overstreet," Carruthers said, correcting him. "Dennis Overstreet."

"The Malibu detective?'"

"Yes. You worked with him yesterday."

"Yes, I worked with him yesterday—"

Van Cleef was about to walk away when the Lieutenant asked, "Is there a problem with Overstreet?"

"No, none other than that the guy thinks he's Denzel Washington."

Lieutenant Carruthers thinking about it said, "Yeah, he sorta does bear a slight resemblance. He's here to pitch in and he's a damn good detective. You worked with him on the Mitrice Richardson case. He wants to be a part of Homicide Special and we're testing him out. Besides... since we're on the subject of Hollywood, rumor has it they call you 'Lee Van Cleef' in the Hollywood division, even do the whistle when they mention your name down there." Carruthers was making a reference to the classic Spaghetti Western, "The Good, the Bad and the Ugly."

"Cute," Van Cleef said, unamused.

"You sure there's no relation?"

"None, just coincidence, like Steve McQueen the director is no relationship to Steve McQueen the late actor or like the late actor Charles Bronson is no relation to that killer creep in the UK."

"But how do you really know?" Carruthers asked, toying with him. "You did go to film school prior to becoming a detective— I mean, have you really talked to your mother…"

"Actually, I'm related to Van Cleef & Arpels, the famous French luxury jeweler, but my mother told me I got cheated out of my inheritance… that's how I wound up here," Van Cleef said, lying through his smile.

Van Cleef was about to walk out when Carruthers got serious and said, "Listen Leo, for what it's worth… I'm sorry about Ed Boots. I know you were one of the few guys that got along with him, and trust me, he was a hard guy to get along with."

Van Cleef reflected for a moment on his recently deceased fellow detective friend. He said, "Yeah, for what it's worth."

Van Cleef walked away from the Lieutenant's office.

"Oh Leo?" Lieutenant Carruthers called out.

Van Cleef poked his head back in the Lieutenant's office.

"Don't forget to use the hand sanitizer," Lieutenant Carruthers said. "Each desk has one."

Carruthers returned to his report. Van Cleef heard Carruthers whistle the theme from the Spaghetti Western and snickered as he reentered the squad room of unfamiliar faces with the exception of Detectives Rodriquez and

Tanaka working the phones. He scanned the room for Overstreet's mug.

There he sat, feet up on his partner Espinoza's desk. There was Overstreet acting as if he had already put in a full day's work. Van Cleef was going to put him to work. *Don't get too comfortable,* he thought. Those oversized feet are recognizable from shoeprint evidence at the crime scene. Van Cleef told him to get his feet off the desk.

Van Cleef pulled his chair out from his desk and noticed a used copy of Stephen King's book *Cujo* on his seat. He scanned the room for the practical joker. All the other detectives were working diligently in their partitioned cubicles, some on the phone, others fixated on their computers. He knew none of the wise guys in the squad room would own up to putting the Stephen King book there, but he had a pretty good idea who it was. Van Cleef had already read the book years ago when it first came out and saw the film, which was equally forgettable.

He tossed *Cujo* on the top of his desk while he got situated and took his seat. He opened a new computer file for Sheila Evans's murder book on his desktop. He logged into his Spotify internet radio and selected one of his favorite stations, the Motown station. Marvin Gaye was singing "Ain't too Proud to Beg," while Van Cleef flipped through his hard copy files and notes. He began the routine process of adding and uploading the files online. He paused for a moment, his thoughts distracted. He noticed his desk plant was dusty. It was a common household "ZZ plant" that could be underwatered and that he jokingly named Stavros after the character on the Kojak series, who had a desk plant named Shirley. He gently wiped off the leaves with a cloth from his desk. He kept his eye out for Lieutenant "Mach" Carruthers and then reached into his briefcase and pulled out some unrelated reports.

Van Cleef started personally investigating the strange

death of his friend Edmund "Eddie" Boots's case one month earlier. Ed Boots, like Van Cleef, was an LAPD Detective. Ed Boots, like Sheila Evans, was killed by a canine. Not on a beach but in the comfort of his own home. Boots worked in Robbery Special Section or RSS. Boots was a hardcore detective by all accounts. The real L.A. version of Dirty Harry. He lasted through Police Chief Daryl Gates and the L.A. Riots, the Rodney King beating, and the O.J. Simpson debacle. He made it through the fire but was not without enemies. Many colleagues supported the opinion that he was a racist dinosaur and needed to go, so when the department decided to investigate and do some reputation management, Boots was on their hit list. Boots retired, albeit forced out and lived in Pismo Beach. He was divorced three times. Lived alone with his 5-year-old purebred pit bull dog named Figaro, which is where things got strange. The death of Eddie Boots first appeared to be an unfortunate accident on the surface until questions and loose ends in the investigation began to resurface in Van Cleef's mind. Boots kept to himself, but wasn't a recluse. Yet, up until the time of his death, several neighbors also reported "sketchy" characters hanging around Boots's residence and several different service trucks on their street at odd hours of the night. Some neighbors even felt that they were also being watched.

Van Cleef reviewed the Pismo Beach divisional detective's notes, and it was clear they ran out of leads and resources. Unfortunately, Van Cleef did not process the original crime scene, and evidence was mishandled, tainted, and even lost. Figaro, Boots's pit bull, was shot on-site by responding officers and his remains were destroyed immediately after the fatal attack on his master Boots.

Van Cleef reviewed the original crime scene photos. He was killed in his kitchen. The theory was that his dog went into a rage and attacked Boots from behind while he was cooking. When police responded, they found charred pasta on the stove, Boots's smoke alarm beeping, and Figaro dragging his owner from the kitchen. The kitchen was a bloodbath and reminiscent of a crime scene like the Manson murder house.

According to neighbors, Boots's pet pit bull spent most of his time in his backyard and did not exhibit aggressive tendencies. Figaro was friendly with neighborhood kids and other dogs, was socialized, and was well adjusted, which bothered Van Cleef. What set the dog off? Also, why was the dog dragging the owner out of the kitchen towards the front door before he was shot? Leg wounds were inconsistent with the torso and fatal throat wounds that killed Boots at the scene. Also, it was noted that the dog's tags were missing.

No shoe or paw impressions were taken of the surrounding area, to make matters worse. Also, no hair fibers were collected. Sloppy detective work, or was it Boots's bad reputation that ultimately led to a careless, swift, and inept investigation? Some fellow detectives joked and called Figaro a hero for taking out the bigoted asshole.

He made a note to place a call to the Scientific Investigation Division, or SID, and ask further questions. He would also fit in a drive out to Boots's residence in Pismo.

Van Cleef paused for a moment and leaned back in his chair, thinking. Two fatal dog attacks with no apparent connection. A celebrity and a retired detective.

Canine Homicides.

His thoughts were interrupted by the voice of Dennis Overstreet. "I heard you got the Murder Books online now and everything is digital down here," he said.

Van Cleef looked up and saw Overstreet standing at his desk. He tucked the Ed Boots file under his keyboard and looked up from his computer.

"Not everything, but we're getting there," Van Cleef

said, studying the file online. "It's a work in progress, but we'll get there. Saves a lot of time."

Overstreet noticed a large, unopened Amazon package on Van Cleef's desk.

"Like Amazon, huh?" Overstreet said, shaking his head in dissatisfaction. "Killing the book business. Everything's digital now."

"Come again?" Van Cleef asked, noticing Overstreet eyeing the Amazon box.

"See, me," Overstreet said. "I'm old school. I like books. I prefer the black and blue binders. I like to have the binder in my hands like a book. Read it like a book. It tells the victim's whole life story. If I read the book online, it makes me feel like I'm reading a news story on Google. I'm not a fan of the Murder Books going digital. I think mistakes are going to be made migrating data."

Overstreet moved up a chair, sloshing coffee from his mug and rolling over the spill. Van Cleef looked around from his computer screen to see if Overstreet was going to clean up his mess. He did not even notice. Instead he rolled up next to Van Cleef, breaking his concentration and space. "You think we got a murder for hire situation?"

"Whatever gave you that idea?" Van Cleef asked, pausing for a moment.

"Husband seems sketchy to me— This your first plastic surgeon?"

"Scuz me?" Van Cleef asked. He thought it was premature to be pointing a finger at the husband.

"We got a lot of plastic surgeons in Malibu. They think they're God. Complete egomaniacs. This guy would be first on my lead list with his San Diego alibi. I don't buy it. The guy is conveniently lecturing out of town while his wife is being eaten alive at home."

Van Cleef focused on the Sheila Evans murder book. He referenced his notes from the Zuma Beach crime scene, creating a new Murder Book and a "To Do" list for the investigation.

Noticing the Stephen King book on his desk, Overstreet said, "So what exactly are we looking at here? Stalker? Serial killer? Cujo?"

"We don't know yet," Van Cleef said, focused on his tasks.

"Sick bastard," Overstreet said, fooling with the plant.

"That's our average customer."

Van Cleef despised Overstreet's presence and the scent of him still lingering at his desk. An Aqua Velva man. Too much Aqua Velva. He moved 'Stavros the plant' away from him.

"Carruthers tell you I got pulled from the celebrity swatter case to work with you?"

"No."

"Man, we gotta stop these assholes. You heard it was Gibson this time?"

"Gibson who?"

"Mel Gibson. Jerk off says they got him at gunpoint. Getting everybody in an uproar over nothing. When I catch the little bastard—"

"What makes you think it's a kid?" Van Cleef said, annoyed.

"Because only an immature kid would be dumb enough to do something like that."

"I've met a lot of dumb, immature adults," Van Cleef said, unimpressed with Overstreet's misguided theories.

Overstreet watched Van Cleef sorting through hard copy files on his desk and said, "I heard you worked the Bryan Stow beating. I'm glad they finally caught those bastards... If it had been me, I would've beat them senseless with that bat, worse than that Negan dude, when I caught 'em. I mean, what's the world coming to when you can't even enjoy a Dodger baseball game without— I hope the

Dodgers have a better year this year than the last with— "

Van Cleef looked up from his notes and cut him off. He said, "Look, Dennis, we've got a lot of leads to work through and I'm the lead investigator on this. I don't talk sports, so save it— if you don't mind, I need you to pitch in and get busy, and if we work hard and fast, we can get you back to Malibu and your celebrity swatter."

"Okay, Chief," Overstreet said, feeling Van Cleef's glacial welcome to the HSS. "Who do we have lined up for interviews this morning?"

Van Cleef pulled out a thick rubber-banded stack of files sitting on his desk and handed it over to Overstreet. The weight of the files surprised Overstreet. "Start with this," Van Cleef said.

"What's this?" Overstreet asked, as he slowly removed the thick rubber band from the hefty stack of files.

"This is what I want you to get started on since you're so interested in Sheila Evans's husband. Recent malpractice suits for Dr. Plotkin. That'll keep you busy. Go through them carefully. Scrutinize. See if you can find anything unusual. Also, since you're fascinated with Dr. Plotkin, I want to put a tail on him over the next few days, just to make sure he isn't on the golf course like a Scott Peterson type, and see if you can obtain an attendee list from his wife's fundraiser. Rodriquez and Tanaka over there on the phone can assist you with all that."

Van Cleef pointed to the HSS detectives working the phones. "We've set up a tip line and are reaching out to the community on social media sites. Talk to them about it. Weed out the cranks and false confessions. I don't expect the killer to come walking in on four legs anytime soon and bark 'I did it' in a Scooby-Doo voice, so that should do it for today and keep you busy. Any questions?" Overstreet had none. Van Cleef took a double-take at Overstreet's notebook that he was writing in. It had to be the most garish, unprofessional notebook he had ever seen a detective use. It had a cheap, silver laminated cover with some trite, embossed motivational saying stamped on the front. Van Cleef tried not to stare at it and let it go.

"Hey," Overstreet said, placing his gaudy notebook in his suit jacket. "Come to think of it... I do have a question—"

"Shoot."

"Where can I get something to eat?"

"Downstairs."

Overstreet stood up and stretched. He said, "No cranks. I'm crossing Scooby-Doo off the list. Got it. Anything else?"

"Yeah," Van Cleef said. "Follow up with your criminalist in Malibu and see if the impression evidence is back. If not, push it."

"You guys don't waste anytime down here do you?"

"No, we leave that to the other detectives. Welcome to Homicide Special."

Overstreet turned toward Detectives Rodriquez and Tanaka, ready to get to work, when Van Cleef called him back to his desk and asked, "Do you want to head over with me to the coroner? I was going to take Tanaka, but he has a weak stomach. You squeamish?"

Overstreet hesitated at first and then decided that would be more interesting than the drudgery of research. He said, "Not in the slightest. Sure. When do we get going?"

"After you get going on getting that attendee list and setting up the tail on Dr. Plotkin."

Tanaka hung up the phone and shouted across the desk at Van Cleef. He was grinning from ear to ear. "Hey, Leo... you're gonna love this—"

Van Cleef waited impatiently for Tanaka to tell him what he was going to 'love.'

"You know that high priced fundraiser that our murder

victim was throwing?"

"Yeah."

"Guess who her Keynote speaker was going to be?"

"Who?"

"Linda Blair."

"Well, that settles it," Van Cleef said, pretending to pack up and put on his suit jacket. "Case closed. We can all go home now," Van Cleef announced to the squad room with a straight face.

Overstreet was caught in the crossfire of their black humor.

"Let me guess," Van Cleef said, beating Tanaka to the punch line, "The only problem is she has a strong alibi."

"Awhhhh... You guessed it. Can't fool old Leo here," Tanaka said, grinning.

"The devil made her do it. I guessed right?" Van Cleef said.

Tanaka chortled as he laughed at his own joke. Overstreet didn't find it funny and Rodriquez covered the mouthpiece of the phone and told Tanaka to "shut the hell up."

Tanaka walked over to Van Cleef's desk, lowered his voice, patted him on the shoulder, and said, "Okay, I'll leave the humor to you." He said to Overstreet, "There is only one stand-up comic in this room. And the Last Comic Standing is this guy right here. Leo here is fucking Robin Williams or Rich Little and can impersonate anyone. Leo, do Peter Falk for our new friend here."

Overstreet waited for Van Cleef's transformation and impersonation.

Van Cleef said, "Some other time. I've got better things to do than stand-up this morning." He tossed the copy of *Cujo* back at Tanaka, who caught the book like a shortstop. Van Cleef said, "Hey Ronnie, do me a favor next time you buy me a book..."

"What's that?"

"Make sure I haven't already read it, or at least get it autographed."

Tanaka said he had not read it and didn't mind being an Indian giver and maybe even read about *Cujo* himself.

He sat back down at his desk.

Van Cleef looked up at the photos on his desk of his two dogs: Bogart, the German shepherd, and Bacall, the Doberman pincher. They were his pride and joy. His concentration was lost on his oldest dog Bogart, who died at age 18. An old-timer for a shepherd.

He wanted to slip away and call his wife. No time. She would still be ticked off about her husband missing their grand dinner at Spago in Beverly Hills with all the big wigs and suits from the studio. He checked his watch and was running behind schedule as it was. He also needed to eat, but as a general rule didn't like to eat before an autopsy. The coffee was churning his empty stomach.

He decided to reward himself afterward with food.

Van Cleef picked up the phone and then hung up. He thought for a moment, his mind troubled and distracted. He pulled Ed Boots's file from under his keyboard and once again sat back thinking about the violent deaths of both victims.

Was there any connection?

He picked up the phone a second time and dialed the L.A. County Coroner's Office. He confirmed his meeting with C.M.E. Ray Driscol.

Van Cleef would attend the autopsy and record his report.

9

VAN CLEEF AND OVERSTREET MET L.A. County coroner Ray Driscol outside the autopsy suite. His eyes smiled behind the plastic shield mask. The door of the autopsy room was wide open. Van Cleef and Overstreet stood outside in their blue scrubs, booties, and plastic shields that surgeon's wear.

"New partner?" Driscol asked.

"Yes," Van Cleef said. "This is Dennis Overstreet."

Overstreet nodded at Driscol and hesitated a moment before entering. He caught a whiff of the repugnant smell of raw flesh.

An Asian female pathologist greeted them and handed Driscol some notes which he examined. They entered the room.

Van Cleef could not believe how ravished and devastated Sheila Evans's body was. It seemed a lot smaller in length on the stainless-steel table than on the Malibu beach the day before. In all his years of detective work, this was the second-worst he had seen. The first happened one month earlier with Ed Boots.

Overstreet stood speechless, regretting his choice to join Van Cleef at the autopsy. He was sorry he ate.

Another male pathologist entered the room and handed Driscol a report. Van Cleef watched Driscol's eyes dart back and forth behind the plastic shield as he read it. He spoke into a suspended microphone positioned over the autopsy table and recorded his findings.

Van Cleef routinely took notes and listened: "Multiple lacerations and puncture wounds to the throat and face…"

Van Cleef noticed Overstreet patting his pockets for a pen while he pulled out his gaudy, shiny silver notebook. Ray Driscol also looked askance when he saw the notebook. Van Cleef caught "Life is…" something on the cover before Overstreet flipped it open and started taking notes with the pen Van Cleef passed him.

"Fatal puncture wound to the right jugular vein," Driscol continued to speak into the microphone, occasionally looking up. "Fracture to the neck region causing dislocation and crushing injury to the larynx… Left hand severed. The criminalist will have a match on the DNA from the hair fibers soon enough. We were lucky to extract them from the medulla of the hair shaft."

"The core around the cortex," Van Cleef said.

"Very good, detective," Driscol said, impressed with Van Cleef's response. "You would know then that the medulla of animal hair is different than the medulla of human hair. It is identifiable because it's one-third larger than our hair—"

Overstreet was still speechless. He would stare at Sheila Evans's body, or what was left of it, then look away at anything other than her around the autopsy room and then up at the fluorescent lights. Van Cleef could see him do this numerous times out of his peripheral vision.

Driscol directed his findings to Van Cleef and continued, "If you'll both follow me," he said.

They took their seats on stools in front of a compound binocular microscope located at another table near Sheila Evans's body. Van Cleef viewed the slides.

"Can we determine or confirm the hair and saliva are canine?" Van Cleef asked.

"Oh, it matched alright and eliminated Sheila Evans's Akita and Black Lab."

"Great, so they're off our suspect list?"

"Free birds... or dogs. Exonerated. Both of them. We are still waiting for a positive ID as to the exact breed, though— You remember the David Westerfield case?"

"Sure, the guy that killed the Van Dam's daughter in OC. What part of it?"

"The dog part of it."

"Help me out a little."

"Well, you see Westerfield did not own a dog. That's why the DNA evidence came back to bite him on the ass."

"Oh yes, now I remember that," Van Cleef said. "They found the Van Dam's family dog hair in his RV, and Westerfield did not own a dog."

"Exactly, and they were able to convict him as a result."

Van Cleef noticed an indentation on Sheila Evans's thigh and pointed it out to Driscol. He commented, "Liposuction."

"Ah, an acute eye you have, Leo," Driscol said. "Yes, that's from liposuction, not a bite mark. She should've asked for a refund from the plastic surgeon. Ms. Evans here has had just about every plastic surgery procedure you can think of done on her. She has transaxillary incisions under both arms from breast augmentations."

"The undertaker is gonna have just as much work if not more," Overstreet quipped as he turned his head the other way.

"What about the trace evidence on Sheila Evans's clothing?" Van Cleef asked.

"Impatient," Driscoll said. "You're jumping ahead, I see."

Driscol switched the slides on Van Cleef's side of the microscope, like a magician with a sleight of hand card trick, and told him to take another look.

Van Cleef hesitated for a moment and then examined the fibers under the microscope.

"We were not able to lift enough fibers from her clothes. Most got lost," Driscol said.

"Blame it on L.A. traffic," Van Cleef said.

Overstreet looked at Van Cleef and said, "I don't get it."

"Time is of the essence," Van Cleef said. "You pass the four-hour mark getting your victim to the morgue and you lose roughly 80% of the fibers. Plus, we were dealing with outdoor conditions and elements."

Overstreet couldn't concentrate or focus.

Driscol produced the sample that Van Cleef had plucked from Sheila's body that day on the beach. "However," Driscol said, "We should have an exact match of the canine fibers soon enough from the criminalist. As I concluded my autopsy, I got the usual nail clippings, scrapings, and well... It's good Leo. Very good. There was a lot to work with. Ms. Evans's hands had a lot of canine fibers on them."

"You should be able to pinpoint the missing animal of interest by the STR markers and the mtDNA—" Van Cleef said.

Driscol paraphrased for Overstreet and said, "The short tandem repeat markers and Mitochondrial DNA?"

Driscol paused, leaned back, folded his arms, and said to Van Cleef, "Are you sure you don't want a job at the lab? You do look handsome in scrubs if I don't say so myself."

Van Cleef joked and said, "Do I get vacation time? All kidding aside, I've spent too much time in court, that's the only reason I know this stuff."

Driscol laughed and said, "I'm impressed. Yes, we'll have the mtDNA processed at another facility that specializes in canine DNA and we'll know soon enough— Here is something else. We also got the results back from the Forensic Odontologist"

Driscol handed Van Cleef a color-coded chart.

"What's this?" Van Cleef asked.

"This is a PSI bite force chart," Driscol said.

"As in pounds per square inch?"

"Precisely."

Van Cleef examined the chart as Driscol explained, "You see we humans have a PSI of about 120 pounds. Lions and white sharks, somewhere in the neighborhood of 600-700. Hyenas 1100 pounds. This PSI I estimated at 340 pounds and that would indicate a large pit, but I can't say 100%. Just guesstimating."

"Can you email me that chart?"

"Have it right over to you when we wrap up."

"Thanks."

Van Cleef made a note to check online for a canine PSI bite force chart and to confer with an expert or specialist on the subject.

"So, you are fairly certain our suspect is a canine?" Van Cleef asked.

"Yes, 99 percent certain," Driscol said. "You can rule out mountain lion, bob cats, wild coyotes, or sharks for that matter — a Rottweiler could be plausible, I suppose. And I was just joking about the shark... Nope, I'd put my money on the pit bull with that kind of bite, but that's not my area of expertise," Driscol said. "I have to say, I've handled fatal dog attacks before— you know, the kind you read about in the papers, but this is one of the worst I've seen. It was a vicious attack. It left little of her body behind."

"How much does an average pit bull weigh?" Van Cleef

asked.

"Again, I'm not an expert," Driscol said. "But I'd say anywhere from 60 to 80 pounds on average."

"Time of death?"

"Just before 6 a.m. 6:30 at the latest."

"Official cause of death?"

"Fatal dog attack."

Van Cleef, Overstreet, and Driscol were about ready to exit the autopsy room when Driscol said, "I do have something neat your friend might be interested in knowing," Driscol said, directing the comment at Overstreet. Overstreet looked stunned like a winning contestant on a game show.

"Me?"

"Yes you, Dennis."

Driscol led him over to a Microspectrophotometer which is used to measure light and color of trace evidence. He could tell Van Cleef's new partner was in over his head and the information overload was overwhelming him.

"We also found out something astounding," Driscol said to Overstreet with no expression.

Overstreet looked up from the machine and said, "What?"

"She's not a natural blonde."

Driscol winked at Van Cleef who was smiling behind the plastic shield mask. Overstreet realized that they were humoring themselves.

Van Cleef took some additional notes and would have a surveillance team at Sheila Evans's funeral checking for mourners who did not belong, running down all the plates on SUVs that parked in the vicinity, and keeping a close eye on Dr. Plotkin, though he was not considered a person of interest at this time.

Van Cleef's cell phone rang. He did not recognize the number, only the area code. It was Long Beach.

"Detective Van Cleef?" the stern voice on the other end asked.

"This is he."

"Regarding the Sheila Evans case... we have a suspect in custody..." the caller said, identifying himself as a Long Beach Detective.

That was all Van Cleef needed to hear.

Van Cleef said he would be right down with his partner.

"Don't interview him until we get there."

10

THE SUSPECT'S NAME WAS Aaron Patterson spelled with double AAs and two TTs etched in hardly decipherable, barely legible chicken scratch on the rights waiver. That was all Van Cleef needed to open their dialogue and get his story legally before a lawyer got a hold of him. Aaron was short. No more than 5'7". Approximately 145 lbs. Bald. Tattoo sleeves. Van Cleef liked to call this tattooed generation "The Illustrated Men/Women Generation," a reference to Ray Bradbury's classic book. Only this generation's tattoos didn't have stories to tell, just another circus in town.

Aaron tried his best to be a hardass; that facade lasted all of 20 minutes before he eventually broke down.

Overstreet teased him and kept calling him "Aryan Patterson."

Van Cleef played the sympathetic detective and told him to "knock it off." A routine they worked on outside the interview room.

"We want to know what you were doing this morning

running your pit off the leash on a crowded beach," Van Cleef asked, reading the arrest report. He towered over the scrawny suspect, intimidating him.

"The police shot my dog," Aaron said, stammering. He had been repeating this phrase since the arrest. He stared down at the table avoiding eye contact with the detectives.

"Your dog was shot because of your carelessness, Aaron," Van Cleef said.

"I wasn't doing anything wrong. Rosie's is an off-leash dog beach… I didn't do anything wrong."

"Rosie's Dog Beach has rules and you didn't follow 'em. Simple rules like keep your dog inside the traffic cones they set out," Overstreet said, examining and flipping through another copy of the arrest report. "Dogs are allowed off-leash inside the traffic cones. You were outside of the traffic cones when your dog killed the woman's pug. That's the way numerous witnesses seen it. They also said you were quote 'daydreaming in your SUV' and it took you a while to react. You on something or what? Medicated? Anti-depressants?"

"No. Look, I thought the traffic cones were for—" Aaron said, looking askance at the two detectives.

"Traffic," Overstreet said in a sarcastic tone.

"I still can't believe you— they shot my dog."

"Your dog killed the woman's pug, Aryan, and would not let go," Overstreet said. "Then went for the officer's K-9 and also injured the officer in the process… do you know what that's called?"

Aaron did not answer. He just sat and scowled.

"I'll tell you what it's called," Van Cleef said. "It's called a Rampage Attack in our book."

"My dog is dead too… I can't believe you killed him."

"Why did it take you so long to react, Aaron?" Van Cleef asked. "Didn't you hear all the commotion?"

"There was a lot of commotion Aryan," Overstreet said.

"Enough to wake the mythical fucking Kraken from the bottom of the sea, and you're trying to tell us you didn't know what was going on or that your dog was missing? C'mon man."

"I already told you," Aaron said, hitting his fist on the table. "And my name is Aaron! Get it right— Look, I don't know what I was thinking or why I didn't react fast enough, okay. I have a lot on my mind to think about, I guess," Aaron said, looking Overstreet right in the eye.

"Yeah well, you'll have a lot more to think about now and a quiet jail cell to think about it in," Overstreet said.

There was a moment of silence. Van Cleef and Overstreet let that thought and image settle in Aaron's imagination. They could see his wheels turning. They were breaking through.

Van Cleef sat down across from Aaron and looked down at the table with a sullen expression, mirroring Aaron. He folded his hands, broke the silence, and said, "Aaron, look... I know you have no reason to trust us under the circumstances, but we're people just like you at the end of the day. We go home to our families— I am a dog owner myself... I recently lost my older German shepherd."

"Someone shoot him?" Aaron said.

"No Aaron, no one shot him. He was old and passed away, unfortunately. Now my partner and I didn't shoot your dog, we just want to find out want happened out at Rosie's. Look, I've been out to Rosie's before, Aaron. My Shepherd used to love to run free on the beach. I can see how the situation might've gone wrong. It's like a big playground for pups. Maybe it was just an unfortunate accident. Is that the way you see it?"

Aaron unconsciously nodded. He kept his mouth shut.

Van Cleef studied Aaron's tattoos. They were not gang tattoos and they certainly were not the famed ink of Mark Mahoney. These were the run-of-the-mill tribal tatts. They had no significance to anyone other than Aaron. Just another pretentious badass billboard. Just another 'Over Illustrated Man.' He went on, "Most people don't know that there are leash laws in California, even at a place like Rosie's. I see it all the time in my own neighborhood, so I understand if it wasn't clear to you."

Overstreet was getting impatient with Van Cleef's approach and wanted to take another jab at Aaron and warned him, "The woman's pug is dead and that can't be replaced. She'll probably sue you."

"I'm suing the city of Long Beach and Los Angeles for killing my dog," Aaron said.

Van Cleef said to both of them, "Guys. Guys. Can we stay outta court for the time being? No one is suing anyone... yet," Van Cleef emphasized *yet*.

Van Cleef referenced the officer's arrest report.

"Says here you live in Simi Valley?"

"Yeah."

"That's a long way to drive just to think. Wouldn't it be cheaper to think at home?" Overstreet asked.

"No, I wasn't just there to think... I wanted to see the beach and exercise my dog."

"Yeah, I know what you mean. My dogs loved the beach. Do you work?" Van Cleef asked.

"Yeah."

"This is a weekday," Van Cleef said. "You work nights or a night shift?"

"No... I was fired last week."

"Sorry to hear. Hard times," Van Cleef said. He stood up to stretch his long legs and leaned against the wall, arms folded. "Suppose you heard about the jogger who was murdered in Malibu yesterday?" Van Cleef asked.

"Hey now... no. no. no...no way," Aaron looked Van Cleef directly in the eye. "My dog did not kill that woman and I was not anywhere in that area that day. You ain't pinning that shit on me."

"Can you prove that?" Overstreet asked.

Aaron thought about it. He was housebound two days ago and didn't go anywhere.

"Yeah, man," Aaron said. "Ask any of my neighbors. I was home all day. Job hunting."

"Job hunting. Craigslist? That sort of job hunting?" Van Cleef asked.

"Yeah."

"Sure it wasn't people hunting like the Craigslist killer?" Overstreet asked.

"Knock it off, Overstreet!" Van Cleef shouted at Overstreet. "Let Aaron explain."

"I didn't kill that woman. I swear to God," Aaron said. He was trembling now.

"No, you didn't," Van Cleef said with a slight sigh of frustration. His lips tightened.

Van Cleef and Overstreet exchanged glances.

"My pit bull was a good dog... I don't know what happened or why that happened... but your police department shot him, and they are going to have to pay for it. I'm going to sue the City of Long Beach."

"Easy Aaron. Just a couple more questions, then we're finished with you, okay?"

Aaron nodded.

"Anything else you'd like to tell us about your dog?" Van Cleef asked.

Aaron was holding back.

"Says here, your dog was named Hitler?" Overstreet said, growing impatient reading the arrest report, "Nice name for a dog."

Aaron didn't answer. He was embarrassed and would have never guessed the day he'd be sitting in the hot seat as a murder suspect. He was sweating now.

"You drive a green SUV?" Van Cleef asked.

"Yeah, it's more like a Ford Bronco."

"I see," Van Cleef motioned to Overstreet to meet him outside the interrogation room.

"When does my lawyer get here?" Aaron asked, watching the detectives on their way out.

"When you call him," Van Cleef said, smiling. He turned to Overstreet and asked him to step outside.

Van Cleef and Overstreet stood outside the interview room with their backs against the wall.

"Well, what do you think?" Overstreet asked. "Early break in the case or what?"

"He's not our guy," Van Cleef said.

"Not our guy?"

"Not our guy."

"Not even a suspect?"

"Not even close."

Overstreet spun around and threw his right hand in the air and dramatically counted on each finger inches from Van Cleef's face. He said, "His dog killed another dog and nearly killed the officer." That was his first point on his right thumb. "Number 2: The guy drove a considerable distance with gas at nearly five bucks a gallon just to 'think,' meanwhile he's been fired and doesn't have a job to afford gas." That was his right index finger now pointing at Van Cleef like he had an imaginary gun. "Three: He drives a friggin' green SUV—"

"According to our 'bonehead' surfer dude," Van Cleef said. "That didn't know shit according to you."

"Whatever," Overstreet said. "And four," Overstreet said. "The freak names his dog Hitler… what kind of sicko would name their dog that? What more do you want?"

Van Cleef was amused and decided to razz Overstreet. "Facts, for starters. Do you have a fifth reason to finish out that hand?" he asked, pretending to be intrigued by Overstreet's fallacious reasoning.

"Yeah…" Overstreet said, his veins bulging in his neck. "Just look at the fucking loser and his gang tattoos. He reminds me of the sicko rotting up in Pelican Bay, that Aryan bastard that was behind the Diane Whipple murder, and you see what happened to her with that dog."

Van Cleef stared long and hard at Overstreet before he said, "You know the name, Giovanni Ramirez?"

Overstreet ran the name through his head and then replied, "Should I?"

"Absolutely. You mentioned the Brian Stow case at the office—"

"Yeah, what about it?"

"Ramirez, like him, was the wrong man. We're careful about making mistakes like that twice."

Two Long Beach detectives interrupted them. Van Cleef said to the taller one, "Have the crime lab finish up with his Bronco."

"He doesn't even have a lawyer, does he?" The shorter detective asked.

"No," the taller Long Beach detective said.

"No priors?" Van Cleef asked.

"Just one other citation for a dog bite, but the party settled out of court."

"Same dog?"

"Yes. Same dog: Hitler," the other Long Beach detective said.

"Bad owner. Bad dog," Van Cleef said. "Get him a Public Defender and call me if you have any more incidents like this."

Another detective from the division interrupted their conversation and handed Van Cleef a report.

Van Cleef examined the report and thanked him. He checked his list as he put on his suit jacket. His next order of business was a private meeting with ASPCA's (American Society for the Prevention of Cruelty to Animals) Behavioral Unit. He agreed to meet with the two investigators, who recently handled the dogfighting raid in Lancaster, at the Seven Grand Bar in Downtown Los Angeles. He instructed Overstreet to continue the investigation back at the Police Administration Building (PAB) and follow up on leads from Sheila Evans-Plotkin's attendee list for her fundraiser event, work the tip line, and check on the status of the impression evidence from the Malibu crime lab. That would keep him busy. Overstreet's comment about the Whipple case bothered him the whole way downtown.

11

"SO, TELL ME EVERYTHING you know about pit bulls," Van Cleef said, as he leaned back in his seat and opened his notepad.

Frank Nelson looked at his partner, Cheyenne Devine, seated to his left, not sure where to start, who should begin first, or how much to delve into on the controversial subject of pit bulls.

Van Cleef noticing their hesitation, clarified, and said, "Just leave out the parts the media tends to leave in."

"You mean the 'dog bites man' parts?" Frank asked, with a slight frown.

"Yeah, those kinda parts," Van Cleef said.

The Seven Grand Bar was a dark, swanky hybrid bar. A combination of Irish Pub and sporting lodge. At 3:15 in the afternoon, it was a ghost town. Patrons still nursing a hangover from the night before. Customers either out of work or avoiding work. Christmas lights and New Year's decorations still hung like the echo of "Auld Lang Syne."

Van Cleef was seated under the giant mounted moose's

head at a corner table with them. He caught Devine staring above his head at the moose head hanging over him. He hoped it was mounted properly. Wouldn't that be a helluva way to go… death by moose head.

Van Cleef listened over the occasional clack of pool table balls and CNN talking heads on the mounted television. The Happy New Year sign reflected in reverse in the mirror behind the bar. It read: "raeY weN yppaH" in the mirror. He rearranged a quick anagram in his mind with the letters and came up with: Weary. Hype. Nap. His state of mind could relate to all three words.

"First off," Frank said. "People loosely use the term pit bull when they don't know what they are really referring to. Is it an American Pit Bull Terrier? A Staffordshire Terrier? An American Stafford Terrier? They don't know the difference. Many people confuse the pit with other dogs. It's not uncommon for someone to mistake a Boxer, Presa Canario, Bullmastiff—- hell they couldn't tell the difference between a pit bull and an Olde English Bulldogge in a lineup."

"Hey, I'm in the business of mistaken identities," Van Cleef said. "I hear it all day long from suspects."

The Seven Grand waitress interrupted their conversation to take their order. She was a gaunt redhead in her early forties. An artistic type. Starving artist. Looked to be surviving paycheck-to-paycheck. Maybe came out to Hollywood with aspirations and drifted further East to the Seven Grand when they didn't pay off.

She focused on Van Cleef to begin the order.

"I'm curious; would you happen to serve Islay Single Malt Scotch Whisky?" Van Cleef asked.

"Did you see it on the drink menu?" she asked with a sardonic tone.

"No, I didn't," Van Cleef said. "Maybe you could double-check with the bartender, see if you ever served it."

"I've never heard of it," the waitress said with a major attitude. "And I doubt she'd know anything about Ismay Malt Liquor. She's only been here a week."

"Islay Single Malt Scotch Whisky," Van Cleef said, correcting her.

"Ah, just coffee for me, please," Frank Nelson said, superficially glancing at the menu.

"Make that two," Cheyenne said, handing the menu back to her.

The waitress walked away. Van Cleef smirked as she walked over to the bar. He liked ordering items that were not on the menu. It drove his wife, Claudia, crazy. For Van Cleef, it was never about the item, it was more about the willingness of a stranger or how curious or perceptive people were outside their daily scripts. In this waitress's case, she didn't give a shit.

Cheyenne Devine picked up the conversation after the waitress walked away and said, "So back to pit bulls. In all seriousness though, it's like dealing with sharks. What's the first shark that takes the rap when there is a shark attack?"

"Great White," Van Cleef said without even thinking about it.

"Exactly. Thanks to Spielberg and Hollywood. When there's a shark attack, the majority of people automatically think *Jaws* and when we think of *Jaws*, we think of Great Whites, but it could be any other species, but since the whole world has seen *Jaws*, we immediately think Great Whites, thanks to the movie."

"And the media," Van Cleef said.

"Sad part is that pit bulls, as a breed, have been demonized like Great White sharks," Nelson said, taking a quick sip from a straw in his ice water in front of him. "They get a bad rap. They just require responsible owners. This thing that happened out in Malibu was not someone's family pet."

Van Cleef's mind drifted for a brief moment to his own dog at home. He thought about Aaron Patterson and his dead pit bull and the Diane Whipple dog attack comment that Overstreet mentioned. He focused on his notepad.

"Is it true that their jaws lock?" Van Cleef asked.

"No," Devine said. "But, having said that… they sure as hell don't let go. They're tenacious. That's the Terrier in them."

Van Cleef focused again and placed two crime scene photos on the table in front of Nelson and Devine.

Frank leaned forward and lifted the photo to eye level examining the animal tracks leading away from Sheila Evans's body. A ruler at the base of the photo depicted the deep and heavy magnified paw prints to be over 4 inches.

"What do you make of them?" Van Cleef asked.

"For one thing, right off the bat… these aren't coyote tracks. Coyote tracks are oval. Approximately 2.5 inches long. 2 inches wide. They have a smaller foot pad in the rear which is typical. But the gait is the main giveaway."

"What about the gait?"

Nelson placed the photo back on the tabletop between them and said, "The coyote has an overstep trot, unlike a dog. You see the pattern?"

Van Cleef examined the paw prints in the photo, noticed a pattern, and said, "These prints are wild, random—all over the place."

"Exactly. Coyote or wolf prints, for that matter, have a distinctive walk almost as is if they are walking a tightrope."

Nelson pulled out a black Sharpie marker from his coat pocket and said, "Can I mark this photo?"

"Absolutely," Van Cleef said. "It's a copy. I have others."

Nelson marked an "X" on the paw print and said, "If this were a coyote track, the X would match up between the pads in this photo, which it doesn't. This is clearly a canine print."

Van Cleef was intrigued, and their assessment supported Driscol's autopsy findings. He asked, "How could a dog of that size just vanish into thin air?"

"It didn't," Cheyenne Devine said. "We were talking about that on the way over and we both agree. It didn't just disappear. That's the part that puzzles us, too. Do you know if it was more than one dog or animal?"

"We still don't know," Van Cleef said. "I'm waiting for more lab results."

"It's possible that the animal or dogs were dumped," Devine said. "We've seen that scenario before. The dogs are dumped somewhere, starving, and then they attack in packs."

"You think this could've been done by strays?" Van Cleef asked.

"They have attacked humans in the past," Nelson said. "Wild dogs are unpredictable."

"The only problem is, we have a witness that claims he might have seen someone around about the time of the murder."

"And you think the dogs belong to that person?" Devine asked.

"I don't know what to think. That's why I'm talking to you," Van Cleef said.

"The media is already screaming pitbulls," Nelson said, skeptical.

"Yeah, well we don't know and we're not responsible for irresponsible journalists—"

"—Or bloggers for that matter," Devine said.

"You got it."

"Y'know the media's jaws lock when it comes to pit bulls," Nelson said. "They get people fired up and hysterical in these situations, then the next thing you know, you get politicians that start witch-hunting again like in

Denver."

"Yeah, I recall Denver banned pit bulls," Van Cleef said.

"They sure did," Nelson said. "Which was a big mistake."

"You said something about 'unpredictable' a minute ago," Van Cleef said, "continue... sorry to interrupt."

"No. No... It's okay. You see when pit bulls attack, they are not in some kind of frenzy or different than any other dog for that matter, contrary to what people think... the Denver court debated that ad nauseam, however, if a pit bull attacks, they are 'in it to win it' as they say.

"Like Mike Tyson," Van Cleef said.

"Ears included," Nelson said.

"Colorado had ten fatal canine attacks over a forty-five-year time span, and guess what?" Devine said.

"What?" Van Cleef asked, not attempting to guess.

"They weren't all pit bulls, but that was the breed that got targeted and that was the breed that got banned. Here, see for yourself. You can have these copies."

Devine handed Van Cleef photocopy printouts of fatal dog attacks ranging from 1978-2008.

"A dog of this size and of this rage would be hard to pull off. It would be like breaking up a dogfight," Nelson said.

"What would make a dog just kill and run off like that?" Van Cleef asked.

Nelson shook his head and said, "Not sure exactly. I suppose if it felt threatened by someone or something, the dog in question could hightail it out of there."

"Like another person intervening to stop the attack?" Van Cleef asked.

Michael Vick, the Atlanta Falcons football quarterback, popped into Van Cleef's thoughts for a moment, then he said, "I know you've done extensive work in this area and I'm going to need your help in establishing a profile of the dogs, or dog, involved. I've got an LAPD psychologist working on the human side of the suspect behind these homicides. I was hoping you could help me on the canine side, since you're working with the FBI on the recent dog-fighting raids."

Nelson and Devine both looked stunned, somewhat surprised, and again not sure how much to say.

"Come on guys, throw me a bone," Van Cleef said, smirking. "The Los Angeles Sheriff's Department contracts out to the sheriff's station in Lancaster. So, I know you can tell me a lot more than you're telling me about pit bulls. So, when I ask you to tell me everything you know about pit bulls, don't be afraid to include the dogfighting parts too."

Van Cleef took a sip of his water and waited patiently for an explanation.

"Yeah well," Frank Nelson said. "The raid was sort of an embarrassment. We kind of came up empty-handed."

Cheyenne Devine chimed in and said, "I'm sure you know we can't disclose too much, Detective Van Cleef, while working with the FBI. You understand we're not in charge—"

"Who's in charge?"

"His name is Warren Slezick. He's heading up the investigation."

Van Cleef knew the name. Guys in the department called him "Sleazebag." He made a note and produced one more photo that he saved for last, hoping Nelson and Devine could identify the fragment of wood found on the side of the road in Malibu, the day of the Sheila Evans-Plotkin murder.

He slid the enlarged photograph across the table, leaned back in his chair, and said, "We got our crime lab analyzing this too. I'm waiting for the results. We found this at the crime scene the day of Sheila Evans's murder. Might have come from the suspect's vehicle. Looks like a piece of a broomstick or splintered wood."

Devine and Nelson exchanged looks again, concerned.

"No," Nelson said as he handed the photo back to him. "More like a breaking stick. This was where you said the car might have been?"

"Yes. What's a breaking stick?"

"They use it in dogfighting; It's used to pry open the jaws of the dogs. Place it between their molars and pop the baby's jaws open. I wish you had shown us a piece of driftwood instead, but that's what it looks like to me."

Van Cleef sat back and imagined the dog jumping out of the SUV and the fragment of wood falling onto the pavement at the top of the bluff where it was found.

"We did not find anyone else's footprints on the beach that day," Van Cleef said.

He observed both of them for a reaction, trying to read their body language. They were both being open and honest he felt.

"Detective," Nelson said, looking over his shoulder and making sure no one at the Seven Grand could hear him. "You might have heard about the multi-state dogfighting raid several years ago—"

"Which one?" Van Cleef asked with a hint of sarcasm in his voice.

"The one down in Georgia, 2013."

"Three states: Georgia, Alabama, and Mississippi," Devine said.

"Didn't they rescue something like three hundred pit bulls?" Van Cleef asked.

"Three-hundred and sixty-seven to be exact," Nelson said. "These creeps had them cooking in the sun in these Southeastern states— deplorable conditions. Chained to tires, starving. It was an abomination."

"You got 'em on felony dogfighting, though?" Van Cleef asked.

"Sure as hell did," Nelson said.

"So aside from money with these guys, what else is at play?" Van Cleef asked.

"They like to think it's a sport," Nelson said, "And will even use bad rational to explain it away, but it's illegal and dangerous and that is what motivates them. You will typically find these suspects have other criminal histories and are involved in drugs, gangs, and other deviant activities outside the law."

LAPD's regular customers.

Van Cleef found himself lost in thought, distracted by a blaring wall-mounted television screen near the bar. Another "Breaking News" story flashed on the television screen and caught his attention. Protestors gathering somewhere in another city. Another black man was allegedly shot dead by a white cop. The black community was screaming about racism. Politicians and talking heads were once again fueling the debate, focusing on racism before all the facts were in. Van Cleef left the Detroit Police Department in 2000 when the United States Justice Department investigated civil rights violations and excessive use of force and decided to reorganize the Detroit PD. The reorganization was an abysmal failure and the Police Chief announced that they would be reverting to a precinct system in 2011. Eleven years later. He found himself ruminating as a present-day Homicide Special detective thinking about his experience as a cop in Detroit when his precinct got the news of the death of Malice Green, a black man, in November 1992. No protests. No rioting like in the Rodney King beating. No bullshit. The officers were convicted, and the City of Detroit behaved itself.

But no one marched for Malice.

"Anything else you can tell me about our four-legged suspect and dogfighting that might be useful?" Van Cleef asked.

Nelson and Devine sat back and shook their heads, finishing their coffee. "We work closely with the Humane Society and some of the cases we see—" Devine hesitated. "You know, when we get reports of dogs missing, we investigate every one of them. Dogs are stolen from their yards, homes, that sort of thing, but sometimes it isn't for money like most people think."

"What's it for?"

"Baiting," Devine said. "Here, let me give you something." Devine reached in her backpack she had underneath the table and pulled out a copy of *Sporting Dog International*, an underground magazine that covers the dogfighting world. She passed it across the table and said, "Here, this is a gift... you'll glean more insight from this."

"What's this?" Van Cleef said, opening the magazine and shifting in his seat. He flipped through the pages with a mixture of intrigue and disgust.

"It's a magazine for creeps. Take it home. Makes good bathroom reading," Devine said.

"Anything else you can give me to go on from the Lancaster raid?" Van Cleef asked.

Nelson and Devine exchanged looks. Devine nodded.

"Check out a pit bull at the Carson shelter," Nelson said. "Police found it in the alley behind a Mexican restaurant, starved to death and beaten."

Nelson leaned back, deep in thought, troubled. His mind was still fixated on the tracks in the photos. He said, "You have one other problem... and it's a big one."

"Oh, and what's that?" Van Cleef asked, looking up from his cell phone while Googling the Carson shelter.

"This animal is bigger than a pit bull," Nelson said.

12

THE L.A. CARSON ANIMAL SHELTER was located on Victoria Street. Van Cleef took the 110 Freeway out to have a look at the pit bull Nelson and Devine suspected was abused and used in dogfighting near Lancaster. He arrived after-hours, just before 7 p.m.

LaDonna Wilson, the Supervisor, was expecting Van Cleef and was told to meet with him before she closed the shelter for the day. She was taking care of business up front at the reception area when he arrived. She let Van Cleef in and locked the door behind him.

"I'm Detective Leo Van Cleef," he said, showing her his LAPD detective badge.

The cacophony of dogs barking echoed in the front lobby area. There was a mixture of canine and feline odors and disinfectant scents in the air.

"Hi, I'm LaDonna," she said. "Nice to meet you. Frank Nelson told me to expect you."

"I'm here to see the pit bull that was transferred from Lancaster."

LaDonna referenced her clipboard and said, "Yes, right this way. Frank Nelson a friend of yours?"

"One of my new best friends," Van Cleef said, half smiling.

They entered the door next to the desk which led to the main pound. Rows and rows of cages like a prison.

Dogs barking, whimpering, and whining.

It broke Van Cleef's heart as he caught sight of a Doberman curled up in the back of a cage, depressed.

The dog reminded him of his dog Bacall, except this one was depressed, withdrawn, and cowering in the cage.

"What is the story with that Doberman?" he asked, pointing at the cage.

"Oh, that's Dakota. His owner lost everything. Job. House. Wife. You name it. He couldn't keep him. He's waiting for a new home."

"How old is Dakota?"

"15."

Van Cleef was afraid to ask any more questions. Senior dogs were harder to find homes for than cute puppies. He turned away from Dakota knowing each cage held a sad story, and he could not permit himself to get involved emotionally at this moment while he was working. He had to stay focused. It was hard with each dog barking, begging, and standing on their hind legs, desperate to get his attention. Desperate to be set free.

They moved along to the cages on the far-right end of the pound.

Van Cleef crouched down to see a frightened black pit bull terrier cowering in the back corner of the cage.

"Where did you find this dog?"

LaDonna referenced a clipboard and said, "Normandie. South Central. And her neighbor in the cage next to her is the pit bull that was found in Lancaster and transferred here. She was eating out of garbage cans in the back of a

Mexican restaurant. The owner was scared out of his wits and contacted animal control. Anyway, they figured she would have a better chance of being adopted on this side of town."

They came to the last cage on the left. He shifted his gaze to the adjacent cage where another gray-colored, disturbed pit bull was curled up in the back licking her left paw, occasionally looking up at Van Cleef.

"There she is," LaDonna said.

"Wow," Van Cleef said. "Pretty beat up and scarred. She have a name?"

"We call her Amelia."

"Amelia, like Earhart?"

"Right on."

Van Cleef put his index and middle fingers through the cage and started sweet-talking Amelia. Saying things like "Poor baby... Where's your home, huh baby? Where'd you come from sweetheart...? Yeah, Amelia's a sweetheart."

Amelia would not come forward. Instead she remained curled up in the shadows of her cage and kept her head down, licking her wounds.

Van Cleef stepped backwards and tried the same routine with Amelia's neighbor, the black pit from Normandie.

LaDonna warned him not to put his fingers in the cage and said, "Ah, I wouldn't put my fingers in that cage if I were you."

Too late.

Van Cleef came a close second to losing the tips of his fingers if his reflexes weren't so good. He snapped his hand back from behind the bars as the black pit bull rammed her face into the cage almost like a shark cage and forced Van Cleef on his ass from the thrust. He examined his fingers. All four, including his thumb, were still on his hand. No blood.

The black pit was nearly twice the size as when it was

cute and curled up at the back of the cage. Van Cleef also got up close and personal and got a good look at the cuts and scratches all over the pit's face.

Then Amelia did something unexpected. She kept viciously barking at the side of the cage where the black pit bull was carrying on, almost as if she were trying to break up a fight.

Van Cleef was intrigued by both pit bulls' antithetic behavior to a stranger. He stood up and brushed himself off, embarrassed by the incident. He straightened his suit jacket and said, "Both dogs are pretty scarred up."

"Yeah, dogfighting. We see it all the time."

"Any chance either dog has a microchip?"

LaDonna gave him a sidelong glance and said, "Yeah, about as good as a chance of finding the real Amelia Earhart."

Van Cleef gave her his card and said, "Contact me if you get any more abused dogs in, especially the ones suspected of dogfighting."

"Sure. Anything you need from us, we're here to help."

Van Cleef looked around the pound at all the dogs. So many of them angry or depressed, not understanding why they were there.

"I guess a lot of them aren't going to make it, are they?"

"No, especially the pit bulls," she said. "Not as long as the local news stations keep reporting negative news," LaDonna said. "It's a shame because they really can make wonderful pets."

"Hey, believe me, I know. Just like people, the formula is simple: Bad owner. Bad dog. It's the owner's fault. I own a Doberman myself."

"Now those are scary dogs," LaDonna said, joking with Van Cleef.

They walked back to the main reception area. "Not in my house," Van Cleef said. "This one is a pampered pooch.

Someone could rob my house blind and she'd sit there and watch. I got her from the Bundy shelter before they closed it."

"It's a childhood thing with me," LaDonna said. "My dad took me to see that movie when I was a kid— and I guess I'm afraid of Dobermans because of that old movie." She tried to think of the title.

"*They Only Kill Their Masters*," Van Cleef said.

"Yeah, that one with the *Rockford Files* guy."

"James Garner."

"Yeah, that's the one. That guy. My dad watched that show too."

"But the dogs were innocent in that movie."

"Yeah, well it was still scary if you were an eight-year-old kid watching the movie."

"Hey, I know what you mean. The '70s were all about demonizing the Doberman. They made quite a few movies. So today it's about demonizing the pit bulls. I'm hoping that once we find these dogs' bad owners, they can trade places with the dogs."

"You mean behind bars?" she asked.

"Behind bars," Van Cleef said. "We'll have a court order for those two pits to spare them while we're investigating. That should buy them time. Thanks for your help."

LaDonna watched Van Cleef saunter out the front door of the shelter. He had a cool badass swagger for a detective who walked like he owned the streets.

She found herself twisting her hair and ogling at him a little too long. She snapped back into reality and returned to work.

He left a message for Overstreet.

13

ALL THE CHRISTMAS LIGHTS were still on at close to midnight when Van Cleef pulled into his driveway. So was every other light in his house. He sat in his car and thought about his wife, Claudia, for a moment before entering their home. She always kept every light on when he was gone and never listened to him when he asked her to turn them off. The reassurance that crime rates were down last year in L.A. didn't help. Being married to a detective and owning a Doberman, whose ears now popped up in the front window, didn't help. Owning a firearm and the latest home alarm system didn't help.

What was she so afraid of?

Their home in West Los Angeles was located on Rochester Street and was within screaming distance of the FBI Federal Building on Wilshire near the 405 Freeway. A nice single-story tract house built in the 1930s. Van Cleef was one of the few detectives in Homicide Special that lived in the city. Not by choice. The majority commuted long distances to get away from their work. Van Cleef's wife, on the other hand, loved her job at one of the major Hollywood studios. She had been after her husband for years to quit and become a consultant like Sonny Grasso. He liked to tease her and say he was going to become an actor instead, since he was often mistaken for one. What Van Cleef really wanted was to get the hell out of Hollywood.

He blamed himself for his wife's phobias. He should have spared her the graphic and gory details of his detective work. He did eventually learn to keep his mouth shut at home and talk about Hollywood, her work, and other mundane newsworthy things like crooked politicians, the stock market, the price of gas, fine dining, or family matters. But he still had to deal with every light in the house burning until he got home to his nightly ritual of turning every one of them off. Maybe he'd leave the Christmas lights up an extra week or two longer this year. Try to enjoy them for once.

He grabbed his paperwork from his seat, placed it in his leather briefcase, and then ripped open the Amazon package sitting on the passenger seat next to him. He smiled when he looked inside. It was an illuminated lawn sign that read:

"Pick Up After Your Dog. It's the Law."

The yellow and black sign had a cartoonish, generic owner doing the right thing, picking up their crap like everybody was supposed to do, and was easy to understand— even if you didn't speak English. Just look at the damn cartoon and pick up your dog shit. The sign came with a little metal stake to drive into his lawn.

He exited his car, hit the alarm, and walked over to the sidewalk in front of his house. Van Cleef tried his best to be discreet, hoping none of his neighbors were watching him. Bacall, his Doberman, was watching him from inside however, quivering with excitement, and intermittently barking and fogging up the glass of the picture window.

He plunged the stake into the ground, then tucked the empty Amazon package under his arm and inspected his front lawn one last time, looking for more Serpico dog shit.

There was none. Just the sunbaked pile of canine defecation left over from earlier. *Maybe Ray Driscol or his new friends at ASPCA could do him an extra favor and get a positive ID on that pile,* he thought. He headed up the sidewalk to his front door. Unswept leaves crunched under his feet reminding him of broken glass he once walked through during a shoot-out in a Venice Beach alley when he worked robbery-homicide.

The minute he came through the front door his female Doberman from the window was all over him on her hind legs. Paws on his shoulder. Licking his face. Bacall always went nuts when Van Cleef came home. Tonight she could smell the scent of other dogs from the Carson pound.

"Easy. Easy. You watch the suit," he said, gritting his teeth imitating Humphrey Bogart, "Down. Down.... I know. I know, Daddy's home. Daddy's home."

He hung his suit jacket up in the front closet and made his way to the kitchen.

The kitchen table was cluttered with scripts, notes, and stacks of books. He zeroed in on a stack of Natalie Wood biographies. He guessed Hollywood was going to take another stab at the mysterious and untimely death of Natalie Wood. A cynical thought passed through his mind: why not just make yet another Marilyn Monroe movie?

Ah, dead celebrities and their untimely and mysterious exits. The gift that keeps on giving in Hollywood.

He caught a note out of the corner of his eye posted on the refrigerator.

It read:

"Hi Honey, another late night.
No time to stop at the grocery store
or pet store on my way home.
I tried to call you to pick something up...
There was nothing to feed Bacall, so I had to give
her your leftovers."

— Love, Claudia

Van Cleef found himself gazing into an empty refrigerator. He felt his wife was being passive aggressive and still angry with him because he skipped out on Spago. He also felt Bacall staring at him gazing into the empty refrigerator, standing by his side hoping for a second helping. Their maid was on vacation for two weeks visiting her family back in Mexico and the Van Cleefs had to tough it out.

"Did you really have to eat the whole thing?" he asked Bacall. "Go lay down. Scat."

Bacall licked her chops and looked away. Guilty.

Van Cleef closed the refrigerator door, grabbed some packaged snacks and a handful of almonds, and began his routine of walking around the house and shutting off all the lights.

Bacall followed him in and out of each of the rooms.

He stopped at his wet bar in the front room next to his entertainment center. He opened one of the glass cabinets. There was an assortment of alcohol bottles, mostly half-empty. Van Cleef reached in and grabbed a vintage bottle of the Islay Single Malt Scotch Whisky. He turned back around with the bottle in his hand, admiring it.

Bacall left the room for a minute.

He flipped on his wall-mounted television without sound. Another buxom meteorologist was sauntering back and forth in her mini-skirt, showing viewers another week of sunny skies. Van Cleef sighed and shut it off. Instead, his attention turned to a CD rack nearby. Just past Montovani, he chose Hebrides Overture to chase away the grim images and ghosts of the day and attempt to catch a few hours of sleep. He put on the CD.

"I'm going to treat myself to a few shots after I close this case," Van Cleef said to himself.

He opened the bottle and took a deep whiff. He closed his eyes, reflecting on the distinctive and stirring aroma of peat.

Bacall sniffed the air and then cowered.

He opened his eyes to see Bacall sitting in front of him with her leash dangling in her mouth.

Van Cleef stretched out his arm, extending the bottle of Islay in front of Bacall's snout.

She dropped the leash at his feet and hightailed it out of the room as if she had just smelt a skunk or sewer gas.

"What's the matter, you don't like the scent of Scotland?" Van Cleef called out, impersonating Sean Connery while admiring the bottle. He twisted the cap back on and placed it back in the cabinet. He picked up Bacall's leash from the floor and carried it into the other room.

Bacall was lying in front of the door, waiting.

"Okay, I can take a hint," Van Cleef said to Bacall.

He opened the closet door, grabbed his gym shoes and his old mid-length leather and gloves, and paused a moment when he glanced down at the folded up handicapped wheelchair that was used for his German shepherd, Bogart, before he passed away. Van Cleef used it to walk his senior disabled shepherd in his final year before Bogart recently and eventually died from Canine Degenerative Myelopathy (DM), a crippling, incurable, and progressive disease of the spinal cord, commonly in German shepherds. His mind flashed to his interview with Aaron Patterson earlier when he told him about his German shepherd passing away. The loss of his dog was fresh in Van Cleef's mind and he still carried a lot of sadness over his death.

He could still see Bogart, his German shepherd, waiting by the door in his wheelchair for handicapped pets, panting, almost smiling with those dark almond-shaped, intelligent eyes that seemed to see and understand things humans didn't. His erect black ears fine-tuned into the buzz word "walk."

He snapped out of it and closed the closet door.

He grabbed his keys, locked the door, and stood on the porch a moment with Bacall. The air was crisp.

Van Cleef and Bacall took it step by step, walking patiently up to the corner of his street and turning on Selby towards the Wilshire Corridor. She stopped and sniffed every tree and bush along the way. The trees were like skeletons bereft of their leaves. The dried crunch of leaves made him think of Detroit this time. The Cider Mill. Henry Ford Museum and Holiday Nights in Greenfield Village.

Van Cleef and his dog spotted another white dog running off the leash ahead of its owner across the street. The owner trailed behind with their nose buried in their iPhone. This irritated Van Cleef. Why didn't owners keep their dogs on leashes? It was for their safety too.

They walked along Wilshire Boulevard, Van Cleef ruminating on the death of Sheila Evans.

The condominium lights on Wilshire Boulevard comforted him. He also noticed many other Christmas decorations still up on tenants' balconies and in windows in the Wilshire Corridor. The Remington. The Carlyle. The Wilshire where Farrah Fawcett died and the paparazzi got one last photo. He stopped at the waterfall fountain in front and looked up. The valet attendant recognized him and said hello. Bacall barked at him. He was always terrified of her and kept his distance. Looked like he was ready to jump out of his skin half the time. Van Cleef's mind flashed back to a moment in time when things were simple. When he used to pick Claudia up from work— as a waitress— in the Ren Cen back in Detroit. He was just a cop then. Van Cleef loved his wife. Even though they rarely saw each other, they had loyalty. Van Cleef's background as a detective was atypical. He was a film nut growing up in Detroit and directed theater classes at Wayne State before he became a police officer. He studied film and wanted to become a director. He even did some acting. Everyone told him he should be an actor. As a kid he was hooked on crime shows: *Kojak, Columbo, Mannix,* it didn't matter, but more than acting the part he wanted to be a real character. *Helter Skelter* was one of his favorite true crime books when he moved out to Los Angeles. He wanted to get into the industry… instead, he got into the LAPD. He made detective in just under five years. He worked down in Hollywood for several more before joining Homicide Special. The Hollywood he grew up on and romanticized had changed and was too politicized these days, so he felt he made the right move. He knew Sheila Evans's work, albeit even the bad B flicks. It was a sad ending and another Hollywood tragedy.

He continued walking down Wilshire Boulevard when his cell phone rang.

"Leo?" The voice on the other end was Frank Nelson.

"Yes, is this Frank?"

"Yes, sorry to call so late—"

"No, no, it's okay," Van Cleef said. "Do you have something for me?"

"Maybe," Nelson said. "I heard you paid a visit to Amelia, our Lancaster pit, at the Carson City Shelter."

"Yes. What a shame. She's a heartbreaker—"

"Well, I can't say too much without it getting back to Slezick, however he has no interest in Amelia and an item we found at the Lancaster raid, so I thought I would run it by you."

"I'm all ears."

"So, we examined the pit bull and found traces of polyurethane.

"What's it used for?"

"Glue. In this case, a chemical substance was used on Amelia to close her wounds."

"What commercial product would I find it in?"

"Gorilla Glue."

"Gorilla Glue?"

"Yep," Nelson said. "It's like Super Glue usually used more for wood."

"I know what it is," Van Cleef said. "I just didn't know creeps used it to close wounds in that way."

"Yessir."

Van Cleef paused for a moment thinking about Amelia. He asked, "What about Amelia?"

"After we evaluate and treat her with behavioral therapy, they'll either put her up for adoption if she can be reconditioned, or they will have to put her down, unfortunately, if she can't be adopted."

Van Cleef thought about Bogart again. He wished Frank had not used the phrase "put down" since it was a sensitive subject with the Van Cleefs. Many people felt Bogart should have been put down even though it was none of their business and he was not in any pain.

"You still there?" Nelson asked thinking the call dropped.

"Yeah, sorry about that," Van Cleef said. "I was thinking about something else. You were saying?"

"There is one other important fact before I let you go," Nelson said.

"What's that?"

"The pit we found at the Lancaster raid—"

"Amelia?"

"No," Nelson said. "Different kind of pit. The pit itself they use to fight the dogs in— it's usually made from wood like a pen—"

"Oh, yeah. Right, go on."

"The wood tested positive for human blood."

"I'll want to get a sample and see if we get any hits back," Van Cleef said.

He ended the call and looked down at Bacall, his Doberman, who was sitting patiently on the sidewalk breathing in the night air. He petted her on the head and they continued their walk down Wilshire Boulevard. He placed a subsequent call to the criminalist in LAPD forensics and gave him Frank Nelson's number to coordinate the blood evidence found in the pit.

14

Jan. 3, 5:30 a.m.
Detroit, MI.

THE LANKY, BEARDED ARAB MAN stood at a pay-phone with his back to the liquor store on the corner of Michigan Avenue. He appeared to be Middle Eastern or Chaldean and was dressed like a medical orderly wearing an old and ill-fitted Army green parka. He occasionally looked over his shoulder at the sizable black male passenger in his van. His cold breath was visible in the sub-zero weather as he exhaled and fidgeted to stay warm. The passenger had the visor down, even though the sun had not come up yet and it would be another overcast, gray day in the Motor City.

The number he was dialing did not connect on the other end. He slammed down the phone once again. Hesitated. Redialed. This happened numerous times before he placed the calling card back in the pocket of his bulky jacket and got back into his vehicle, a midnight-blue Dodge Caravan with the blue handicap placard hanging from the rearview mirror.

"Something went wrong," he said with a Middle Eastern accent. "This I know. I feel it."

"So, what chu' wanna do," the large black man asked, cranking up the heat on the dashboard.

"He's my brother," the Arab man said, anxious, thinking too many morbid things. All bad. All negative. "I should have gone myself," he said.

"So, what chu' wanna do 'bout it?"

"He's in trouble... I feel it. I think we got burned."

"Nah man, we ain't got burned."

The Arab man turned to the black passenger, icy air and steam emitting from his mouth when he spoke. "You said this was a sure-bet. Those were your words, not mine."

"Easy brother, we gonna get our bread and the dog back."

"Screw the dog... and I'm not your brother. My brother is what matters and he is missing."

"Look man, I just breed 'em... I don't care what they do with 'em once they leave my domain. Dude out in L.A. say he lookin' for a good dog for protection and he came from a reliable and verifiable source, so I delivered."

"Wrong," the Arab man shouted. "My brother delivered and now he is not answering. It is not like him. We have to find him... he is in trouble, something is wrong... this is unlike—"

"Look man, I can't leave my dogs, man, or my situation, you know that. Hell no."

"Then I go alone. Get out."

The large black man stared straight ahead and yelled back, "Hell no, wind chill is 10 below... drop my ass off— You on your own. Tell you this much tho'... You get busted, you don't say shit 'bout Kali. Nothin'. Like I say, what people do is they own business. I'm just a breeder— And drive slow man, y'all upset and shit... gonna get us a ticket."

The Arab ignored him and sped out of the lot and pulled a U-turn out onto Michigan Avenue.

15

January 3rd, 8:30 a.m.

PEARL & EARL'S DRUGSTORE was a local Lancaster shop that was just what one would expect to find in the middle of nowhere. It was the classic mom and pop store with the owner, Earl, behind the register being the only employee, and the owner's wife, Pearl, working in back. The specials were painted on the glass of the windows just like the old days and Van Cleef imagined the owner probably had a feather duster hanging out of his back pocket.

Van Cleef entered the store. First customer of the day. Maybe the only customer of the day. It felt like he stepped into the Twilight Zone, or another dimension, or another time. They even had a little bell jingle above the door.

The sounds of Merle Haggard, Johnny Cash, or some other country singer, played over a small transistor radio near the counter.

The owner was weather-beaten, pushing 80, and looked up at Van Cleef once or twice. He was busy working the numbers for this weekend's SuperLotto like it was a Sudoku puzzle.

Van Cleef walked the three aisles of the drugstore and

took a mental inventory of the products stocked on the shelves.

The owner eventually acknowledged him and came out from around the counter. Van Cleef was wrong about the feather duster.

"Can I help you?" he asked.

"Yes," Van Cleef said. "I see that you sell hydrogen peroxide, Elmer's Glue, Vaseline, sponges, and dish gloves... those sorts of things."

He learned about these common, store-bought items from one of the dogfighting magazines Nelson and Devine gave him at the Seven Grand. The article was entitled, "Dogfighting on the Run."

Earl, the store owner, had a dumbstruck look on his face and just listened.

"Do you sell Gorilla Glue?" Van Cleef asked.

"What kinda glue?"

"Gorilla Glue. It's like Super Glue. Has a Gorilla on the tube?"

"Dunno, my wife does the ordering around here. I'd have to check with her."

Van Cleef assumed the wife probably ordered more around there than just products.

The owner observed Van Cleef's suit and stature with skepticism. He didn't dress like a local.

"I'll check with her on the Elephant Glue."

"Gorilla Glue," Van Cleef said, correcting him.

"Gorilla Glue, right. Be right back."

Van Cleef superficially browsed up and down the aisle, arms folded, overhearing Earl repeat his question to Pearl, his wife, in the backroom. The wife didn't answer his question, instead began nagging at him about something he forgot to do when he closed the store the other night.

Earl returned from the backroom. He looked at Van Cleef, who was patiently waiting for an answer, and then turned back around and asked the Gorilla Glue question again. Pearl said to "tell the guy yes, but we don't carry it on a regular basis and we don't carry it now." Then she started ranting about a customer when Earl returned to the front.

"Well, yes... we do," Earl said, tuning out Pearl in the backroom, still ranting. "We're a drugstore and drugstores tend to sell those sorts of things. We don't have a local Walmart here for miles... oh, they'd like to get me out of here and take away all my business, but I ain't selling—"

"Listen, I'm Detective Leo Van Cleef, Homicide Special division."

He handed the store owner his card. Earl, the owner, tried to authenticate it, holding it up to the fluorescent light as if it were a counterfeit bill, squinting at it.

"Someone murdered?" Earl asked.

"No, not here," Van Cleef said. "I would assume you know most all the locals?"

"Yep," Earl said, proud of himself. "That's how I knew you."

"Knew me, what?"

"Knew you weren't one."

The owner gave Van Cleef back his card and said, "I don't know anything about any murders."

"I'm not here about a murder."

"Says on your card you're a homicide detective and you just—"

"Yes, it does. Look, can you try to recall anyone recently, within the last few months, that was not a local or regular like me?"

Earl thought for a moment. His forehead wrinkled up. "No. No. I can't say that I have. I woulda remembered," he said.

"No one that bought those kinda items I pointed out... the gauze, Gorilla Glue, hydrogen peroxide?"

The owner hobbled back behind the counter and sat down, his forehead wrinkling up more than before. He reminded Van Cleef of a Walter Matthau type. He returned to the back room. Van Cleef could overhear him discussing the subject of murder with his wife who finally emerged. Pearl looked like a Haight-Ashbury relic from the '60s. Maybe a Grateful Deadhead, for sure a Janis Joplin fan from long ago with her mane of gray hair pulled back in a rubber-banded ponytail worn down to her waist, overhauls, and tie-dye shirt with a big yellow smiley face. Her face was withdrawn and miserable from years of hard living and belied the t-shirt. Van Cleef overheard her say to her husband, "I ain't talkin' to no cops," like it was the '60s and she was taking a stand against "The Man." He followed her as she disappeared again in the back room.

After several minutes of bickering, the husband reappeared and informed Van Cleef, "There was a white gentleman, come to think of it. Tall like you. Nice guy," he said sarcastically. "Came in about two weeks ago and did buy some dish gloves and Gorilla Glue. We don't normally carry it, but our supplier was out of Super Glue and sent us that kind instead. I remember because it was the last one on the shelf – had to reorder – and he had on one of those hoodies and dark shades like that Unabomber nut... what was his name?"

"Ted Kaczynski."

"Right. Like that guy. All the kids wear 'em nowadays. Can't tell 'em apart."

"But you referred to him as gentleman, not a kid."

There goes that forehead again. He said, "Guess I did."

"Paid cash?"

"We don't take credit cards. We're not Walmart here. Oh, Walmart would like to take over here, but they aren't gonna, and we aren't selling out to them. No way. No how."

Van Cleef smiled politely and tried to keep the interview on track. "Anything else you recall about the hooded man?" he asked.

"Nothing. Just an average white guy. Really tall. Maybe even taller than you. Didn't see much of his face."

"Do you remember the type of car he pulled up in?"

"Wasn't a car. Was a truck of some sort. See, that was the other thing I was trying to remember."

"The truck?"

"Yeah, it was a white kinda truck. He wasn't a trucker. I get some of them in here that are just passing through, but ah, this wasn't one of them. And it wasn't a UPS truck neither. Something in between, size-wise, but like a kinda truck I'd seen before somewhere. Like a box truck, you know the kind I'm talkin' about?"

"Like a U-Haul?"

"I guess you could call it that."

"You remember the color?"

"White like I said— I think."

Van Cleef took a few notes and then looked around at the ceiling. "You don't have video cameras here either, do you?" he asked.

"We're not like Wal—"

"I know, you're not Walmart," Van Cleef said, stopping another Earl rant. "I thank you for your time. Here's my card again. Let me know if you recall any other details about the truck."

"I do have one question for you, Detective Van Cleef—"

Van Cleef turned around hoping that Earl recalled more details.

"Are you any relation to Lee Van Cleef, the actor that was in all those spaghetti westerns with Eastwood?" Earl asked in a serious tone.

Van Cleef paused, smiled, and then politely answered, "None whatsoever."

Earl was disappointed. He returned to his SuperLotto numbers instead of his work.

Van Cleef took a moment outside the store to digest what the store owner told him. He thought about the type of vehicles that fit the general description. Not much to go on, but it was the little things that can add up in an investigation.

16

VAN CLEEF CALLED OVERSTREET from the car on his way back over to Beverly Hills from the drugstore. He wanted to catch Dr. Plotkin alone at his office, if he could, and run some more questions by him about his wife's murder without his attorney guarding him. He was about an hour and twenty minutes away in good traffic. In L.A. there was never "good traffic." He padded in an extra hour.

"Overstreet, are you finished reviewing Dr. Plotkin's files?" Van Cleef asked.

"You gave me a lot of files to review," Overstreet said.

Van Cleef also knew that even his best detectives wouldn't finish in such a short time. He just wanted to keep Overstreet distracted.

"So, tell me where you're at so far."

"Well, for starters, I can tell you our celebrity doctor spends as much time settling out of court as he does doing cosmetic surgery."

"Malpractice isn't murder," Van Cleef said.

"Yes, but there's where your boy Goldstone comes in."

"Makes sense," Van Cleef said, without giving it much thought and not too impressed with Overstreet's findings. "Goldstone is his right-hand man when it comes to litigation. His practice is well-versed in this area. Here's the thing: most of these malpractice cases are too expensive to litigate, somewhere in the neighborhood of a hundred Gs to go to trial, and the juries don't sympathize with a wealthy woman who made a costly vanity mistake. California law won't allow damages exceeding $250,000 for pain and suffering unless it involves gross negligence. It's a proverbial exercise in futility— So, nobody is going to become an overnight millionaire off a bad facelift. I also found out that Goldstone had a practice in Colorado before going Hollywood, but I'm still digging," Overstreet said.

"Where'd you find that out?"

"His website."

"Look, Overstreet, just finish the malpractice files on Plotkin and check his wife's attendee list for the fundraiser," Van Cleef said. He figured that would keep Overstreet busy until his regular partner, José Espinoza, got back.

"Did you know Marilyn Monroe had plastic surgery?" Overstreet asked. "Man, that blows my mind."

"That's old news, Overstreet. Dr. Gurdin on Bedford Drive revealed that several years ago," Van Cleef said, matter of fact. He was more concerned with the case at hand.

"Well, that was new news to me," Overstreet said. "Man, that just blows me away. I thought she was a natural beauty. It's getting to the point where you can't take anything at face value… literally, and appearances are more deceiving than ever."

"That's the smartest thing you've said on this call."

"Well, I think Plotkin's a damn good suspect. Guys like Plotkin always get away with murder because of guys like Goldstone. They get their celebrity attorneys involved and they go scot-free. And Goldstone reps some of the biggest names in sports and entertainment."

"So, what else do you have?"

"Well, I think our doctor is a breast man," Overstreet said.

"'Breast man'..? You lost me..."

"You see Dr. Plotkin's website?" Overstreet continued, "Man, it's pretty graphic."

"I haven't been on it, but try and keep focused and keep your mind on your work, will 'ya?"

It was clear to Van Cleef that Overstreet spent more time on the doctor's website than the files he gave him to investigate.

"Man, this guy is referred to as the Picasso of Plastic Surgeons. I've seen before and after shots on his website and they look Photoshopped if you ask me. Did you know this guy can charge up to a hundred grand on a single facelift and still he is near bankrupt? How is that even possible? I'm in the wrong business—"

"Longstreet, listen—" Van Cleef liked toying with Overstreet by mispronouncing his name. It was an inside joke to humor himself with 'Longstreet' since this new case involved a dog, and he liked the blind character James Franciscus played in the television series about the blind insurance investigator and his white German shepherd named Pax who was his seeing-eye dog.

"Overstreet," Dennis said, correcting him.

"Overstreet, sure," Van Cleef said. "This is L.A. and people live beyond their means. That is not unusual, even for the mega-rich. People also don't grow old gracefully here, they grow old shamefully.

Overstreet switched topics and asked, "So, do we have a name for this case yet?"

"Come again?"

"I was thinking on my way over to the PR firm about

the name of our murder case… a name for the pit bull attack in Malibu. Like the Homicide unit has interesting case names like: "The Grim Sleeper," "The Hillside Strangler," or "North Hollywood Shootout," y'know names like that for this case we're working on."

"Don't worry about that."

"I'd like to offer a suggestion. Who would I speak to in the department?"

"Never mind about that nonsense. You don't speak to anyone. We have a PR department to handle the media." He instructed Overstreet to interview the Plotkin's PR firm in Beverly Hills, Everleigh & Associates. Both Sheila and her husband, Dr. Jordan Plotkin, hired the prestigious PR firm on retainer. They got a two-for-one deal for five thousand a month. Some deal. Van Cleef was ready to disconnect when Overstreet said, "I think I know how the dog got away."

Van Cleef went silent on the other end of the phone, waiting to hear Overstreet's theory.

"It's like this," Overstreet said. "It's two guys right, two-man team—"

"Two gangbangers?"

"Yeah, something like that. They're working as a team. In concert together. One of 'em has a boat. They see their victim jogging along the shore. She doesn't give it a second thought because the boat is supposed to be there, and then all the sudden, Bam!" He could hear Overstreet hit his fist on some object to exaggerate his point. He blathered on, "They let the rabid dog loose along the shoreline. They got him on some kind of heavy-duty fishing line like the kind you use while fishing for Marlins, Great Whites, or deep fishing shit, and when the dog is done attacking they just reel him back in and take off in the water."

"Just reel him in like that, huh?" Van Cleef said, cranking an imaginary fishing reel in his mind.

"Why not?"

"Your boat theory is filled with holes, that's why."

"What do you mean?"

"The dog's paw prints left a trail back to the highway. That much we know, and the other problem is we've got a witness that says he saw an SUV around the time of the murder. The missing dog and the guy in the SUV go together."

"Yeah, well, I wouldn't bank on that bonehead surfer."

"I'm not banking on anything at this point. Keep focused on those files and let me know what you turn up."

Van Cleef instructed Overstreet to continue checking out the PR firm that represented the Plotkins. That would keep him busy. He also asked to be transferred to Detective Ron Tanaka. Van Cleef was still waiting on impression evidence from him.

Overstreet transferred the call.

"Ron, it's Leo."

"Hey man, I'm still waiting on the impression evidence for the tire treads," Ron said. "However, I spoke with the events manager at the Four Seasons. Her name is Amy Tang, chatty Cathy type. Anyway, she confirmed contacting Sheila Evans the afternoon of her death. She said the phone rang, someone picked up, and then hung up."

"Did you get the cell phone records yet?" Van Cleef asked.

"Yessir," Ron said, tapping away on his computer keyboard at his desk. "I'm still reviewing her call log, but her phone was still in use in Malibu that afternoon. Same area."

"Her husband, I'm guessing," Van Cleef said.

"I also ran the vehicles that were parked at Dr. Plotkin's estate when you notified him of his wife's death," Ron said.

"Lay it on me," Van Cleef said.

"I confirmed the maid, Monique Chavez, drives the

Toyota Camry. The black SUV, which was not the wife's, with the license plate number: 4RAM229 is registered to a Justin Young in San Diego, and I took it a step further and found out that the vehicle was sold to him by a Lisa Comstock. Found her on LinkedIn, and guess who she works for?"

"I'll take a wild guess," Van Cleef said. "Dr. Plotkin."

"How'd you guess?"

17

THE GOLDEN TRIANGLE section of Beverly Hills is home to some of the wealthiest seven commercial streets in the world, Rodeo Drive being one of them. The triangle consists of Wilshire Boulevard, Santa Monica Boulevard, and Canon Drive. Dr. Plotkin's office was located in the heart of Rodeo, overlooking the boutiques and clothing stores that require reservations to shop and a Platinum card to charge it on.

Dr. Plotkin's office manager, Lisa Comstock, greeted Van Cleef and offered him coffee. He declined. He took a seat and waited for the doctor. Lisa had a Midwest vibe about her. She probably still used a curling iron on her blonde cascading locks and had too big of a smile to have been a long-time resident of California.

Van Cleef watched out the window overlooking Rodeo Drive in Beverly Hills. He observed the tourists window shopping and the red TMZ double-decker bus pass down below. The rented Ferraris, Maseratis, and Teslas sped by with their paper license plates.

Van Cleef looked at his watch. It was almost 11:00 am.

The soothing mixture of a Zen water fountain and yacht rock played throughout the sterile office waiting room while Van Cleef thought over his questions for Dr. Plotkin.

He grabbed a random, glossy lifestyle magazine on the table. He was just about to superficially read a cover story about yet another celebrity split-up when Dr. Plotkin entered the room.

"Sorry to keep you waiting, Detective. Please follow me back to my office," he said as the two gentlemen walked down the hallway to his back office.

Van Cleef noted the hall walls hung with framed news articles and autographed photos of the doctor posing with various celebrities, all thanking the doctor for his fabulous work.

Dr. Plotkin closed the door behind them and took a seat behind his large mahogany desk. The blinds were closed. Van Cleef looked around the room at all the various framed diplomas, certificates, and photos. None of which included his wife.

"Any progress on my wife's killer?" Dr. Plotkin asked.

"We're making significant progress," Van Cleef said. "Leads continue to pour in."

"Great, go on," he said. "I'm anxious to hear what you have."

"For starters, we found your wife's iPhone."

"You did?" he responded uncomfortably.

"Yes."

"Where was it? Who had it?'

"You had it."

"What?"

"Yes. You had it."

"Why would I have it?"

"That's what I came here to find out. The day your wife was murdered on the beach and I came to interview you at your home, her missing iPhone was still being used. At first, we thought it got lost in the sea, perhaps washed away in the attack. Or maybe even eaten by the beast that attacked her, but the cell phone kept transmitting because you were using it. Right in front of us while we were interviewing you."

Dr. Plotkin's eyes darted back and forth. Small beads of perspiration began to form on his head. He leaned back and stroked his chin pretending to weigh the situation, but Van Cleef could see the only weight was on his head and shoulders, like an anvil was just dropped on him.

"It was obviously a simple mistake," Dr. Plotkin said, a slight sigh of relief. "We both have iPhones and I had hers by mistake. That has to be it."

"But then, why would you also be communicating on yours in San Diego?" Van Cleef asked. "You see the problem we have here?"

"Detective, again it is simple. My wife had left it behind at the house. I obviously picked hers up by accident or inadvertently took both with me to San Diego. That must be it. I'm afraid you made a mistake and your progress is hardly what I would call 'significant.'"

"No, sir," Van Cleef said. "You obviously made a mistake. The hotel event coordinator was trying to reach your wife that afternoon. Last minute logistical items. You inadvertently picked up and hung up on an incoming call during the interview. We confirmed that. You knew which phone you had."

"Detective Van Cleef," Dr. Plotkin said, taking a deep breath and then exhaling as if he were meditating. "Considering the grim circumstances... I didn't want to get into all this in front of my attorney and I don't intend on getting into this in absence of him, but I had become very suspicious of my wife recently and did not feel it was right, or respectful, to get into this the day of the interview.

However, I have evidence that she may have been cheating on me, which was why I had her phone."

Van Cleef nodded and said, "If you suspected her of having an affair, couldn't you have just as easily looked at her cell phone records in the history on the phone or bill? That's what I would've done, if it were me."

"You're not me," Dr. Plotkin said. "I guess I was impatient and wanted to catch her in the act."

"Dr. Plotkin, I'm afraid I don't believe you."

Dr. Plotkin's distraught face turned to anger in a split second. He said, "I don't care what you believe, Detective. That is my personal business."

"Any ideas on who she might have been involved with?" Van Cleef asked.

"Not a clue. She would get some hang-up calls late at night. She would say 'another robocall' and then act distant. Things like that. Not quite herself in the days leading up to her death, but again... I have no clue who she was seeing or if, in fact, she was involved with anyone else. She knew so many people and was a social butterfly. It would be impossible—"

Doctor Plotkin was interrupted by his office manager, Lisa, informing him that his next appointment had arrived.

Van Cleef wondered if Lisa Comstock was also Dr. Plotkin's personal business. He asked, "Why did you lie to me the day your wife died about who owned the SUV?"

"Excuse me?"

"I asked you who owned the SUV parked in your driveway and you replied, "My wife," Van Cleef said as he referred to some notes.

Dr. Plotkin sat bewildered and said, "But, my wife does own an SUV. A black SUV."

"Yes, she does. But not the one that was parked in your driveway that day.

"I'm afraid I don't follow."

"Your deceased wife's SUV is a black Mercedes Benz Hybrid X6 model, is that correct?"

"Last time I checked."

"Well, that's a problem because the black SUV that was parked in your driveway that day was a black Cadillac Escalade."

"You're sure about that?"

"Yes, I tend to notice things like that."

Dr. Plotkin rolled back his chair and rolled his palms over his tired, bloodshot eyes. Then he was checking his iPhone again. His carotid artery in his neck was visible and rapidly pulsating.

"Detective," he said. "I have been in surgery all morning and was called out of surgery this morning to meet with you. You have offered me nothing new and I have answered all your inane questions. I work very hard, long hours, and I am dedicated to my patients and practice. My practice is my life. I don't care if you're incredulous about my misperception of a black SUV in my driveway after rushing home to an emergency all the way from San Diego. My wife, Sheila, also had many frequent and random guests over… it could have been anyone's SUV. I had one-hundred-and-one things on my mind that day."

"Sure, I understand. We all make mistakes. But the question still remains: who's black SUV was in the driveway that day?"

"I didn't know that there was one. You say there was. How should I know? Maybe it was my maid's—"

"No, your maid Monique drives a Toyota Camry. We checked that out."

"Then maybe it was one of her friend's—"

Van Cleef referenced some notes and said, "It is registered to a Justin Young. Does that name ring a bell?" Van Cleef asked.

"No. Should it?"

"If it doesn't mean anything to you, it should mean something to your office manager."

"Why do you say that?'

"It's her boyfriend's vehicle," Van Cleef said. "She borrowed his SUV over the New Year's weekend while he was up in Big Bear with some friends for the week. We checked 'em out and he's not a suspect or person of interest in this investigation."

"That's easy to explain," Dr. Plotkin said. "My office manager drove down with me to San Diego and left her car in my driveway. I don't know what kind of car or vehicle she drives. I guess I am guilty of that absent-minded fact. You see, I offered to drive since she would be handling my presentation for the medical conference and figured we could also save time and discuss patients and office matters on the way down. We have new policies and procedures and typically meet weekly. She can confirm that fact, and you should be speaking with her about that and not me, since we are finished."

Dr. Plotkin sat tapping his pen, fidgeting with papers and charts. He said, "I think we're finished here."

"Just about," Van Cleef said, referencing some additional notes from his notebook. "You drive the lime green Jag?"

"Yes."

"Your attorney, Gordon Goldstone, who was with you that day drives a midnight blue Jag?"

"Yes, yes I believe so. Look, Detective, for the last time, I asked you if you had made any progress on my wife's murder and you said, 'significant.' You have failed to bring anything significant to the table, and I have patients to tend to as we speak. I was obviously in a state of shock the day of my wife's murder and don't remember a whole lot. Her funeral is this weekend, and I have not even processed that she is gone. I'm sure it would be easier for you if I confessed that I had my wife murdered and you could wrap this investigation up like they do in some inane one-hour television show, however, I'm afraid you have your work cut out for you elsewhere. Now leave and talk to my attorney should you have any additional questions. I have patients waiting and a funeral to prepare for."

Dr. Plotkin came out from around his desk in a forceful manner and thrust open his office door, his hand trembling on the handle. He stood to the side and pointed in the direction of the hallway.

The door slammed behind Van Cleef. He could already hear Dr. Plotkin speed dialing his attorney, Gordon Goldstone.

***

Van Cleef stood in front of Lisa Comstock's reception desk. Lisa was arguing on the phone with a patient about coding and some billing issues, Affordable Healthcare, and what the caller's insurance did not cover. He got to see an ugly side of her personality which was the polar opposite of the perky receptionist façade.

Did she have it in for Sheila Plotkin? he wondered.

Lisa slammed the receiver down on the distraught patient, disconnecting the call. She smiled through her gritted teeth and said to Van Cleef, "Sorry about that. Some people are just so nasty."

Van Cleef smiled and said, "I know what you mean."

The office phone was ringing again. More-than-likely the disconnected patient calling back to finish the billing debate.

"I'll let it go to voicemail," Lisa said, glancing up at the clock on the wall. It was 11:30 am. "We have to break for lunch soon anyway and put the phones on service. Her bad timing."

Van Cleef checked his watch and thought, *early lunch*.

He introduced himself again, gave Lisa his card, and asked if he could speak with her privately over her early lunch or coffee break.

There was that look again. She tried to cover it up with a smile, but her eyes did not lie. They darted back and forth like a caged rat looking for an exit.

"Me?" she asked, shocked.

"Yes."

"But I don't have anything—"

"It's okay, Lisa. You're not a suspect or anything like that. I just need to ask you some additional questions, privately."

"A restaurant wouldn't be too private at this time of day in Beverly Hills."

"We can walk across to the Beverly Canon Gardens if that makes you more comfortable."

She thought about it for a moment, looking over her shoulder for Dr. Plotkin.

"He knows that I want to interview you," Van Cleef said. "It's okay."

Lisa let out a sigh, put the phones on the answering service, grabbed her purse, and said, "I've never been over there. Sure, why not. I need a cigarette."

18

THE BEVERLY CANON GARDENS mirrored the Montage Hotel gardens across the street. There were blissful water fountains reminiscent of the 1920s and '30s, and rows of sycamore trees. Van Cleef escorted Lisa Comstock to a corner table removed from nearby conversations of money, fashion, and superficial relationships. Van Cleef pulled out a seat like a gentleman for Lisa, which she seemed uncomfortable with. She did not bother to thank him and appeared offended. He noticed she was not carrying a purse, but instead wore a black fanny pack like a tourist.

"I never knew this existed," Lisa said, looking around. "I mean, I've been to the Montage before across the street—everybody's been over there, right? But I didn't know this was over here. I should come here more often to get away. I usually eat lunch close by our office or sometimes order in."

Van Cleef had never been to the Montage himself, but did not believe Lisa had never been here before. He was amused at her nervous rambling. He said, "Tell me about it... L.A. is like that... I discover new places every day that were right under my nose, even though I've lived here longer than I'd like to admit— How much time do you have?"

Lisa looked at her fancy expensive wristwatch and said, "Not much. Twenty minutes, tops."

Van Cleef took note of her Cartier style watch which would've cost him a year's salary. He opened up his notebook and said, "That'll work. Lisa, I am just confirming a few facts in Sheila Evans's homicide, then I'll be on my way."

Lisa nodded as she watched a woman and her Yorkie walk by.

"Dr. Plotkin told me that you two drove down together for the medical conference in San Diego the night before Sheila was killed, is that correct?"

"Yes. That is correct."

"And the conference was for telehealth and plastic surgery applications, is that correct?"

"Yes, the doctor was the keynote speaker and has developed an app for reconstructive surgery. He's really brilliant with technology. I had to prepare his presentation for him."

"When did you leave for San Diego?"

She sat thinking for what seemed like several minutes and said, "We left the night before."

"Sunday?"

"Yes. We had an early morning on Monday, so the doctor thought it was best to get there early. As I said, I had to prepare his presentation and slide deck for the keynote."

"Slide deck?"

"Sorry, PowerPoint."

"What time was that?"

"Around 9 p.m."

"Where do you live?"

"Oh, I live in Westwood."

Van Cleef pretended to make a note. He already knew

she lived in Westwood on Le Conte near UCLA. He also knew it didn't make sense to backtrack to Malibu. It would have made more sense for the doctor to pick her up along the way. Overstreet had checked out her home address.

"Do you own a black SUV?"

"Practically."

"Pardon me?"

"It's my fiancée's vehicle, but I'm the one making all the payments. It's mine as far as I'm concerned."

"I see. What does he do for a living?

"Justin?"

"Is that his name?"

"Yes. Justin Young," Lisa said, turning her head away from the conversation. This was a sore subject for her. "Right now, he makes a pretty good living, living off of me."

"I see. Where was he when you went to San Diego?"

"Where else? With his friends. He went up to Big Bear with them. Skiing or something."

"Do you ski?"

Lisa laughed and blew air as she said, "Are you kidding me? I'm not into any of that snow or outdoors shit—" Lisa corrected herself and apologized. "Sorry Detective, I meant stuff. He's into all that adventurous outdoorsmen 'stuff.' I came to California, from Chicago, to escape the cold and all that. He's into all that outdoor crap. You know, Detective, I once thought I wanted a rugged guy like Rambo... an outdoorsman type. The type that can hunt with a bow and arrow and save us if we ever got lost in the woods or wilderness, or ever had to wrestle grizzly bears or worse yet, deal with a zombie apocalypse— and Justin is all that, all Alpha-male. He's just more into himself and his buddies than he is me. I call him 'Ramble.' He sure loves to hear himself talk. He's always got these big ideas and likes to talk a lot about what he's gonna do. But he never does what he says he's gonna do. Big dreamer. Big loser. Anyway, I don't think he goes there to ski anyway."

"How do you mean?"

"What I mean is when I met him, he was married."

Van Cleef decided to let that one go. He switched his line of questioning to Sheila Evans-Plotkin.

"Did you know the doctor's wife personally?"

Lisa seemed surprised at the question and asked in a raised tone of voice, "Sheila?"

"Yes, Sheila."

"Sheila was the one who hired and trained me, so I guess you could say I've known her as long as I've known the doctor. About seven months, I'd say."

Van Cleef already knew her employment background. The question was rhetorical.

"Would you have called her a friend?" he asked.

"No," Lisa said, unable to frown due to Botox. "And that's a shame. I mean I could've been a good friend to her, but she could be—"

Van Cleef waited for her to complete the sentence, but she never did. Instead, she unzipped her fanny pack and pulled out a pack of Virginia Slims Ultra Light 120's. Van Cleef thought about those catchy Virginia Slim commercials that said, "You've come a long way, baby..." Yes, Lisa Comstock did. All the way from Chicago to Beverly Hills to the middle of a homicide investigation. He glanced across the crowded street, getting the instinct that someone was watching them. He decided to move on to another question and asked, "Did you go over to their house in Malibu often?"

Lisa was not sure how to answer and wasn't sure what Van Cleef was after. She checked her watch and said, "Why sure. I had been over there quite often."

"How often?"

"Y'know. Business. Parties. Special holidays. Things like

that. The doctor runs a very busy practice and does a lot of business. They're both socialites."

"Did you see Sheila the night before her murder on Sunday?"

Lisa winced and shifted in her seat. A pigeon strutted along the edge of the fountain near them, occasionally pecking a drink. That broke her concentration. She seemed to have a childlike fascination with the bird. Her profile was flawless and the morning sun was highlighting her face just right, washing out any traces of stress like an actress well-lit on a movie set. Van Cleef wondered if Dr. Plotkin gave her the same nose job as his maid, Monique, and if Lisa even knew about Monique. She finally looked up from the pigeon and said, "Detective, I can't comment on the doctor's personal life. It wouldn't be ethical, nor would it be right, and it would only be my opinion."

"I'm not asking for your opinion."

"Then what exactly are you asking me?"

There it was. The cracking of the façade. Van Cleef had broken through that cute little "daddy's little girl" bullshit. Her true colors were shining through and her eyes had daggers in them.

"You probably know this," Lisa said, standing up and taking another drag on her cigarette. "The Plotkins were in the process of filing for a separation, and that is none of my business. I think I have probably talked enough to you, and my little smoke break is over. Nice to chat with you."

Lisa stormed off back to the office, disappearing into a crowded street of tourists.

Van Cleef people watched for several minutes, making some additional notes and observations and then walked back to the 2 Hour Free Public Parking structure on Rodeo Drive. He was five minutes over and had to pay the parking guard the difference. He decided to drive out to Pismo Beach. The long drive would give him time to digest the facts so far in the Sheila Evans-Plotkin canine homicide, and he could also start retracing Ed Boots final days before his family pit bull turned on him. He placed a call to Boots's ex-wife, Carol Jones. It had been a while since they spoke to each other. Good detective work involved having genuine empathy and being there for the survivors. Van Cleef was always there for them. The families.

He took the US-101 N route out to Pismo Beach and would pass through Oxnard and Santa Barbara along the way. Van Cleef would also make a quick 'pit stop' in Solvang on the subject of 'pits' where he could still catch a windmill, grab a quick bite to eat, and step back in time for a brief moment.

19

PISMO BEACH IS FAMOUS FOR many things. In the '50s it was considered the 'clam capital of the world.' Joe Friday once said in the *Dragnet 1966* film that, "It was a good place to retire." Ed Boots would have agreed with Joe Friday. *The Big Lebowski* was also filmed there. Van Cleef thought about The Dude, *Dragnet*, and Ed Boots on his afternoon trip out to the Boots's residence to search for any additional clues of his mysterious mauling.

He exited Highway 1 and turned onto Wilmar Avenue where Boots used to live. The single-story home had a blissful seaside charm with a white picket fence and an American flag wafting in the wind. The kind of place a single guy could retire to. The mortgage was even paid off, completing the American Dream.

Van Cleef parked the car and listened for a moment. It was serene. He entered the yard through the small, waist-high white picket fence. Before he went inside, he walked around back to the yard and looked around. There was visible evidence of Figaro, his family pit bull, still in plain sight: dog toys, tennis balls, a hand-crafted dog house, and dog dishes for food and water. He crouched down and examined the torn-up grass and paw prints scattered on some of the dirt patches next to the dog house.

Van Cleef reached inside the empty dog house and removed a hidden spare house key hanging from a hook inside. Ed Boots once joked about it and told Van Cleef that Figaro had the only other key to his house. Van Cleef remembered and figured it out. It bothered Van Cleef that it was still there, and it proved what an inept and superficial job the detectives did investigating his mauling. He stood up, stretched his back, and listened for a moment to the sound of peaceful wind chimes in someone's yard nearby.

He decided to use the back door to enter. When he entered, he found himself in the kitchen. The place where Boots died. There was a window above the sink overlooking the backyard. Boots would have been looking out it while he was cooking. He could still see Figaro's food dishes near his dog house from the window. He removed some crime scene photocopies from his pocket and crouched down to examine the cheap linoleum floor for scratches. He noticed numerous scratch lines etched into the linoleum towards the front room area, consistent with nails dragging on the floor. The Pismo Beach detectives did not bother to take photos or videotape these scratch marks. His crouching turned to a crawl as he studied the linoleum near the cupboards, hoping to find any hair fibers that were not collected the evening of the pit bull attack.

He stood up in front of the refrigerator and removed a photo attached by a promotional magnate for a local cable company. The photo was of Boots's dog Figaro with a red bandanna tied around his neck. Van Cleef noticed the dog's tags; the metallic dog bone type with the owner's number and dog's name stamped on them. There also appeared to be another strange looking collar on the dog. *Why two?* San Luis Obispo County Animal Control that picked up the dead dog after the attack claimed the collar and tags were missing. No mention of either of them was in the report.

Van Cleef did not think that they came off in the attack. At this point, he was still uncertain Figaro killed his master.

A door slammed shut in the other room and startled him.

Van Cleef froze. He looked up from the photo, gently placed it inside his suit jacket pocket, and pulled out his .38 revolver. He turned his back on the refrigerator and crept along the kitchen wall until he could peek around the corner into the front room where he heard the door slam.

He watched a large figure with a hoodie hurdle over the front yard picket fence. The parted Venetian blinds were still swaying back and forth in the front window. The suspect must have bumped into them or brushed by them on his way out. A loud crash of garbage cans reverberated outside.

Van Cleef moved quickly through the front room and ran outside after the suspect

He noticed the large, dark figure hightailing it down Wilmar Street and then cutting between the nearby houses heading over to Franklin Street, the street behind Boots's residence.

Dogs were barking and growling at the noise and disruption.

Van Cleef pursued him on Franklin Street and was gaining on him. *The sonofabitch was lightning fast*, Van Cleef thought, as it had been a while since he had a good foot chase.

He watched the suspect make a sharp turn left and cut back in the direction of Wilmar Street. The suspect jumped on top of a BMW parked four houses down and leapt over the iron gate the Beamer was parked in front of.

An attractive blonde woman talking on her cell phone,

dressed like a Real Estate agent, emerged from her house screaming, "Hey asshole—" and something about a car wash as Van Cleef ran past her. Van Cleef followed the suspect, running a short distance behind and catapulting himself over the fence. He almost lost his balance, but regained his momentum and continued sprinting after him.

He caught sight of the suspect heading towards the end of the street and down to the beach.

There was a wooden staircase at the end of the road that led down to the ocean. The iconic Pismo Beach Pier could be seen in the distance.

Van Cleef called for backup on his cell phone while he ran down the wooden staircase, intermittently bumping past beachgoers, residents, and civilians. Most of them were oblivious or slow to react to what was going on around them.

He jumped off the last three stairs and picked up his speed running towards the shoreline.

He noticed the prints of the suspect's shoes were large. The suspect was now running through the edge of the tide along the shoreline and through the ocean tide washing in.

There was a scattered crowd of people milling around on the beach. The suspect kept zig-zagging in and out of the crowd as if he were in the Super Bowl. *Damn this bastard is fast, and he isn't stupid*, Van Cleef mumbled to himself, running out of breath.

There was now a good one-hundred yards between the suspect and Van Cleef when he vanished into the crowd.

Van Cleef lost the foot chase and the suspect. He was winded and sweating profusely, and he felt cramping in his gut. He slowed down to catch his breath and decided to backtrack and work with what he had: footprints in the sand and maybe the possibility that the suspect could've dropped something along the way during the chase.

20

"**THE SUSPECT WAS SMART TO RUN** along the shoreline and through the crowd," Van Cleef commented to the crime lab technician that was taking shoe impressions near the bottom of the wooden stairs that led down to the beach. The stairs and surrounding sand path the suspect ran through was now barricaded with crime scene tape.

The crime technician began pouring the dental stone plaster inside the large shoeprint around a metal frame. Dental stone is a common plaster that is used in sand, snow, and outdoor conditions where shoeprint evidence was challenging. The lab tech methodically mixed up the powder into what resembled pancake batter. Van Cleef interrupted him.

"Can you please spray those prints with shellac or something before you cast the mold?" Van Cleef asked, looking over his shoulder. The crime lab technician seemed a bit put off or insulted by Van Cleef's request, but he knew Van Cleef was right to ask. He didn't want the shoe impression deformed and this extra step would help preserve the print.

The crime scene photographer noted the large print size of the shoe in the ruler next to the print. Van Cleef also interrupted him and insisted that he use a tripod, a 45-degree angle, and to shoot at several different points to get the best results. The photographer agreed it was a good idea and followed orders.

The suspect left a large, heavy, and deep print. Between the impression and his encounter with the suspect, Van Cleef estimated his suspect to be about 240 lbs. and at least 6'3". The sole of the print did not have a logo of a brand; however, it did have flat ridges. The suspect placed most of his weight on the balls of his feet, and the stride between steps would also indicate a tall man.

The Pismo Beach police were busy questioning witnesses that had seen the suspect race past them, or were either knocked or pushed out of the way by him. No one gave them much to go on other than that he was a large, tan guy. Athletic attire. Hoodie, shades, dark clothing. The Pismo police and detectives were terse and were wrapping up their questions when they ran into witnesses reversing the questions and asking more questions than the police.

Van Cleef requested an officer meet him over at Ed Boots's residence to examine any signs of forced entry. It became apparent to Van Cleef that the officers shared a mutual disdain for Ed Boots.

On his way back over to Boots's residence, he made a quick stop at the house on Wilmar Street where the woman encountered the fleeing suspect running over her car and through her yard. It turned out she was not a real estate agent, but a local divorce and family law attorney. Van Cleef noticed she was vigorously scrubbing off her BMW in her driveway, still upset by the incident and erasing what evidence the suspect may have left behind.

Van Cleef approached her and said, "Ma'am?"

She looked up from her car with an agitated look as if Van Cleef were a panhandler.

"Do you want something?" she yelled in a defensive tone over the running water.

"Yes," Van Cleef said, approaching her with his detective badge out. She seemed skeptical of the badge and Van Cleef.

"I was the person chasing the man through your yard today."

"Were you also the one that left three large dents in the roof and hood of my car?" she asked, turning off the hose and tossing it on the side of the house. She walked over to get a closer look at Van Cleef and his badge.

"No," Van Cleef said. "That would have been the suspect I'm looking for."

"Well, you won't find him here. He came charging through here like a goddamn bull in a China shop. I had just gotten my car detailed, and now look at it. He ruined it. I swear... you can't have anything nice anymore—"

She threw the rag on top of the hood of the car, all worked up and perspiring now, her heels clicking on the cement as she walked around the car examining every detail. She sprang open her trunk and took out some additional cleaning products like Armor All and a Microfiber car mitt and kept complaining and carrying-on to herself.

Van Cleef felt she was exaggerating. The dents were minor dings. She did not care that Van Cleef was a detective.

"Did you happen to get a good look at him by any chance?" Van Cleef asked.

"Yes, I did," she said.

Van Cleef took out his notebook.

"He looked like an asshole."

"Could you be more specific?" he asked, ready to put away his notebook.

"Okay, a big asshole."

"Do you mean large?"

"Yeah, large. Big head. Big body, and big feet— a big Gorilla that damaged my car. Who is going to pay for this damage?"

"You have insurance."

"You want me to file an insurance claim for your mistake?"

"Miss," Van Cleef said in a calming tone, "I think we're getting off on the wrong foot."

"Wrong foot?" she mocked, with a hateful look in her eyes. "The wrong foot is all over my car and he'll pay for this— what is he, a rapist on the loose? Burglar? Homeless person?"

Van Cleef was polite and said, "I don't know who he is yet, that's why I was hoping you could help me out."

He noticed her trash cans were lying on their sides in front of her gate. He also noticed there appeared to be blood on the gate.

"I'd like to send an officer over and the crime lab to see if—"

"Crime lab?" she said, cutting him off. "I have clients booked throughout the day and don't have time, nor do I want to get involved—"

Van Cleef passed her his card and said, "Please don't touch that gate. I promise I'll be right back."

She noted "Homicide Detective" on his card and did a 360 with her bad attitude.

"Detective Van Cleef," she called out in a sweeter tone of voice.

Van Cleef turned around.

"Sorry we got off on the wrong foot," she said. "My name is Debra Woods—"

Van Cleef walked away raising his hand in the air in a dismissive gesture. He said, "Please, Miss Woods, don't touch the gate or anything else. I'll be right back in two minutes."

Debra Woods stood in the driveway with the garden hose in one hand and Detective Van Cleef's card in the other. The water was running down the pavement in the direction of the street. He figured her to be the type that could care less about conserving water during California droughts. She muttered something else to his back about her precious BMW. He ignored her comment.

Van Cleef walked back to his car. Popped open his trunk. Grabbed a couple of items and returned, as promised, in under two minutes flat. He passed Debra Woods, still angry standing in her driveway, rag in hand.

Miss Woods watched Van Cleef put on a pair of latex gloves and swab her fence. He then placed the sample in a small vile.

"Excuse me, Det—?"

"Van Cleef."

"Van Cleef," she said, her voice trembling. "What if that gorilla comes back to kill me?"

"He won't be back here, Miss Woods."

"How do you know?"

"He's not after you?"

"But how do you know?" She said, not convinced.

"It's my job to know these things. He won't be coming back."

Van Cleef walked away once again and then stopped and turned around, "The lab and police officer will be over here soon. Please try to remember any details you can about the suspect."

21

VAN CLEEF MET THE PISMO BEACH crime lab over at Ed Boots's residence. They were finishing up.

"That was fast," he said to the crime technician that was examining the door locks.

"No signs of forced entry," the technician said, standing up from a crouched position in front of the deadbolt. He was a heavyset Hispanic man with a neatly trimmed mustache and sensitive eyes. Van Cleef heard his knees crack when he rose to greet him.

"No picks, prints, nothing?" Van Cleef asked.

"Nope," the lab technician said, adjusting his pants around his fat waist.

"Windows?" Van Cleef asked.

"They are locked," the lab technician said. "The back door was open. That's how he got in is my guess. Maybe used a bump key... I see it all the time."

He closed his toolkit and walked with Van Cleef through the kitchen and to the backdoor.

Van Cleef did not want to tell the tech that he entered through the backdoor and that the backdoor was locked when he arrived. Did Boots know the suspect? Did he have a key?

"I'd like to get some additional shoe impressions from inside," Van Cleef said. "Is the other crime scene technician on his way?"

"Yes," he said. "We are short-staffed, so the technicians at the beach said they will be here after they finish up."

Van Cleef felt they were more than short staffed, they were short sighted and deprioritizing the situation, or stalling for whatever reason.

The crime lab technician shook his head as he stared down at the kitchen floor and asked, "Is this where it happened?"

"You mean where I saw the suspect?"

"No, I mean the deadly dog attack."

"Oh?" Van Cleef asked, surprised by his question.

"Yes. The dog attack," the crime technician said, adjusting his crooked pants up around his waist. "I would never own a pit bull. You can't turn your back on them. Can't trust them. That was his last mistake. Glad they shot the dog. I told my wife that I have a rule: never to own a pet with a bigger mouth or appetite than mine."

Van Cleef did not comment. He was interested in finding out what the suspect was after and how he got into Ed Boots's house. He started in the front room where the suspect fled from and began going through drawers, closets, and Ed Boots's desk for clues. What would the suspect be interested in stealing?

Boots had a few framed pictures in cheap discount store frames. Lots of photos with Figaro the pit bull. This dog didn't look aggressive to him. He stopped and smiled at a movie poster Boots had hanging in his hallway. It was from the Clint Eastwood movie, *The Eiger Sanction*. There was a caption on the poster that read: **HIS LIFELINE –Held by the Assassin he Hunted.** Van Cleef smiled as he remembered some of their movie conversations about Eastwood's films, and he recalled one in particular about *The Eiger Sanction*," because Boots investigated the horrible death of Jack Cassidy— Eastwood's co-star in the movie.

A neighbor pulled up and got out of her car, an older model Ford Escort. Van Cleef referenced a note from his notebook. He spoke out loud to himself, "Good afternoon, Mrs. Hackett."

Van Cleef ceased his search. He stepped outside to greet her. He said, "Mrs. Hackett?"

Mrs. Hackett put her hand to her heart and nearly jumped out of her skin. She said, "You scared the living daylights out of me."

"I'm sorry, Mrs. Hackett. I'm Detective Leo Van Cleef from LAPD Homicide. Do you mind if I ask you a few questions?"

"Certainly," she said, fishing her house keys from her purse and opening the door for him. "Come inside, please. It's been so quiet around here— You'll have to excuse me about the mess... I live alone."

Van Cleef entered the house. The place was not in any detectable mess that Van Cleef could see, maybe a stray magazine here or there, or a single coffee cup on the table from this morning. She had faded morning makeup and a creased suit that she probably purchased over a decade ago. Her shoes would suggest she was on her feet a lot. They were well-worn and several steps away from the dumpster. She was one of the unable-to-retire seniors that would be working until the day she died.

Van Cleef got to the point, "You're an RN over at the Spyglass Drive Wellness & Retirement Home, is that correct?"

"Yes, been there since 1982. Would you like some coffee?"

"Sure," Van Cleef said to be polite. He expected her to

be a Folgers gal.

"Did you know your neighbor Ed Boots very well?"

He was wrong about the Folgers. She was scooping out coffee from a Maxwell House can and opening every cupboard in the kitchen in search of an extra coffee cup.

"Like I told the police officers and detectives," Ms. Hackett said as if sharing a secret, "Mr. Boots was a very private person. Not unfriendly, just private. Y'know the old saying, 'Good fences—'"

"Make good neighbors," Van Cleef said, completing the old cliché.

"He was always polite and waved hi whenever I did see him."

Van Cleef was referencing the detective's notes from the Boots crime scene. He asked, "Did you have any issues with his dog?"

"Issues?" she asked, poking her head out from the kitchen.

"I mean that it was a pit bull, or any complaints in general that neighbors sometimes have, like the dog barks a lot, or that it was aggressive, those kinds of issues."

She stopped rummaging through the cupboards, turned towards Van Cleef and said, "See, that's the thing I told the detectives. That dog was so quiet, I did not ever even hear him bark. Frankly, when I found out he had a dog, I was shocked because the dog was as quiet as a cat. I'm not a 'dog person' myself, but when I found out it was one of those pit bulls— Then to find out that that dog—"

She turned her attention back to the coffee pot and turned it on.

"You were gone when the incident occurred?"

"Yes, we had a retirement party for one of our staff members, so I got home later than usual. That was around 8:30 that night and there were police, fire trucks, and paramedics all over the place when I arrived home. You have to understand this is a pretty peaceful community and usually very quiet."

Van Cleef noted Mrs. Hackett's consistent statements in the report. He did not expect to uncover any new insights, but was more interested in the personal observations of Ed Boots and his dog. "Did you know what had happened to Mr. Boots when you arrived home?"

"At first not," she said, handing him his Maxwell House coffee in a faded old Catalina Island tourist coffee mug. She set down cream and sugar in front of him, but Van Cleef always drank his black. She continued with her story, "At first I thought Ed had a heart attack and nobody really knew, but then I saw the Animal Control vehicle outside and for the first time ever, I heard his dog barking like I had never heard him bark before. Then I heard a shot fired, then it was quiet... and well... no more barking. "

"But you didn't see the dog?"

"No sir," she said, without any doubt in her mind while sipping her Maxwell House like it was '*good to the last drop.*' Van Cleef could not get past the first gulp; the coffee was weak and acidic. More water than coffee and might as well have been decaf. He hoped she did not make coffee for her co-workers.

"So, to be clear," Van Cleef said, standing up from the small floral printed loveseat. "That was the first time ever that you heard Ed Boots's dog Figaro bark, is that correct?"

"Yes, barking and whimpering like it was hurt or distressed."

Van Cleef noticed that the beach crime lab tech pulled up outside in Boots's driveway during their conversation. It was the same shoe impression guy that gave him a slight attitude at the beach that was now lumbering up the driveway. He thanked Mrs. Hackett for the coffee and the interview and asked one more question on his way out, "Did you ever happen to notice any unusual guests at Mr.

Boots's house, or anyone that sticks out in your mind?

She took another commercial-style sip of her rancid Maxwell House and thought carefully as she swallowed. She said, "Aside from the usual postman, UPS or FedEx guy, or an occasional repairman… like I said, he kept to himself. It's funny, I always felt safe with him around—someone down the street later told me that he was a detective, and then I also read it in the newspaper and heard it on the news to know it was true. But I could've sworn he told me he was a retired garbage man."

Van Cleef held back from laughing as he walked out the door. That was how he remembered Ed Boots. Always putting people on and humoring himself. He was never honest with outsiders about his real work as a detective. He would lie with a straight poker face. His comment about his job to Mrs. Hackett was also typical cynicism for the way Boots felt about detective work and being forced into retirement. Garbage man was appropriate for him. He loved Eastwood's *Dirty Harry* character. The department even got him an autographed photo of Clint as *Dirty Harry* that Boots had proudly displayed in a steel frame on his desk. He always liked to quote Clint's famous line from *Magnum Force*: "Man's got to know his limitations." He once heard him tell a woman at a party that he was an Animal Control Specialist for the city of L.A., which was sort of true when it came to criminals, but on another note, Van Cleef always found it interesting when jokes became reality with people. Often the thing that people would joke about could be a factor in their death.

Life's irony.

In Boots's case, "Animal Control" was a joke that had a strange punch line at the end of Boots's life.

Van Cleef stood in the driveway and paused for a moment. He heard a dog barking in the distance and the peaceful sound of wind chimes once again. The aftertaste of bad coffee and lingering questions were still bothering him.

He sensed someone staring at his back. He glanced over his shoulder to see Mrs. Hackett quickly moving away from the window trying to avoid detection, the blinds still swaying.

He wondered for a brief moment why Mrs. Hackett wasn't a 'dog person.' *Was she ever?* So many dogs in the city need homes. So many lonely people.

He got his briefcase out of his car and walked back over to Ed Boots's house. *Yes, the neighborhood would be less safe now without a guy, or an old watchdog, like Boots.*

One thing was clear to Van Cleef: Whoever killed Boots knew when Mrs. Hackett was gone, knew the neighborhood and people's patterns, and evidently returned back to the house to retrieve something.

22

VAN CLEEF RECEIVED AN INCOMING call from an 805 area code. He answered. The caller was Monique, Dr. Plotkin's maid. She asked if she could meet privately with him. He agreed and suggested Paradise Cove on PCH in Malibu near the Plotkin's residence. He could hit it on the way back from Pismo.

He continued to search Ed Boots's home for anything out of place. It was possible that the suspect was a burglar, but none of the typical items in the house were disturbed. Ed Boots also had several firearms in the house: a .357 Magnum (yeah, he loved *Dirty Harry*), a Glock, and a rifle. Van Cleef found it odd that the suspect left them behind. That was atypical if he was there to just burglarize Boots, or was it that Van Cleef caught him in the act and didn't give him enough time to make off with the weapons? One cabinet drawer in the hallway caught Van Cleef's attention. It was slightly open and out of joint. Aside from a few bedraggled hand towels, it was empty and uneventful. Van Cleef called out to the shoe print technician and asked him to try his best to lift some impressions from the hall carpet to see if they were consistent with the prints on the beach to link the suspect. The lab tech grumbled something about having to go get his electromagnetic lifting device out of his vehicle.

Van Cleef shook his head as he referenced a copy of a report from his briefcase. It figured this was the same lazy lab tech that mishandled the original print evidence the night of Ed Boots's death. This guy really needed to find a new line of work, Van Cleef thought. Maybe with a pest control company or something less demanding.

Van Cleef's cell phone rang again. This time it was the somewhat familiar, but barely recognizable voice of his bedridden partner, Jose Espinoza.

"Leo?" Espinoza asked in a strained, hoarse voice, almost like a Mafioso.

"Is this Don Corleone?" Van Cleef asked, knowing it was his partner.

Espinoza tried to laugh, but choked and coughed instead. "Any luck with the dog or our murder suspect?" he asked.

"Well, he hasn't bit me on the ass yet, but I'm still optimistic."

"Give him— it time, sooner or later they'll step in shit."

"You're right, maybe he just did."

Van Cleef walked out through the kitchen and to the backyard for privacy. Boots did have a nice wood fence surrounding his whole yard. Good fences made good neighbors.

"How are you feeling, buddy?" Van Cleef asked.

"Horrible," he hacked, sneezing over the phone. "Anyway, I had an epiphany about the case."

"Great, lay it on me," Van Cleef said, as he ambled around Boots's backyard.

"So, I'm bored out of my mind. Sick as a dog. Lakers are losing—"

"José—"

"I know, I know," Espinoza said. "I know you don't give a shit about sports. I'll get to the point. So, my wife keeps telling me to turn off the sports and get some rest, but I couldn't sleep, so I thought I could binge watch something on Netflix, and then I came across the old *Columbo* TV show. So I read the description and there is this one episode that caught my eye about a dog.

"Columbo's dog?"

"No, the one about the killer Doberman dogs."

That made Van Cleef laugh when he thought about his pampered pooch at home. He recalled the episode with total recall, which always amazed Espinoza.

"You're referring to '*How to Dial a Murder*,'" Van Cleef said, "with a young Kim Cattrall where the psychologist kills his best friend because he's having an affair with his wife, and he owns the two killer Dobermans: Laurel and Hardy. You know, it was that episode that inspired me to name my dogs Bogart and Bacall. Anyway, that's another story— go on..."

Van Cleef walked along the edge of the inside of the fence as he listened, checking the ground and grass for any evidence.

"Your memory astounds me," Espinoza said, suppressing another sneeze. "Well, that episode got me thinking about our mysterious, missing 'Giant Hound' and the subject of conditioning and command words."

"And you think our killer's master used a word like 'Rosebud,' like in the episode, to call off the dog?"

Espinoza was disappointed that Van Cleef stole his payoff. "Sure, why not?" he said, covering the phone as he coughed.

"Not a bad theory, Espinoza, but in our murder the dog was a considerable distance from his master from what we can tell so far."

"Yes, but if you remember, so was the psychologist in the episode, and he used a phone. He got the victim to use the word on the phone—"

"There's no phone booth on the beach, Jose, or anywhere for that matter these days—"

"C'mon Leo, you're always razzin' me. I'm just saying, maybe our killer got Sheila Evans to say the kill word on her cell or used some kind of transmitter or something on the dog—"

Their phone conversation was interrupted by Espinoza's wife yelling at him in the background to get some rest and hang up the phone.

Van Cleef noticed the lab technician looking for him out the back kitchen window. Van Cleef thanked Espinoza for his input and urged him to get over his influenza and back to work. He wanted to get Dennis Overstreet out of Homicide Special and back to Malibu where he could deal with occasional celebrities and privileged offspring bored by affluenza.

Van Cleef thought about the Columbo episode and blurted out loud to himself, "Rosebud," imitating Peter Falk. He wrapped up his search and headed out to Paradise Cove.

As he drove up the coast, Peter Falk came to mind and he remembered meeting him one time at a Los Angeles book signing at Book Soup on Sunset Strip where Peter was promoting his book "Just One More Thing." Peter Falk was a true legend and a real funny guy. He liked Van Cleef's sense of humor, and many of the detectives had great respect for Columbo.

The irony was that years later Van Cleef would lay his own dog to rest at the Los Angeles Pet Memorial Park in Calabasas where the late Peter Falk's dogs were also resting in peace, and Peter's widow, Shera, was the Board President of the cemetery. Van Cleef wanted to stop by there, but there was no time today.

He would make the time after he wrapped up this case.

23

PARADISE COVE IN MALIBU was a beach café less than three miles from where Sheila Evans-Plotkin was murdered. It took Van Cleef nearly two and a half hours to get there. He apologized for being late.

Van Cleef sat outside with Monique on the plastic chairs with umbrella tables where they could speak in private, listen to the surf, and watch the seagulls scavenge for scraps of food on the private beach and cove. Monique kept her sunglasses on and her hands in her lap underneath the table. They ordered coffee for openers. Van Cleef broke the ice by talking TV and films. He informed Monique that they shot some famous television shows there like *Rockford Files*, *Baywatch*, and *Gidget*. Monique only knew of *Baywatch* with Pamela Anderson. After moments of silence and people watching, she began the conversation. "I really liked Ms. Plotkin," she said, gazing down into her coffee cup.

"She was very well-liked from what I understand," Van

Cleef said.

"She was a very nice lady. Always good to me."

Van Cleef nodded and listened, giving her plenty of time to reflect.

"They were both very good to me," Monique said.

"You mean Dr. Plotkin too, when you say both?"

"Yes."

The waitress came by and asked if they were ready to order. Van Cleef asked if they could have a little more time. She told them to take all the time they needed since it wasn't very busy at 3 pm in the afternoon. Van Cleef could tell she was more interested in chit-chatting with her co-workers and checking her Android phone.

"In some ways," Monique said, "I sometimes think he treated me better than her."

"In what ways do you mean?"

Monique looked over her shoulder and across the restaurant, paranoid as if Dr. Plotkin or Gordon Goldstone was going to show up and silence her.

"Well, not always," she said. "But on many occasions, he would buy me things and tell me not to tell her about it. Expensive things. Jewelry from trips they would take. He would sneak gifts to me and keep it secret. At first, I refused, but then I figured I had earned them over the years. He said they were just gifts. He would say Ms. Plotkin would get mad if she found out about it and not to ever tell her about them or else I would be fired."

Van Cleef was skeptical and wondered what she did for those gifts and if they were having an affair behind Sheila's back.

"You see, I came to this country with no money," she said. "When I got hired by the doctor, it was like I won the lottery or something, do you understand?"

Van Cleef nodded and asked, "So, how long did you work for the Plotkins?"

"Four years this past August."

"Okay, about four years, four months."

"Yes, something like that— I feel bad for even thinking this—"

Monique broke down. Van Cleef passed her a napkin. She motioned that it was okay and removed her sunglasses while dabbing her eyes with a Kleenex from her purse. She must've worn waterproof mascara. Her large doe eyes were staring at him, now glassy. She continued, "I feel bad to even think of myself at this time. It's selfish, but I am worried now that I am going to lose what I have."

"Why would you worry about that?"

"I don't have any money saved— I have a child back in Mexico that, well, I've been sending money home to over the years—"

Van Cleef got the picture. Dr. Plotkin and Monique were using each other. The question was, was Sheila Plotkin aware of it?

Van Cleef knew Monique was censoring her thoughts and words. Omitting details, as people being interviewed by detectives often do. Worried about saying the wrong thing or saying too much.

"It's okay, Monique," Van Cleef said in a reassuring and calm tone. "You are not a suspect in this case and will not lose anything, or your situation, by speaking with me. It's confidential.

She continued, "Dr. Plotkin is very good at what he does— his work," she said. "The best. He made me look like a movie star. I get a lot of attention now, more than ever before. I was such an ugly duckling when I was growing up, you should've seen me—" She laughed, thinking about herself and then got real serious and said, "He fixed that part of me."

"What part was that?" Van Cleef asked, leaning forward.

"He fixed what was inside."

"Your self-esteem."

"Yes, my self-esteem," Monique said, enunciating the word, emphasizing the "e."

"You're a beautiful woman."

She took the compliment, flirting with Van Cleef. He noticed her examining his wedding ring.

"Can I ask you a personal question, Mr. Van Cleef?"

"Sure, go ahead."

"What is your wife like?"

Van Cleef was rarely asked that question, so it caught him off guard. He was flustered and said, "Well, she is a wonderful person."

"I'll bet she's beautiful?"

"Inside and out. We've been together for a long time and are still happily married whenever we get a chance to see each other."

"Do you think it's wrong to change your appearance?"

Van Cleef smiled, sat back and said, "Only if you're wanted by the law."

Monique did not get his dry wit and attempt to lighten up the situation. She looked at the ocean and her eyes welled up. She repeated once again, "I really liked Ms. Plotkin and can't believe this happened to her... it's horrible—"

"It is horrible. Do you have any idea who might've wanted to do that to her?"

"No," Monique said with a firm undertone. "Never... everyone loved Sheila. I don't know why anyone would've wanted to do that to her."

"Do you think her husband—"

"Never," she said again, emphasizing the word.

"Did you ever use her SUV, or did anyone else?"

Monique thought for a few minutes and she again said, "No," in a firm tone.

"I want to see her killer locked up, Monique. Anything

you can tell me, even if you think it's trivial, might be of help to me."

There it was. That decisive moment in an interview where the detective breaks through and reaches inside, or the interviewee decides it's time to confess.

"Well, Dr. Plotkin was not alone in San Diego," she said in a quiet voice.

Van Cleef played dumb and said, "You mean, he was with his attorney?"

"No," she said. "He was with his office manager. He took his office manager with him."

Van Cleef already knew this, but played along and took out his notebook and pen and was prepared to write it down.

"You won't say I said anything will you?" she asked innocently. There was that paranoid look again as she looked around the restaurant.

"No, you have my word," Van Cleef said.

"Her name is Lisa."

"Lisa Comstock?"

"Yes, Lisa Comstock," Monique said, surprised and slightly angry. "You spoke with her?"

"Yes, earlier today."

"She does not know that I am talking with you?"

"No Monique, this is a private conversation between you and me."

"And Dr. Plotkin does not know that we are talking?"

"No Monique, Dr. Plotkin does not know."

"His Lisa does not like me and told me so to my face," she said, getting angry.

"You said, 'his Lisa,'" Van Cleef said, writing it down on his notepad.

"Sorry, it's my English."

"Your English is fine."

"I meant to say, this Lisa."

"I understand." Van Cleef said. "Why do you suppose Lisa Comstock does not like you?"

"I don't know because she doesn't know me, and I never did anything to her. But Mrs. Plotkin definitely did not like her, and I know why she did not."

Van Cleef waited for her to fill in more blanks, but then Monique pushed away from the table, upset. She ripped open her purse and pulled out a fistful of keys.

"Did I say something wrong, Monique?"

Monique stood up from the table. Van Cleef stood up from his seat and said, "Monique, you asked me to meet with you today. Is there something you would like to tell me?"

"I guess I just wanted you to know that the doctor has his problems and he is under a lot of pressure, but I believe he did love his wife—"

Monique was being respectful and did not know that Lisa Comstock had already broken the news to him earlier that day about the Plotkins' pending separation. She was also trying to say in a roundabout way that Lisa Comstock was the cause of their pending separation and troubles. Monique had told him enough without saying much. Dr. Plotkin was philandering with two women, maybe more, but Van Cleef still did not believe he was responsible for his wife's murder.

He watched Monique pass through a crowd of people as if she were someone else. She was more than Dr. Plotkin's maid or plaything; someday she would come to realize this.

24

VAN CLEEF CUT ACROSS to Sunset Boulevard from Pacific Coast Highway. He figured the long and winding road would be less congested and give him time to process his conversation with Monique. He thought about the strange love life of Dr. Plotkin and Sheila Evans-Plotkin's corpse at the morgue. His mind was also still reeling on the recent incident in Pismo at Boots's residence.

His cell phone startled him. It was the forensics lab tech from UC Davis, the only qualified and accredited lab in the country that dealt with animal DNA profiling.

"Detective Van Cleef," she asked, in a voice as soothing as the drive. "This is Gloria Tannenbaum, the Director of the lab."

"Nice to meet you, Gloria. Are the lab results in?"

"Yes, and the conclusive result is that the dog you are looking for is not a pit bull of any kind."

Van Cleef kept his eyes on the road and continued to listen. She confirmed what Frank Nelson had speculated back at the Seven Grand meeting. It was another type of dog. A much larger breed.

"So what type of dog are we hunting?" Van Cleef asked.

"It's a Pakistani Bully Kutta breed."

A Harley Davidson motorcycle blasted by Van Cleef and cut in front of his car. He hit the brakes and then sped back up.

"Sorry, I didn't catch the second part... a Bully what?"

"Pakistani Bully Kutta, or PBK breed for short. It's like a large Bulldogge. Typically found in India and Pakistan. Highly aggressive. We also managed to extract the DNA and saliva from the piece of wood that you sent us."

"The break stick?"

"Yes, the break stick," she said. "And that also confirmed our findings that it was a Pakistani Bully Kutta breed. We'll have the results faxed over to you and send the hard copies in the mail."

"That's great. Thank you, Gloria."

"You're welcome. Anything we can do to help."

Van Cleef had an odd thought and hesitated to ask another question for a moment, then asked the question anyway. "Do you ever test dog feces for DNA?" he asked.

"Absolutely. You'd be surprised just how accurate we can trace it to the breed. Not to get too graphic, but after the dog feces passes out of their colon, the dog's DNA is found on the epithelial cells. Why?" she asked. "Did you also find canine feces at the crime scene? Because we can also process—"

Van Cleef laughed uncomfortably as he thought about Serpico, the miscreant whom he had suspected of leaving the large piles of dog crap on his lawn. That conversation could wait until another time, he thought. But he had a reliable source now and could settle the shit on his lawn mystery as a bonus. He politely said, "No, we didn't find any canine feces at the crime scene, but it's good to know for future use in the event that we ever do."

He hung up with Gloria, enjoying the scenic drive back to West L.A.. He was passing through Pacific Palisades now.

Frank Nelson from the ASPCA was dead right that day at the Seven Grand when he and his partner, Cheyenne Devine, reviewed the crime scene photos and he remarked that the dog that killed Sheila Evans was bigger than a Pit. Van Cleef muttered again to himself the famous Sherlock Holmes line from *The Hounds of Baskerville*, "They are indeed *'the footprints of a gigantic hound.'*"

He dialed Frank Nelson's cell. Frank answered.

"Hey Frank," Van Cleef said, "We got the DNA results back from the lab, and you were right. Our murder weapon was not a pit bull."

"Lay it on me," Frank Nelson said. Van Cleef could hear a door close on Frank's line.

"It appears we are looking for a Pakistani Bully Kutta or PBK breed, so now tell me everything you know about our latest suspect."

Van Cleef could hear hesitation on the other end of the phone. Nelson said, "Well, some call the dog 'the Beast from the East' because of its roots in Pakistan and powerful game hunting abilities. Like the pit bull, this breed is confusing because of labeling or mislabeling: Bully Gull Terr, Gull Dang, Pakistani Bull Dog, Pakistani Bully Kutta, or PBKs are a mix of three-quarters Gull Terr and one quarter Bully Kutta. This breed was also used for dogfighting. Great protector. Extremely dangerous dog for the wrong owner or criminal mind. Not a domestic dog or what you'd exactly call a family pet. Bigger than a Rottweiler and much more aggressive. Weighs about 140 pounds. About 40 inches in height. The good news is that they are not as common as pit bulls in the U.S., and that should enable us to track a breeder or suspect easier."

"That's solid info, Frank. Appreciate it," Van Cleef said.

Van Cleef swerved away from another driver in a blue Toyota Prius that almost side-swiped him by drifting into his lane.

Frank Nelson could hear tires squeal over the phone. He said, "I'd better let you go before you get into an accident."

Van Cleef said, "Thanks. Yeah, see what you can find out about any local breeders, and I'll also want a sample of the blood from the wood pit you mentioned that was found at the FBI sting in Lancaster. I'll have our guys run it and see if we get any hits."

"You got it," Frank said. "I'll call and coordinate with the lab and we'll narrow it down. They maintain the canine DNA database, and we work with them all the time on animal cruelty and dogfighting cases."

"Oh, and there is one other favor I have to ask of you," Van Cleef said.

"Let me take a wild guess," Nelson said. "Does it involve Agent Slezick from the FBI?"

"You're good Frank, very good," Van Cleef said. "Yes, please keep our 'Gigantic Hound' out of his gunsights until Sherlock here gets confirmation of what exactly we are dealing with."

"Sure thing," Frank said, quoting from the famous book by Sir Arthur Conan Doyle, "*The world is full of obvious things which nobody by any chance ever observes.*"

Van Cleef disconnected and continued his blissful drive with a nice flow of light traffic until he approached the 405 near the Getty Center. The blue Toyota Prius that cut him off was now in front of him stuck at a traffic light.

He took a deep breath and told himself to relax. One pair of footprints had now been identified, the others would follow, and the proverbial "other shoe" would drop on the real killer.

25

VAN CLEEF WAS JUST ABOUT to crawl into bed when his cell phone rang. He recognized the caller. It was Lieutenant Carruthers from Homicide Special.

"Leo," Carruthers said in a disturbed tone of voice. "You spoke with Dr. Plotkin today?"

"Yes, why? What's up?"

"Well, it looks like you won't be speaking with Dr. Plotkin anymore."

Van Cleef's mind instantly reverted to his interview with him earlier that day at his office in Beverly Hills. The doctor warned him to back off and that he would be dealing with his attorney from now on. But now that would not be the case.

"He's dead," Carrurthers informed him.

Van Cleef slowly sat down on the edge of his bed, rubbing the tension in his neck with his left hand.

"I don't understand, I just interviewed—" he said.

"I know," Carruthers said. "Goldstone, his attorney, is already claiming we put the gun to his head. He was found dead, apparently from a self-inflicted gunshot to the head.

The Beverly Hills police are at his office right now."

"Where did they find him?" Van Cleef asked, still not wrapping his mind around the situation.

"Parking lot in his car."

"I'll head over there right now."

Carruthers informed him that Dennis Overstreet was already there with BHPD Chief, Paul Kuznick, and would meet him on site. Van Cleef informed Carruthers that he did not want Overstreet interviewing anyone or talking to the media until he got there to supervise.

"I think Overstreet has spent too much time in the office, Leo," Lieutenant Carruthers informed him. "I want you to show him the ropes until Espinoza gets back, is that clear?"

Van Cleef said it was crystal clear, paying him lip service. He hung up the phone.

He slowly rose as his wife rolled over to the empty side of the bed, reaching for her husband. She muttered in a sleepy voice, "You got home late again... Don't tell me you're leaving already—"

Bacall, their Doberman, jumped up and took his place in bed.

"You have your own bed, Bacall," Van Cleef said to his Doberman, who was now sleeping in his place. Bacall ignored him.

He kissed his wife on her forehead and whispered, "Sorry, honey—"

He fixed his tie and left the house.

Another sleepless night.

26

"**SORRY TO GET YOU OUT OF BED, LEO,**" Beverly Hills Police Chief, Paul Kuznick, said as he greeted Van Cleef at the crime scene while pushing back reporters and lookie-loos from the roll-up gate at the entrance of the monthly parking structure.

"It's okay, Paul," Van Cleef said, signing the crime scene logbook, entering his badge number, and ducking under the yellow tape. "You made my Doberman happy. She's keeping my bed warm until I get home." He patted BHPD Chief Kuznick on the back and shook his hand. They had worked together and coordinated efforts back in 2010 when the well-known celebrity publicist Ronni Chasen was murdered and more recently when the owner of a Beverly Hills Rolex store was robbed and the suspects got away.

"How's Claudia?" Chief Kuznick asked.

"She's still keeping the other side of the bed warm."

"How's Bogart these days? He's gotta be—"

Van Cleef tightened his lips and shook his head, implying that Bogart, his dear canine, was no longer 'these days.'

"Sorry, Leo. Very sorry to hear... I didn't hear —"

"It's okay. Thank you," Van Cleef said, walking together to the side of Dr. Plotkin's lime green Jaguar, their footsteps echoing in the parking garage. Van Cleef spotted Dennis Overstreet engaged in a conversation with the Community Relations Sergeant, Kyle Caleb. Van Cleef recognized him from the past.

Overstreet did not notice Van Cleef.

The front of the Jag was facing in. The reserved parking placard read: **Dr. Jordan Plotkin.**

The doctor would have a grave reserved in less than a week.

Van Cleef crouched down eye-level like a traffic cop would do issuing someone a ticket. The driver's side window was down. There was Dr. Plotkin slumped over the console. Van Cleef noted the burn mark and star-like wound with a stellate pattern that resembled a jagged star that would typically indicate that it was a self-inflicted, close contact shot.

"I think this one is pretty clear-cut, Leo," Chief Kuznick said, talking over Van Cleef's shoulder. "One fatal shot."

Van Cleef recognized the lead investigative lab tech as Julian Yang. Yang was finishing up with the interior of the Jag, collecting samples and lifting prints from the .38 in Dr. Plotkin's dead left hand that had gunpowder residue on it. Van Cleef noted that and nodded at Yang.

"The gun is registered to the doctor," Chief Kuznick said. "It checks out."

Van Cleef noticed the car was in neutral, the heat was turned up all the way, and the engine was off.

Van Cleef checked the temperature on his smartphone. It was a cool 52 degrees. The Jag's white diamond stitch quilted leather was now marred with blood in various areas, some even visible in the rear cargo area where the lab tech was searching for additional evidence.

"The window was rolled down when you found him?" Van Cleef asked.

"Yes," Chief Kuznick said. "Officer Jones was the responding officer. Your partner Overstreet—"

"He's just filling in until my regular partner gets back," Van Cleef said, setting the record straight.

"Like I was saying," Chief Kuznick said. "Officer Jones was the responding officer."

"Who called it in?"

"Parking attendant, over there," Chief Kuznick pointed at the glass booth flanked by the entrance and exit gates. "You can see the upward angle of the shot which also would indicate—"

Van Cleef glanced up at the concrete ceiling of the parking structure and interjected, "Are there any surveillance cameras in this lot?"

"No," Chief Kuznick said. "We also did not find any suicide note—"

"Why would you?" Van Cleef said. "His wife is dead, and he was pretty much married to his work. Who would he leave it for?"

Van Cleef walked around the Jaguar away from the Chief. He began inspecting and scrutinizing the body of the car and pavement, looking for anything unusual. The car was immaculate, recently washed and waxed, and did not appear to have a single imperfection. That was until Van Cleef zeroed in closer on the driver's side door near the handle. There appeared to be tiny scratches surrounding the handle and lock.

He stood straight up and examined the bottom of his suit jacket and then stood back and reexamined the tiny scratches near the door handle. Chief Kuznick curiously observed Van Cleef. The Chief was ruminating on Sheila Plotkin and finally asked, "So, how is your case going with

Plotkin's wife and the pit bull attack in Malibu?"

There it was again, Van Cleef thought. Even the City of Beverly Hills and the Chief of Police were fixated on pit bulls in the Sheila Evans-Plotkin murder. He didn't correct the Chief that pit bulls were not on his suspect list. Instead, he changed the subject and asked, "Has anyone checked the stairwells yet?"

"I'm sure one of our detectives would have," Chief Kuznick said.

Van Cleef was not reassured. He pointed to the tiny scratches on the door and said, "I want multiple photographs of that."

Chief Kuznick squinted at the door handle and said, "I can hardly see anything. It looks like normal key scratches. Everyone has those— y'know my wife got her car keyed the other night at the Rite-Aid over here on Canon, right in the parking lot. No reason for it, just some asshole keyed her brand new Lexus and we gotta pay for it. Looks like someone keyed the Doc's car if you ask me."

"Paul," Van Cleef said in a smiling, matter-of-fact tone, "I'm not asking for Annie Leibovitz, just multiple photos. I am checking the stairwell. Have another tech meet me over there."

Van Cleef walked away from the Chief in the direction of the stairwell. He pulled a pair of latex gloves from his pants pocket and carefully turned the knob. It was open.

He entered the stairwell which reeked of a recent homeless person, booze, and urine. There were a few scattered cans: one Red Bull and two Coors Light beer cans. Some fast-food wrappers and some random cigarettes. Van Cleef would have the detectives collect all of them into evidence just to be safe.

Dr. Plotkin parked on the first level of the six-level parking structure. After Van Cleef climbed to the top, he walked back down and out to the alley behind Rodeo

Drive and the doctor's office. The door leading to the alley was open to the public and did not appear to be broken. He came back in the first level door where the crime scene was located and walked over to the parking attendant in the glass booth. Van Cleef identified himself to the thin Nairobi man working the booth.

"I'm Detective Leo Van Cleef from LAPD Homicide," he said. "I understand you were the person that found the doctor and contacted the police?"

"Yes," he said. His deep-set eyes with dark circles stared in the distance at the Jaguar with the dead body of Dr. Plotkin. His tone of voice was meek and effeminate. "I would see him every day, sometimes late at night like tonight. He would always nod to me, but never talked to me. He was always there, now—"

"Is this garage closed to the public after a certain time of night?"

"Yes, no one after 11 o'clock," he said, raising his voice out of defensive habit as if Van Cleef were a tourist parking in his lot and debating the lot hours. "No one can park here without a keycard after 11 o'clock."

"I understand," Van Cleef said in a more relaxed tone to calm the parking attendant down.

"Are those stairwells locked after 11 o'clock too?"

"No, they are never locked. We have tried in the past, but people keep breaking them and the owner does not care to lock them anymore or pay for new ones. Besides, if your car is parked overnight you will pay the maximum fee." He pointed to the maximum fee of $26.00 on his sign next to his booth. "The owner will get his money from you or you will not get your car."

Van Cleef felt like the parking attendant was personally attacking him. People had strange ways of reacting around detectives and crime scenes. This poor gentleman was hostile for some reason. Judging by the circles under his eyes, it was due to sleep deprivation.

"One last question," Van Cleef said, slightly turning away from the glass attendant booth. "Do you have video cameras anywhere in this parking lot?"

"Video cameras?" he asked.

"Yes, like mounted video cameras for monitoring the garage, like surveillance cameras for safety."

"No sir, the owner would never pay for that. He is greedy and just wants to collect the money and extra charges. He pays me minimum wage and has me working seven days a week like a dog. When I ask him for a raise he always says he can't, but I see how much money he takes in. Dr. Plotkin and the other doctors pay top dollar for parking here. When I tell the owner he is making lots of money, he lies and says he is not making any money, but I know better. I have eyes. So, what can I do? He makes excuses and says he has to compete with all the other free lots around here and tourism is down, and he has other businesses to run and nobody wants to—"

Van Cleef cut him off, tuned him out, and said, "Thank you for your time." He walked back to the crime scene. The parking guard needed to find a new job or line of work and spend more time out of that little booth. Van Cleef thought he must get lonely in there all day, which explained why the poor guy emotionally unloaded on him.

"I see you spoke with our parking guard friend," Chief Kuznick said with a slight smirk. *He must have already had a similar encounter with the guy,* Van Cleef thought.

"Yeah, got his whole life story and the owner's too," Van Cleef said, less amused. He continued to watch the technicians photograph, videotape, and collect evidence. They were doing a good job and taking their time since it wasn't every day that someone was murdered in Beverly Hills, and it was certainly more exciting than the occasional assault, robbery, or property crime.

"I'm going to head over to Dr. Plotkin's office," Van Cleef said.

"Do you have a warrant?" Chief Kuznick asked.

"I didn't say I was going to search it, Paul. I'm just checking over there to see if anyone at his building had seen anything unusual tonight. Oh, also run the last numbers in his cell phone and check the GPS on the Jag, and let me know what you come up with."

He turned back around, observing Overstreet taking notes and acting official. Van Cleef lowered his voice and said to Paul, "Do me a favor."

"Of course, Leo… anything you need."

"Keep Overstreet over there and away from the media."

Chief Kuznick gestured an okay sign with a grin. He shouted at Van Cleef as he walked away, "Hey, we've got your Leibovitz photos too. We'll have them for you tomorrow."

Van Cleef sauntered out of the parking garage, signaling back an okay gesture over his shoulder. He signed out of the crime scene logbook, entered the time, and went next door to Dr. Plotkin's office. The media, including TMZ, was swarming outside the parking garage gates. Reporters attempted to interview Van Cleef.

He ignored them.

27

"YOU BETTER HOPE TO GOD you've got a warrant."
Gordon Goldstone said, emerging from Dr. Plotkin's office. Van Cleef closed the door to the reception area behind him and entered.

"I didn't come here to search—"

"You're damned right you didn't," Goldstone said. He was now standing toe to toe with Van Cleef, only Goldstone was a good five inches shorter.

"Frankly," Van Cleef said. "I was surprised the door was unlocked. I was hoping—"

"I know what you were hoping, Detective Van Cleef, and I'm hoping to hang this on you and your department before this nightmare is over."

"Hang what on me, Gordon?" Van Cleef said, taking the same seat in the waiting room area opposite where Lisa Comstock sat earlier that day.

"Dr. Plotkin's death."

"You think I was responsible for pushing Dr. Plotkin over the edge?" Van Cleef asked.

"I warned you, Detective Van Cleef, not to speak with him any further without my involvement, did I not?"

Goldstone was now pacing back and forth with all the fury of a trial attorney. His histrionics were almost amusing.

"He spoke to me of his own accord. You know that's legal," Van Cleef said.

"It might be legal, but it was unethical, and you knew what the hell you were doing. It was devious."

"What was I doing?"

"Don't play stupid with me, detective," Goldstone said. He took a seat and stabbed the print button on the desk printer with his index finger. Paper started spitting out the top tray. He brought his melodramatic tone down a few notches. Looking Van Cleef square in the eyes, he said, "You did what detectives do best. You backed him into a corner. You implied certain things with those petty mind games that cause weak and vulnerable clients to crack and cave in and eventually capitulate to untruths until they begin to believe they are guilty and are coerced into a confession. That sir... is what you did."

Van Cleef examined Gordon Goldstone's hatred in his eyes. He kept his tone calm, talking over the sound of the printer and said, "You got me and my motives all wrong, Gordon."

"Do I?"

"You do," Van Cleef said, standing up now and staring down Goldstone. "It might come as a shock to you now that I thought Dr. Plotkin was innocent. Someone murdered his wife in Malibu, but he had nothing to do with it, not even indirectly, as far as I can see at this point in my investigation."

"That is not the way my client interpreted your visit here today. He was completely distraught and contacted me after you questioned him."

"Dr. Plotkin's stress had little to do with my appearance here today, and I was the least of his concerns."

"Detective Van Cleef, you are really going out on a limb here. Dr. Plotkin believed you were close to making an arrest and targeting him in your investigation."

That statement disappointed Van Cleef. He bit his lip and looked down at the table scattered with tabloids and fashion magazines. "So, your theory is that he committed suicide rather than go to jail for murder, is that correct?"

"Yes, he was panicked about a false arrest, his reputation, his business to run—"

"Dr. Plotkin was a basket case when I first interviewed him with you the day of his wife's murder."

"And that is unique?" Goldstone asked, turning his head as if someone were sitting next to him, throwing up his arms for drama while still talking over the sound of the printer. Whatever Goldstone was printing seemed like one-thousand pages and was eating up all the paper over their conversation. "Dr. Plotkin was well respected," he said. "He was loved by his patients and everyone that knew him. You and your department could only view him as another Scott Petersen."

Goldstone began arranging and sorting the printed pages from the printer tray, occasionally breaking his concentration to give Van Cleef the evil eye. He said, "Detective Van Cleef, exactly how much do you know about me?"

Van Cleef was not sure how to answer Goldstone. He knew more than he was letting on and had checked his background and clients early on in his investigation. He just simply said, "I know the basics."

"Basics?" Goldstone repeated in a mocking tone. "You mean who I represent, what good or bad press I've received over the past decade, or if I'm in financial trouble like my deceased client, Dr. Plotkin?"

"If you say so," Van Cleef said, getting bored with the

guessing game.

"Were you aware of my practice in Colorado and how I personally fought to have pit bulls banned in that state?"

"Yes, it was brought to my attention recently."

"Was it also brought to your attention that I had been a proponent of SB861 and BSL in California?"

"BSL?"

"Breed Specific Legislation."

"I know the acronym, I just—"

"What you could not know is that I happen to be in the minority in my opinion, however, I believe that pit bulls, as a breed, should be banned. They are violent, vicious predators. It should also not surprise you that in a two-year period: 2006-2008 pit bull type dogs killed 52 Americans and accounted for 59% of fatal attacks. Did you also know that from 2005 through 2015 that canines killed 360 Americans? That's nearly one a day. And of those 360 lives lost, pit bulls contributed to 64% of those deaths. It is all in this report. Keep it for your edification."

He dramatically dropped a ponderous, rubber-banded stack of papers that thudded on Plotkin's desk between him and Van Cleef. "Read it. Keep it for your investigation. I have multiple copies for the trial."

Van Cleef eyed the stack, but did not touch it.

Goldstone continued his rant, "Senior citizens killed in their own backyard. Killed taking a walk or getting the mail by some pit bull running wild through the streets. Your own department even lost a detective just last year to a pit bull attack. His pet pit bull. Some pet."

"Yes, but—"

"Yes, but what? Sheila Plotkin was murdered and you have yet to find the dog or the killer."

"It doesn't alter my opinion or stance on BSL."

Goldstone packed up and stood by the door, suggesting Van Cleef do the same.

"So, you think we should legislate the breed to extinction?" Van Cleef asked.

Their conversation was interrupted by Chief Kuznick. He entered the office and asked Van Cleef to step outside for a moment. They closed the door to the office.

"We ran the Doc's cell and GPS. Nothing remarkable. Looks like he was headed over to the Beverly Hills Hotel over on Sunset. That was the last number he called."

Van Cleef looked away for a moment from Kuznick, deep in thought. Kuznick attempted to read his face and said, "Does that mean something to you?"

"Yeah," Van Cleef said. "I think I have a pretty good idea."

"Well, Malibu is a long trek back," Kuznick said. "With his kinda money I guess you can afford to stay anywhere when you need rest."

"Yeah," Van Cleef said, skeptical. "I guess so."

Van Cleef rode the elevator back down with Chief Kuznick. Moments later Gordon Goldstone opened the door to discover both men were gone. He stood alone with his 500 plus page dog bite report wedged under his arm like a bulky package. He would FedEx it to Van Cleef in the morning, whether the detective wanted it or not. He returned to Dr. Plotkin's office and tossed the report on the waiting room sofa. He sat in silence for several minutes listening to the calming water fountain in the waiting room. He grabbed the phone receiver like he was choking the life out of it and then started stabbing numbers on the phone, dialing anyone he could to yell at... at that time of night. He finally woke his legal secretary out of bed and demanded she take dictation.

Goldstone needed someone to bully since Van Cleef 's equanimity rattled him.

28

VAN CLEEF DROVE TO the famous Beverly Hills Hotel. It's true that a detective's shoes, aside from his instincts, are one of the most useful items he owns. Van Cleef spent a lot of time on his feet when he wasn't behind the desk. He cut through the gardens near the peaceful bungalows on his way to the hotel front desk. It was so quiet; he could hear crickets, an uncommon sound in the city. Bright red Bougainvilleas and Banana plants were illuminated on his path, and he could smell a strong scent of Hibiscus.

He showed his detective badge to the attractive young Asian desk clerk who nervously nodded her head and cooperated with him. She pointed back in the direction he just came from.

He got off the elevator, walked down the silent hallway, and located the room number. He paused a moment before he rapped on the door. For some odd reason, he thought of a '60s Milton Bradley board game his sisters used to play called "Mystery Date." There was a commercial and jingle that advertised the game, something like: "*Open the door... it's mystery date...*"

There was a dream date, and of course the dud, which is how you lost if you opened the door and got the dud. There was no detective in "Mystery Date" because that would have taken all the fun out of a young girl's game. He guessed why he had the random nostalgic thought about mystery date. It was all about the element of surprise, which was the selling point and excitement of the game. He was about to take the fun out of an older girl's game in less than a minute. He rapped on the door, using a little more force.

Lisa Comstock did not even bother to ask who was on the other side knocking because she wasn't expecting a mystery date. She figured she had the dream date wrapped around her little finger. Imagine her surprise when detective Van Cleef was standing in front of her instead of her dream date and she was dolled up in her Victoria Secret's lingerie.

Lisa's flushed red face drained of color within seconds. She froze standing in her high-heels, blocking the door.

"May I come in?" Van Cleef asked politely.

She turned her back on him and grabbed a robe on the edge of the king-sized bed. Van Cleef took note of the flowers and *Congratulations* balloons on the coffee table.

He stepped inside and closed the hotel door. Lisa grabbed a cigarette and sat on the edge of the bed, covering her legs and chest with the large robe. She went for the phone and rang the front desk for security.

"Have you been here all night, Ms. Comstock?" Van Cleef asked.

"Yes, I never left this room," she said, blowing smoke in his direction. "Security is on their way up."

"That won't be necessary."

"What the hell is this about anyway? I told you everything I knew earlier— stalking's against the law..."

She caught Van Cleef staring at the floral bouquets on

the coffee table. He asked, "Any particular occasion?"

"Just a private celebration, that's all."

"A celebration with Dr. Plotkin, your employer?"

"Detective, you'd better leave," she said, bolting up from the bed and walking back over to the door to show him out. "I told you earlier—"

"I'll be on my way in a minute," Van Cleef said, not standing up or moving from his seat. "You said you've been here all night?"

"Yes."

"Anyone that can verify that?"

She thought about it for a minute and said, "Room service, I suppose. If you must know, I just binge watched some shows and stayed in. I had a very long day at the office."

"What time did you check-in?"

"Right after work."

"And what time was that?"

"Oh, I don't know. 6:30-7pm. Somewhere around there."

"Was Dr. Plotkin still working at the office when you left?"

She walked back over to the bedside and poured herself a glass of champagne from an open bottle sitting on the nightstand.

"He was finishing up in his office when I left. What is this all about anyway?"

"Did he seem troubled or upset, anything like that?"

"Not at all. What is this about? Is he in trouble or something?"

Van Cleef caught her looking at the clock several times, her face turning from anger to concern.

"No, nothing like that," Van Cleef said, referencing some notes in his notebook. "Have you spoken to your boyfriend, Justin, this evening?"

"He's not my boyfriend."

"Okay, have you been in communication with him?"

"No, he's out of town with his buddies again. This time in Las Vegas."

Van Cleef made some additional notes and would verify her statements later.

"Lisa, I'm afraid I have some bad news for you," Van Cleef said. A hulking figure came barging through the door. The hotel beefcake security guard was bulging out of his suit jacket ready to escort Van Cleef out when Van Cleef flashed him his detective badge without saying a word.

The beefcake security guard bowed out of his way.

Van Cleef informed Lisa of Dr. Plotkin's death and contacted another Beverly Hills detective on his cell to come over to the hotel to ask some additional questions.

The morning papers, local news, and the internet would know Dr. Jordan Plotkin intimately in several hours as every aspect of his life would be reported, misreported, and dug up.

The story would go something like this:

BEVERLY HILLS
CELEBRITY PLASTIC SURGEON
FOUND DEAD IN BEVERLY HILLS
OF APPARENT SUICIDE

Dr. Jordan Plotkin, whose name was synonymous with many of Hollywood's famous aging faces, was found dead this morning in Beverly Hills by an apparent self-inflicted gunshot wound.

Dr. Plotkin, 48, was recently in the spotlight when his wife and known actress, Sheila Evans-Plotkin, was fatally attacked by a pit bull. The dog, or owner, responsible has not yet been found. The investigation is still ongoing.

Dr. Plotkin practiced in Beverly Hills for nearly a decade and was highly recognized as one of the best. Dr. Larry Stroud, who also practices in Beverly Hills and knew Dr. Plotkin, said he is "shocked" and that "no one took more pride in their work than Dr. Jordan Plotkin. He was an artist when it came to our field. He will be missed."

Dr. Plotkin was also on the Board of Plastic Surgeons at UCLA...

***

PART TWO:

SCRATCH

LINES

29

THE INDUSTRIAL SECTION of Fontana provided the perfect facade for dogfighting. A city in the County of San Bernardino, Fontana consistently manages to make the Top 10 Worst Cities to Live in California list. The noise of the factories and the filth and neglect of nearby abandoned warehouses were home to many stray dogs and homeless squatters.

Van Cleef and his team received a tip through the LAPD tip line. He had a search and arrest warrant in hand signed off on by the Superior Court Judge Richard J. Fogel.

The police, San Bernardino sheriffs, and the L.A. Dept. of Animal Control rolled up to *Sang & Son's Tire and Auto Body Repair* just before the smog of dawn. The rusted, faded, and dilapidated sign looked like it was used more for target practice instead of advertising.

The LAPD waited, armed and ready, outside the gated fence. The commercial building wasn't on any realtor's list and didn't look like it had seen a customer in the last decade. It was an abandoned tire warehouse in the middle of nowhere with the usual gang graffiti sprayed anywhere there was a wall. The machine shops sounds, the constant rush of traffic from the freeway in the background, and the hum of a loud generator, masked the barking dogs.

The entire warehouse was surrounded within five to seven minutes with teams in tactical gear and loaded weapons.

The officers could see fences and make-shift kennels in the back behind the building and could also see about a dozen pit bulls chained to stakes and axle rods in the yard.

They waited for their cue to enter from the Captain.

Cracks of fluorescent light could be seen through half-open windows.

The raid was well orchestrated with the exception of:

First obstacle: The pit bulls were staggered like bumpers on a pinball machine. There was no way around them to enter in the back of the warehouse.

Second obstacle: The front was the only way in.

The officers used bolt cutters on the chained gates behind the warehouse and stood motionless waiting for a signal.

The pit bulls were in attack mode, abused and hungry. They lunged forward on their hind legs, barking and snapping their jaws at the perceived presence of strangers.

At the front, the signal was issued to move in.

A shadow inside passed by the window for a brief second.

The shadows outside froze.

The fluorescent lights inside were snapped off and everything went pitch black.

The hum of the generator stopped.

Lieutenant Garrick Cartwright placed a call to the number inside the warehouse.

No one answered.

A loud clanking sound like an old wooden roller coaster cut through the barking chaos.

One of the officer's night goggles caught sight of movement on the back-loading dock gate. He watched six pit bulls launch off the dock like rockets and headed straight in the direction of the team of officers in the back.

A short Asian suspect was seen ducking back inside the warehouse away from the loading dock.

The pit bulls charged toward the officers giving the little man a chance to flee.

Lieutenant Cartwright grabbed three of his officers, and rushed to the back of the building.

Several rounds of gunfire erupted from the rear.

Van Cleef joined Lieutenant Cartwright at the side, and they emerged and sprinted to the front.

The suspect was hanging out of a broken window, and unfortunately for him dropped flat on his back and landed right in front of them. He was met with two automatics leveled at his face. The suspect froze, trying to catch the wind that was knocked out of him.

He was identified as Kim Sang, the owner, and was arrested on the spot.

The unleashed and aggressive pit bulls were shot on sight and Animal Control and the officers were swiftly rounding up the others using catchpoles and putting them in cages.

"Hold up a moment, officers," Van Cleef shouted at them as they wrestled the vicious pits.

Van Cleef examined the catchpole, standing far back from the teeth of the pit bull.

"Do you have an extra one of those I could take a look at?" Van Cleef asked.

"The dog?" One of the frazzled officers asked, struggling to control it.

"No, not the dog… the pole."

The Sheriff jerked his head over his shoulder in the direction of the Animal Control truck, as if suggesting to talk to one of the workers.

Van Cleef walked over to the truck and asked to see one of the catchpoles. The Animal Control worker handed him one out of the back of the truck. Van Cleef extended the pole to his left, and then to his right, and walked along as if he had an imaginary dog beside him in the catchpole. He then extended the pole in front of him like he was fishing. The animal control worker just watched him out of curiosity, which Van Cleef noticed, and then he kindly handed the catchpole back to him and thanked him for his help.

Kim Sang, age 42, would be charged with: dogfighting, animal cruelty and neglect, possession of weapons, possession of controlled substances, and dogfighting paraphernalia.

Van Cleef's cell phone rang. He picked up. It was Frank Nelson.

"Leo, it's Frank," he said in an excited tone.

"Wow, that was fast," Van Cleef said.

"I might have a lead on your PBK breeder... Do you have a minute?"

"I'm all yours, go ahead."

"There is this breeder we traced back to Florida," Nelson said. "People call him Gator."

"Gator? Like Alligator?"

"Yeah, Gator. That's what his alias is anyway."

"Sounds like a character."

"For sure. A character that is off everyone's radar right now. Florida authorities have tried, unsuccessfully, to link this 'Gator' to dogfighting, but nothing sticks and they can't even get a real name on him, but what makes this Gator dude interesting is that he likes to breed a certain type of Bully Gull Terr."

"Very interesting. Does he still reside in Florida?"

"No, not since 2011. He's been missing ever since. No one knows how to locate him."

"You think he was killed?" Van Cleef asked.

"Not likely."

"Maybe he got out of the dog breeding business."

"Not likely," Nelson said. "That breed has turned up recently in your old stomping ground."

"Detroit?"

"Yes, sir."

"You have any description or anything else to go on?"

"For one thing, sources say if you see this guy you won't forget him."

"Why's that?"

"Rumor has it, that he's badly disfigured."

"Disfigured how? From a fire or something?"

"No, not the way some people tell it, which is why they call him Gator. He likes to tell the story that he tangled with a real gator in a Florida swamp and it took half his face off. I suspect it was probably from a dog attack. He's described as a large man at least 6'4, African-American and typically wears hoodies to cover most of his head up."

Van Cleef wondered if this Gator sought out reconstructive surgery at some point, or if there was a plastic surgeon connection.

"Your biggest problem is that this guy is like a ghost. Like a phantom. Nobody knows how to locate him. He's a recluse. He never meets with anyone and no one will give him up.

"We can get next to him," Van Cleef said. "I can get some undercover guys on it. Listen, call me if anything else turns up on Gator."

"Of course."

"I meant to ask… Does Warren Sleezbag and the FBI know anything about this Gator?"

"They're aware of him—" Nelson said, with a frustrated tone.

"And?"

"They don't care."

"Figures," Van Cleef said.

Van Cleef hung up with Frank Nelson and entered the warehouse which was swarming with police and sheriffs and newly arrived San Bernardino detectives. The warehouse was gutted and stunk of garbage, stale food, urine and feces. There was no evidence of legit business dealings, just the vestiges of dogfighting. Van Cleef noticed some coloring books and grimy toys on a cheap folding card table. He placed a call to Overstreet and filled him in on the suspect they were bringing in for questioning, Kim Sang, and asked him to prepare some additional background information before the interview. Overstreet did as he was told, no questions asked. Maybe the latest occurrence of recent events with Dr. Plotkin's death and the extra work and duties would make Overstreet reconsider Homicide Special.

He could only hope.

30

VAN CLEEF AND OVERSTREET stood at opposite ends of the interrogation room at the LAPD Commerce Division. Kim Sang sat in silence at the table with a Dr. Pepper and a blue pack of American Spirit cigarettes in front of him. He chain-smoked half the pack in silence before he asked to see his lawyer.

Where'd you get the dogs?" Van Cleef asked patiently, knowing this was going to be a long night.

"I no talkie to you or him," Sang said, scowling and flicking his cigarette ash at Overstreet.

Kim Sang's English was as broken as most of his teeth. Overstreet cautioned him to watch where he flicks his ash.

"Who sold you the dogs?" Overstreet asked.

Sang ignored the question and demanded, "When my lawyer get here?"

"He's on his way," Van Cleef said in a calm tone.

"I talkie to him now," Sang said. "I talkie now to him. Not you. Just lawyer."

"Your lawyer isn't going to be able to help you with the

dogfighting charges," Van Cleef said. "It's a felony, you know that. Don't be stupid. Just help us out and answer a few of our questions. We know you have kids. You're going to lose contact with them over this if you don't cooperate with us here."

Kim Sang pretended not to care, but Van Cleef knew he struck a nerve.

"We're asking you to help us out here and help your kids out," Van Cleef said. "If you even give a shit about them... it's time to consider what their life is going to be like without you."

"I dunno who the hell you talkie about," Sang said.

"I think you do," Overstreet said, referencing a file.

"Stop bullshitting us," Van Cleef said. "Where did you get the dogs?"

Overstreet slid Sang's rap sheet across the table. Sang looked away and pushed the sheet back to him.

"Look, we've got all night," Overstreet said. "Lots of people want to talk to you. The AGU, the FTA, the DEA, the FBI... hell Charlie Rose might want to interview you before the night is through."

Van Cleef liked that one. Overstreet was getting in his groove as detectives do. But Kim Sang did not care about the barrage of acronyms and never heard of Charlie Rose anyway. He just wanted to go to sleep in a warm jail cell.

"C'mon, work with us, Sang," Overstreet said, leaning across the table almost whispering in Sang's ear.

"It's so easy," Van Cleef said. "Your lawyer can plea bargain with the D.A. and we'll let them know that you cooperated. We know you don't want to be talking to us all night. I get it, you're the strong, silent type. You're not going to roll over on your buddies. Let's just tie up the dog nonsense you got mixed up in, okay?"

"No," Sang shouted. "Why the fuck I cooperate with you?"

Overstreet placed a photograph in front of Sang from a family picnic featuring Sang, his ex-wife, and their two children.

Sang stood up and looked over his shoulder. Still no lawyer.

"Where did you get the dogs?" Van Cleef asked.

"I dunno."

"Did the dogs just find you? Bunch of stray dogs show up on your doorstep?" Overstreet asked, being sarcastic.

This amused Sang for some reason, and then he got serious and said, "He find you. You don't find him. He find you."

"Okay then, who's he and how did he find you?"

"Ah, some driver."

"Driver?"

"Yeah, ah-ha driver. Likie limo driver."

Van Cleef and Overstreet exchanged looks again, their curiosity burning.

"'Likie' what else do you know about him?" Overstreet asked, mocking Sang.

"I dunno anything. I told you last time."

"We're just talking about the driver," Van Cleef said.

"Oh, ah-ha," Sang laughed.

There was a long moment of silence as Sang sipped his Dr. Pepper. Sang lit another cigarette. He didn't finish the first one. He was nervous. He eventually said, "Ah, I remember now... he famous for something."

"Famous for what?" Van Cleef asked.

"Don't cover for him," Overstreet said.

"I told you, I thinkie."

"Yeah, well 'thinkie' faster," Van Cleef said.

"Okay. Okay," Sang said as he put out another unfinished cigarette in the ashtray. "He famous fighter, ah at one a time."

"Dogfighter?" Van Cleef asked, raising his eyebrow.

"No, boxer... y'know," Sang said, motioning with his fists like he was shadowboxing.

Van Cleef enjoyed the shadowboxing with the interview process. He never tired easy and would go all night to break a suspect.

Another detective entered the room and informed Van Cleef that FBI agents were on their way in. Van Cleef whispered under his breath to Overstreet, "Keep on him until his attorney gets here. Try to get more out of him about this driver. Also, work with Tanaka back at the office and run down a list of limo companies that our boxer drove for and see if Sang's story checks out or if he's lying to us."

Van Cleef waited outside the interview room for FBI Agent Warren Slezick and his agents.

31

"WE'LL TAKE OVER FROM HERE," FBI Agent Slezick said, staring down Van Cleef.

"This has nothing to do with your investigation," Van Cleef said in a calm tone.

"If it involves dogfighting, it has everything to do with our investigation, you know that. Now step aside," Slezick said, moving past Van Cleef and going for the door. He hesitated a moment before opening it and asked, "Is there anything you want to tell me now that he told you?"

"Not a damn thing," Van Cleef said, without even considering sharing information with him.

Slezick took his hand off the door handle and said, "The suspect you have in there is working as our informant. Did you know that Detective Van Cleef?"

"I did not," Van Cleef said.

"I wouldn't think you did," Agent Slezick said, "You also wouldn't know that he lied about a recent dogfighting raid that made me look like an asshole, to send us in the wrong direction. Now, how in the world you wound up with him on your suspect list and without consulting me first is beyond me, but your Captain will hear about it and it ends here... Is that clear?"

"Crystal," Van Cleef said.

"Can I ask you a personal question, Detective Van Cleef?" Slezick said, his arms folded with a slight smirk on his face.

"Am I related to Lee Van Cleef, the Spaghetti Western actor?" Van Cleef said.

Agent Slezick hadn't thought about that before and only gave it half a thought now, but the amusement quickly dissipated from his face. He said, "Seriously, why are you doing this? I checked with your superiors... your record is impeccable. You have a solid reputation in your department and colleagues rave about you like you're the famed Jigsaw John. You've cooperated with us before without incident, so why damage your stellar rep? Smart guy like you...Stick with celebrity homicides and let the big boys handle this one, huh... This dogfighting ring supersedes your Malibu mauling, and I can assure you that there is no connection."

"You're sure about that?" Van Cleef asked, expressionless.

"100 percent. There's no connection, detective," Slezick said, grinning. "Besides, the FBI runs on a much longer leash."

Van Cleef kept his mouth shut and decided to let Slezick take a crack at Kim Sang. He motioned for Overstreet to leave the interview room.

Overstreet strolled past Slezick not saying a word, just staring at him on the way out.

They walked down the hallway together. Once Van Cleef was certain the door was closed and Slezick and his FBI pals were sweating out Kim Sang, he stopped dead in his tracks and turned to Overstreet confidentially and said,

"Do me a favor and find out everything you can about this retired ex-boxer turned driver, and find out who he is and what his connection is to Sang."

"You got it," Overstreet said. "Shouldn't be too hard to narrow down."

"Thanks."

Dennis Overstreet started to walk in the direction of the elevators when he noticed his partner, Van Cleef, was heading for the door. He asked, "Hey, where are you headed? I thought we were becoming a team?"

"Checking out some more leads, Dennis," Van Cleef said. "Let me know what you turn up on our ex-boxer suspect."

They went their separate ways.

32

LARRY AND ELLEN JACOBS STOPPED dead in their tracks along the dirt road at Malibu Canyon State Park. Exhausted and parched they finally reached their parked car, a classic cream yellow Volvo. Larry continued to complain the whole time about why they should have just paid the $12 parking fee and would not have had to walk an extra mile back to their car just to save twelve dollars. Ellen Jacobs reminded him that it was his idea to save the twelve dollars. Deal with it. They were both in their mid-sixties, slightly overweight, and looked pale from too much office work. Larry was more hunched over from computer necking than Ellen, and Malibu was their rare and annual dose of Vitamin D.

They were loading their trunk with their hats and backpacks when Ellen started complaining about her bladder and how she should have stopped at the restroom on the way out. She suggested going back, but Larry threw a fit and demanded she stop at a restroom on the way home.

Larry insisted on driving and said to hurry up because he was hungry. He unlocked the car door and collapsed into the car seat, sweating profusely. "My chest hurts. My legs hurt... I'm getting too old for this shit," Larry said.

Ellen was about to open the passenger side door of the car when she caught a glimpse of something odd in the brush. She moved closer to inspect what looked like a large animal carcass and covered her mouth with a bandanna she had in her pocket.

Larry rolled down the passenger window and shouted at her, "You can't go to the bathroom out there, Ellen. What the hell are you doing? Get in the car, I'm hungry. I told you I was hungry, didn't I tell you that?"

She grabbed a stick and huddled over what appeared to be animal bones of some kind, poking at them like a dying campfire.

Malibu Canyon was known for its wildlife, and part of the allure to hikers was seeing an occasional wild animal; it added an extra sense of danger. A dead animal would be disturbing enough, but Ellen's intuition was that it was covered up for some reason, and Ellen Jacobs watched too many crime shows to not think it could even possibly be human bones.

Larry bolted from the driver's side and walked around to the other side of the parked Volvo to where Ellen was poking around. "What the hell did you lose this time, Ellen? I told you I was hungry, and you need a restroom, don't you? It stinks like a sewer over here... C'mon, let's get the show on the road."

His anger turned to disgust as Ellen brushed more of the leaves away and uncovered what appeared to be a large mountain lion or canine carcass.

The presence of flies and maggots quickly suppressed Larry's appetite.

She dropped the stick and turned, covering her mouth trying not to vomit. The stench smelled like a city dump rotting and decaying on a hot summer's day. Ellen reacted quickly using her cell phone to contact the police.

33

SHEILA EVANS-PLOTKIN'S FUNERAL was at the famed Hollywood Forever. The cemetery was becoming more of a tourist attraction these days. They even have their own Movie Night and music events. The most recent big celebrity event here was the famous grunge singer and frontman Chris Cornell who died in Detroit and was now resting next to Johnny Ramone. Van Cleef and several other homicide detectives were undercover to pay their last respects and look for potential suspects. It was not uncommon for a killer to insinuate themself into a public funeral and try to find out more details.

"So, I hear the bonehead surfer consented to a polygraph," Overstreet said, observing mourners passing by and occasionally nodding at an attractive one.

"That's the plan," Van Cleef said, paying attention to a tall, athletic man that was bulging out of his suit. He was standing alone with dark shades and appeared to be upset.

"Is that Tom Selleck over there in front?" Overstreet asked.

"Yeah, don't ask for his autograph or anything stupid, Dennis," Van Cleef said.

"I still think you're wasting your time with that bonehead

surfer if you ask me," Overstreet said.

"I didn't ask you and remember, you're working here," Van Cleef said. "Keep your eyes peeled."

"I guess Linda Blair is gonna get up and say a few words," Overstreet said.

Don Johnson brushed past them and gave them a nod.

"Was that who I think it was?" Overstreet asked.

"Yeah, Kurt Russell," Van Cleef said, toying with him. Van Cleef kept his sights on the muscular athletic man near Sheila Evans's closed casket.

"I heard someone in the can talking about Tarantino showing up."

Dennis, we're not here to stargaze."

"Just making small talk s'all— Man I hate these things," Overstreet said under his breath. "Suppose we have to attend the husband's now too?"

"Yep," Van Cleef said. "Don't worry, you'll get a breather while we wait for his official autopsy report." He motioned to Ron Tanaka to come over.

Tanaka squeezed past a row of mourners standing in the aisle way. He met Van Cleef and Overstreet at the back of the room.

"Hey Leo," Detective Tanaka said. "What's up?"

"The big guy to the front left, you can't miss him," Van Cleef said.

Detective Tanaka stood with his back against the wall and zeroed in on the big guy in front. He said, "Yeah, I have my eyes on him. I overheard him say he was a friend of the family, only no one seems too friendly with him and I haven't seen one member of the Plotkin family come up to him since I've been here."

"Tail him and let me know who he is," Van Cleef said.

"You got it, man," Tanaka said, patting Van Cleef on the shoulder as if to console him. He walked back up to the front of the wake expressing his best somber face.

Van Cleef turned to Overstreet and said, "Why don't you grab some fresh air. Looks like it's getting stuffy in here." This was also Van Cleef's code phrase for Overstreet to walk the lot and look for a black SUV.

"Sure thing, boss," Overstreet said with one foot out the door and ready to bolt. "Anything else?"

"Yeah, check with the valets and engage them in some car talk. Maybe ask a few sensible questions while you're at it. Maybe somebody lost their keys."

Van Cleef was speaking code again and "lost keys" meant they had an eye on a suspect.

Van Cleef received a call on his cell. He recognized the call coming from the ballistics unit. He stepped outside the parlor and looked for a private space to talk.

"Detective Van Cleef?" The man's voice asked on the other end.

"Yes, this is he."

"This is Jack Halliwell from the ballistics unit," Halliwell said.

"Yes, I recognize your voice and your number."

"Oh?" Halliwell said, surprised.

Some people were good at remembering faces, names, and voices. Van Cleef was excellent at remembering them all. He thought Halliwell sounded a bit like Christian Slater.

"Well," Halliwell continued. "We identified a bullet that was found in a canine carcass up in Malibu Canyon. An old couple was hiking up there earlier today, discovered the remains and called it in— could be connected to your case."

"Great," Van Cleef said as he pulled his notebook out of his suit jacket. He wedged his cell phone between his neck and shoulder while he took notes.

"It matches a Sig-Sauer 9mm P226—"

Van Cleef interrupted as he wrote down the gun model and commented, "Interesting— could suggest a left or right hand… or even a Navy Seal."

"True," Halliwell said. "You would also know, Detective Van Cleef, that it has an X-Change kit, so it can be converted to 9mm—"

Van Cleef now knew that Sheila Evans's killer had a more interesting background, maybe even military.

"There's more," Halliwell continued. "We also found a mangled fragment of metal bearing some numbers," Halliwell said. "Most likely a serial number of some sort."

"You'll email me a photo of that, too?" Van Cleef asked.

"I'll have it right over to you."

"Good work, Jack. Appreciate it," Van Cleef said.

"Anytime, Leo," Halliwell said.

They disconnected before Van Cleef returned to the parlor to continue his surveillance. He ducked into a nearby alcove and dialed another number to make a private call to his wife, Claudia.

34

TAD KELLER FAILED THE POLYGRAPH, plain and simple, the morning after Sheila Evans's wake. He was brought back into the interview room with Van Cleef and Overstreet already seated waiting for him, arms folded for dramatic effect. Cold coffee and legal pads were in front of them on the table.

Tad knew he failed it, and it was all downhill from there. Tad's friends referred to him as Tad Cooler. Yeah, he was a tad cooler in another situation, but in the present circumstances, he was screwed.

"Why'd you lie to me, Tad?" Van Cleef asked, disappointed.

"I didn't lie," he said.

"That's not what the polygraph said, and the polygraph doesn't lie like you do," Overstreet said, looking him square in the eye.

"You can't use it in court. Like, everybody knows that. So what," Tad said with a stupid grin on his face.

"You weren't there to surf the day Sheila Plotkin was murdered," Van Cleef said.

"Ah, I had my surfboard with me—"

"You weren't there to surf."

"You don't know what I was going to do," Tad said on the defense.

"No, we don't," Van Cleef said. "We only know what you did do."

"What did I do? I still don't understand."

"I spoke to your buddies, Tad," Overstreet said. "Funny thing is, they told us you haven't dipped your board in the Pacific since you dropped out of college four years ago."

"Those aren't my friends."

"They're your friends if they're on your cell phone every day texting you and Facebooking you every half hour— when you gonna start leveling with us and stop wasting our time?"

"Like, I'm tryin' to—"

"You weren't there to surf, Tad. You had rock climbing shoes in the backseat of your car," Van Cleef said.

"So?"

"So, you are an experienced rock climber according to your friends, and I think that you were on the rocks that day with a pretty good vantage point of the murder and the highway, almost like sitting up in a crow's nest."

"That's crazy, dude," Tad said as he played with his Guy Fieri spiky, frosted hair. His scent of Patchouli mixed with stale cigarette smoke and incense was nauseating.

"You know what a lookout is, Tad?" Van Cleef asked.

Tad played stupid and said he didn't know.

"I'll tell you," Van Cleef said. "A lookout is someone who watches out for cops. Makes sure the coast is clear during a commission of a crime. A lookout is an accomplice and what you were on the day of Sheila Evans's murder— You know she was buried yesterday. Beautiful woman. Still had a lot of living to do."

"Look, I didn't know she was going to be murdered or

anything sick like that."

"Who paid you to lookout?" Van Cleef asked.

"Some guy," Tad said.

"Some guy you know?" Overstreet asked, getting impatient.

"I didn't kill anybody, man!" Tad yelled out at Overstreet. "Get it straight. I was just told to keep an eye out for the CHP while the guy ran his dog on the beach."

"How much did he pay you?" Van Cleef asked.

Tad hesitated for a few minutes and then blurted out, "A thousand bucks. He paid me one thousand bucks, that's all."

"A thousand bucks for a woman's life," Overstreet said, wanting to spit on him. "Didn't a damn light go on in that dim brain of yours that it wasn't just to run his dog off the leash for that kind of money?"

"Look, he didn't say anything about killing anyone," Tad said. "He said he just wanted to run his dog on the beach and that there were no dogs allowed... some rich stranger dude... I swear I hardly knew him, or what he—"

"And you believed him?" Van Cleef asked.

"Yeah," Tad said.

"The guy you hardly knew," Overstreet said.

"Yeah, that's what I said," Tad said. "I didn't really know him. I don't know him," he insisted.

"You're an accomplice," Overstreet said. "Do you have any idea the penalty for lying to detectives or police during a murder investigation?"

Tad had no idea.

"It looks bad for you, Tad," Van Cleef said, standing with his arms akimbo. "This 'rich stranger dude' that you claim just drove up and wanted you to watch for the CHP while he ran his dog off the leash is bullshit— We know you used a burner phone, Tad... a disposable phone, and he called you to meet him that day in Zuma. "Big question is: where is he now?"

"I don't know him, dude. I don't mess with people that are dangerous. He told me he would let the dog loose on me if I ever ratted on him."

"We've got bigger dogs down here, Tad," Van Cleef said. "And when we find these people, we are going to eat them alive. You can count on it. You also lied about the type of vehicle this guy was driving."

"Look," Tad said as he stood up to stretch his lanky legs. He was fiddling with his spiky hair again. "There was so much confusion that day. Police and helicopters were everywhere because of that Mel Gibson thing."

"What Mel Gibson thing?" Van Cleef asked.

"The celebrity swat thing—" Tad said.

Tad didn't realize that the LAPD stopped reporting and publicizing the celebrity swats back in 2013 to cut down on the publicity that fueled them and the copycat sickos that perpetrated them. The Mel Gibson celebrity swat never made it into the papers or evening news.

"Now that's a funny thing, Tad," Van Cleef said. He leaned against the wall, folding his arms and sighing. "Unless you were the one that was responsible for the prank call, no one knew that it was at Mel Gibson's place. Now, you mind telling us how in the world would you know such a thing?"

The interview was over at that point. Tad might have been stupid, but now he was smart enough to keep his mouth shut and get a lawyer.

Overstreet flashed Van Cleef a look behind Tad's back. He fanned his face with a report he was holding and opened the door ajar to air out the stink of Tad's Patchouli.

"You were a lookout, Tad," Van Cleef said. "He used you. You were an accomplice to murder. You lied to us. You called the police the morning of Sheila Evans's murder after 'this guy' and his killer dog hit the road, but you also threw in another obstacle to confuse the timeline and that was a celebrity swat, which gave the killer and his dog enough time to hightail it out of there. Don't say another word. You've told us everything we need to know."

"We found the dead dog," Overstreet said, "But I'd still like to know how the killer made the dog vanish— tell us how he did it."

Tad would not say another word. Van Cleef and Overstreet were done sweating him out. The interview was over. Van Cleef connected Tad Keller to the killer but needed more proof, more time, and a little luck.

"I'd like to speak with an attorney now," Tad said.

35

VAN CLEEF WORKED MOST of the afternoon in his office at the Police Administration Building (PAB) downtown. He continued to compile and organize data and evidence for the Sheila Evans's murder book. He was reviewing Tad Keller's failed polygraph with the examiner when he got a call from Lieutenant Carruthers to meet in the conference room. He took his brief case and file boxes of photos with him.

Captain Thomas Ware of robbery-homicide stood at the head of the conference table. He removed his reading glasses and pushed back from the table, unimpressed. Lieutenant Carruthers sat next to Van Cleef equally unimpressed.

"Your number one suspect is dead," Captain Ware said.

"He was never my 'number one suspect,'" Van Cleef said.

Captain Ware glanced at Van Cleef with a confused look. Carruthers looked down and scribbled some notes and just listened.

"The D.A. thinks he was involved in his wife's murder and then he committed suicide, plain and simple," Captain

Ware said. "Let's wrap this thing up."

"I'm going to need some more time, Captain."

Captain Ware flashed Lieutenant Carruthers a look and sighed.

"Your time is needed elsewhere," Carruthers said. "You're running out of resources and leads."

"Is this about Warren Slezick?" Van Cleef asked.

"What the hell does he have to do with anything?" Carruthers said, standing up and stretching his back. He faced the window overlooking the downtown Civic Center.

"You tell me," Van Cleef said. "Look, Sleezebag and his team are the ones running out of leads on their dogfighting raids, and now I got him breathing down my neck with one of my suspects. I'd say—"

"Dogfighting is the FBI's business and none of our concern," Captain Ware said, standing up and pacing. "It is our understanding that you are crossing lines with the FBI's current investigation of dogfighting rings in several counties. Now how you think that ties in with a celebrity mauling and her now deceased plastic surgeon husband, is beyond my wildest imagination. However, that will stop today. You've been warned by Agent Slezick to keep your nose out of his dogfighting investigations. Do not interfere."

"Sheila Evans's husband had nothing to do with her murder," Van Cleef said, raising his voice from across the table. "Other people are involved."

"Dogfighting people?" Carruthers asked, troubled, turning away from the window and facing Van Cleef.

"It's a distinct possibility," Van Cleef said.

"You're reaching, Leo," Carruthers said. "Let's wrap it up."

Van Cleef studied Lieutenant Carruther's face for several minutes. He felt something was being withheld between the three men.

"Why did you assign me to the Evans murder case, Mike?"

"We had our suspicions early on with her husband," Lieutenant Carruthers said confidently.

"C'mon Mike, you can do better than that," Van Cleef said.

"Look Leo, just trust we had our reasons."

"Give me the real reasons."

Captain Ware and Lieutenant Carruthers exchanged glances.

"Your buddy, Boots," Captain Ware said.

"Boots?"

They both nodded.

"What the hell does he have to do with this?"

Lieutenant Carruthers sat on the edge of the conference table and said, "Why don't you tell us, Leo?"

"I wish I knew."

"You seem to be wasting your personal time on his mauling," Carruthers said. "Aside from you being one of the few friends he had, what is your special interest in his accidental and unfortunate death?"

"I'll answer that Mike," Captain Ware said, checking his watch and cutting him off.

"Ed Boots was sniffing around like you, Leo," Captain Ware said. "He started crossing the line with Agent Slezick and his dogfighting investigations, like you are. Now Slezick told us to inform you to back off and you will back off."

"With all due respect, Captain," Van Cleef said. "I think Ed Boots was onto something."

Carruthers interjected and said, "Yeah, Agent Slezick—and we sure as hell don't need you following Boots's blind alley."

"I wouldn't call this a blind alley, sir," Van Cleef said.

"No?" Captain Ware asked in a demeaning tone of voice.

"No," Van Cleef said. "Let's start with the murder weapon... a Pakistani Bully Kutta."

Captain Ware shuffled through some reports in front of him and said, "I thought it was a pit bull that mauled Sheila

Evans."

Lieutenant Carruther's said, "Ah, it could have been a pit bull, still—"

"It was most definitely not," Van Cleef said. "The DNA came back and confirmed the PBK breed."

"You're talking in circles, Van Cleef," Carruthers said, pacing. "Look, why don't you let Warren Slezick and the FBI do what they do, and you do what you do best and wrap up the murder investigation."

Captain Ware lowered his voice, reviewing Van Cleef's reports. He suggested Van Cleef relax.

Van Cleef eased back into his chair and softened his tone. "Look, Sheila Evans wasn't murdered by her husband," Van Cleef said. "That much I know. I think the same person or persons that killed Sheila killed her husband. The dog was used as a murder weapon, and this is a clear-cut case of canine homicide."

"Jesus, Leo," Carruthers interjected again, "These pit bull attacks are an everyday occurrence across the country... what makes this one unique?"

"Well, for starters... it wasn't a pit bull."

Captain Ware shot a confused look at Van Cleef.

"We are looking for a rarer breed known as a Pakistani Bully Kutta, or PBK for short," Van Cleef said. "This is a powerful and dangerous animal. We are not looking for a common pit bull. Furthermore, whoever murdered Dr. Plotkin— and he was murdered— could likely be, or be linked to, the same person who killed Sheila Evans. They're still at large. While the Evans-Plotkin murders seem clear cut on the surface, I can assure you that the dog that was used as a murder weapon was born, bred, and sold to fight and kill... that was this beast's sole purpose. There is a dog-fighting connection."

"Then all the more reason you should let Warren Slezick and the FBI handle it," Carruthers said.

"It's the wrong move," Van Cleef said.

"Leo, you're running out of time and resources on this one. Let's wrap it up and call it a day," Carruthers said in a calming voice of reason. "We've got Goldstone up our department's ass now, and you know he is a reputable attorney with plenty of clout who would welcome the media attention."

Captain Ware added as he reviewed several notes, "As I see it, Detective Van Cleef... Dr. Plotkin was financially insolvent. His practice was nearly bankrupt and he was in collections with most of his creditors. What's clear cut is: You have a celebrity doctor who's in over his head— he doesn't want to pay his wife alimony and just wants to run off with some pretty young thing, so he kills his wife and then he can't live with the guilt, so he kills himself. It's that simple."

"Yeah, that simple. Too simple," Van Cleef said. "Except you forgot the part about the rare breed of dog, the affair the wife might have been having, and the other accomplices involved— Look, I'm getting real close."

"Is it your theory, Detective Van Cleef, that maybe the husband got involved in dogfighting because he was so deep in debt?" Captain Ware asked.

"Not at all."

Van Cleef got up from his seat and was ready to walk out. He had had enough.

Lieutenant Carruthers ordered him to sit back down. Van Cleef remained standing.

"Now, Lieutenant Carruthers here is right," Captain Ware said. "I'm sure you're well aware of the problems Gordon Goldstone, the Plotkin's family attorney, can cause for the LAPD. He's a media whore and is threatening harassment— claims you personally pushed his client over the edge."

"Well aware," Van Cleef said. "Goldstone is another attorney after the media attention and the money. He could give a shit about the real killers out there. The canine homicide in Malibu and the made-to-look-like-a-suicide in Beverly Hills—" Van Cleef censored himself. He did not want to talk himself into a hole. He took a deep breath and exhaled and said, "Now this is a real switch."

"What's a real switch?" Lieutenant Carruthers asked.

"Usually it's the other way around," Van Cleef said. "Usually, I'm the one trying to convince you or some other deputy district attorney on a suspect— I told you I'm real close to wrapping it up."

Captain Ware rose from behind his desk and said, "Close is not good enough. You know that, Leo. You are one of our best detectives, but you have not produced one viable suspect, and you don't even have a murder weapon."

"Correction," Van Cleef said. "Oh, we have the murder weapon. It was discovered recently up in Malibu Canyon with a .22 caliber bullet in its massive skull. That dog was the canine that killed Sheila Evans and the owner happens to be a semi-famous heavyweight boxer. Now this is no common pit bull that was used. This unique dog is used in Pakistan for hunting and bear-baiting. I have confirmation from the lab that this dog did in fact murder Sheila Evans. I also have confirmation that those bones are that of what some call, "The Beast of the East." We got a 'lookout' from the day of the murder who just failed his polygraph… Now, Slezick and his team can hunt down and bust all the dogfighting rings they want, and I applaud them for that, but this is one Pakistani Bully Kutta that is not on his suspect list. It's on mine, and I am going to find its owner come hell or high water."

Lieutenant Carruthers asked in a meek tone, "This Bully Kunta monster—"

Van Cleef corrected him and said, "Bully Kutta."

"Whatever the hell the thing is— You say it's capable of

taking down a bear?"

"Their reputation doesn't lie. They are as tough as advertised."

"Jesus," Lieutenant Carruthers said, while he reflexively caressed his neck.

"Here's something else to chew on while you're at it," Van Cleef said. He tossed several gruesome and graphic crime scene photos on the conference table in front of Carruthers and Ware. "Sheila Evans was a meager 120 lbs. When this monster used her as a chew toy, she looked like she had been put through a garbage disposal. Now, the maniac that turned it loose on her is still out there, and he either got bored with traditional blood sports or someone paid him a lot of money and went through a lot of trouble to send the FBI barking up the wrong tree… and I don't think we want him walking the streets. This creep isn't part of any dogfighting ring Slezick is looking for."

The room fell silent. Van Cleef won his case to carry on. No more negotiating. He did not have to say another word.

"The press— "Captain Ware interjected.

"No one knows about this breed that was used in the murder, except the killer," Van Cleef said. "I'd appreciate it if you keep it that way until I wrap this up."

"The public thinks it was a random pit bull attack as far as I have seen or heard reported," Lieutenant Carruthers added.

"Great," Van Cleef said. "Let 'em continue to think that."

"Now that's a switch," Lieutenant Carruthers said, chiding Van Cleef.

"What's a switch?" Van Cleef asked, packing up his briefcase and file boxes.

"I thought you were out to save the reputation of these precious pit bulls and didn't want the media misleading—"

"Save it, Lieutenant, will you?" Van Cleef said, reflecting on his outrage about the media misreporting Sheila Evans's murder.

Captain Ware checked his watch and moved around to the front of his desk. He patted Van Cleef on the back, showing him the door and said, "I know you want to tie this case up, but I need more from you and know that you will deliver the goods quicker."

Van Cleef exited the conference room dejected and lost in thought. He heard a door shut behind him and Lieutenant Carruthers emerged and asked, "How's Claudia?"

Van Cleef continued to walk back to the squad room, ignoring Carruthers's small talk.

"Leo, hold up a minute."

They both stood outside the squad room door, which was closed.

"I'll see what I can do to correct the—"

"Don't bother," Van Cleef said, twisting the handle on the door. He sensed the Lieutenant still wanted to talk or felt bad about their interaction. "Is there something else you'd like to discuss?"

Lieutenant Carruthers invited Van Cleef to join him in a peaceful discussion back at his office. Van Cleef agreed. He sat down, and as Carruthers closed the door, he said, "I heard about the ruckus at Boots's place."

"Ruckus?" Van Cleef asked. "Maybe attempted robbery, that's a whole 'nother story."

Lieutenant Carruthers took a seat behind his desk and said, "I could use a good bedtime story." He kicked his feet up on his desk and folded his arms behind his head with his big ears hanging on every word.

"Isn't it past your bedtime?" Van Cleef asked.

"I'm not sleepy— go on... so, the detectives down in Pismo tell me you were spending quite a bit of time investigating at Boots's place."

"I would've been in and out faster, but Boots had a guest."

"A guest with a key?"

"More like an intruder that had access to a key and then fled the scene."

"Boots had several families over his lifetime. Maybe you scared one of his family members or relatives off."

"Then I should have been the one fleeing, don't you think?"

Lieutenant Carruthers thought about it and nodded. He said, "This bedtime story is gonna put me to sleep. Why don't you get to the good parts?"

"Sure, why not," Van Cleef said. "So, since we're on the subject of big bad wolves, unicorns, and silly bedtime stories, why was Boots really forced out?"

"Come again?"

"C'mon Lieutenant," Van Cleef said. "Everyone in the department knows Boots was forced into retirement. But why?"

Lieutenant Carruthers leaned forward and said, "Dirty Harry is a bad bedtime story, Leo," Carruthers said, rising from his chair. "Let's call it a night."

"I'm not sleepy, either. Go on," Van Cleef said.

"We had our reasons, Leo, and I understand he was a friend of yours, but like I said, we had our reasons and it was time for Boots to move on and enjoy retirement and his Golden Years."

"Doesn't look like he got to enjoy them, if you ask me."

"He can thank his dog for that."

"And you believe that?"

Lieutenant Carruthers stared at Van Cleef long and hard in a concerned way. He said, "Leo, either you're getting a touch of that nasty flu or you've been working too much overtime on this canine-homicide, but you can't possibly think Ed Boots was murdered too like Sheila Evans, do you?"

Van Cleef didn't answer.

"My God," Lieutenant Carruthers said. "You do. That's insane."

"Is it?"

"It is."

"What if Boots's intruder was our 'boxer-man' suspect?"

"With a key?"

Van Cleef was lost in thought, half listening.

"Boots certainly had more enemies than friends, that's for sure," Lieutenant Carruthers said.

"Most of them were his co-workers."

Lieutenant Carruthers came out from around his desk and showed Van Cleef the door, not out of courtesy, just to let Van Cleef know that the meeting was over on his terms.

"Look Leo, I see it like this... the intruder was probably a random petty thief on a hot prowl, nothing more to it. Key bump. No forced entry. I just fail to see any connection with Evans's case and Boots."

"I don't buy it."

"I'm not asking you to," Lieutenant Carruthers said. "Don't lose sleep over it, and let me let you in on a little secret, my friend, that's not so secret... I know Boots was a wiseass.. Loved putting people on. I never knew when to take him seriously, quite frankly. He could lie straight-faced and could ace a lie detector, which made him a damn good detective." I also know Ed Boots had a thing for women of color, and from what I understand he had quite a few kids out of wedlock, which may predate your friendship with him. Some of us used to tease him about his second wife. We used to call her 'Cleopatra Jones.'"

"Bad movie," Van Cleef said with a smirk.

"Bad marriage, too," Lieutenant Carruthers said, swallowing a gulp of coffee. "Boots was a hard guy to live with from what I understand. Anyway, half his paycheck was spent on child support and running around. I'm surprised he wound up with a home in Pismo... he must've been stashing money from the D.A. and his ex-wives. Ed Boots, a racist? Not on your life... the department was changing, that's all, and it was time for him to retire."

Van Cleef still wasn't buying it.

"Look Leo," Lieutenant Carruthers said. "I'm not denying it was politics... look, there was politics involved. It was a political thing."

"Politics."

"Yeah, yeah, politics."

"Dirty politics?"

"Do you know of any other kind?"

Van Cleef did not, and he decided to end the discussion there. His mind was drifting to Ed Boots's crazy life and ex-wives. He had heard rumors that Boots was screwing around with the DA's wife. Those kind of "politics" could have cost him an early retirement. He also had his own suspicions that the so-called intruder was not a friend of the family and that Figaro was taking the fall like Dr. Plotkin.

Both innocent and both now dead.

36

"YOU REMEMBER MCGRUFF?" Van Cleef asked his wife, Claudia. "Y'know… the way he used to say: *Help take a bite out of crime…* in all those PSA commercials when he'd nab the bad guy." Van Cleef did a spot-on imitation of the character that sounded like the commerical.

Claudia lay across the couch reviewing a script for a new film that was in pre-production at the studio. For a moment she fantasied about what it would be like if they were more like *McMillian & Wife*, the '70s television police procedural starring Rock Hudson and Susan Saint James. But Van Cleef wouldn't ever let her solve anything in real life.

"You're talking about the cartoon?" she asked, glancing up from a movie script.

"No," Van Cleef said, slightly annoyed. "He wasn't just a cartoon like *Underdog*. McGruff was more of a PSA to deter crime and teach kids not to steal, not to commit crimes, and not to bully other kids. He even had songs kids could sing." He imitated him again, pleased with his own impersonation which was starting to sound more like Jimmy Durante as McGruff.

"I don't remember singing any of his songs," Claudia said, teasing her husband.

"It wasn't like McGruff was Paul McCartney or Michael Jackson and on the Billboard 100. He wasn't known for his hit songs. He was known for his message."

"What was his message?"

"Stay outta trouble. Don't break the law. That kinda message— Look, Claudia, I'd love to get into some trouble with you tonight, but I gotta lotta work to do here."

Claudia started teasing her husband thinking it was cute, as wives sometimes do, twisting her hair and batting her eyelashes. She was asking him what breed of dog McGruff was and whatever happened to him. Silly questions that Van Cleef got tired of and eventually suggested she should go look on the internet and YouTube if she was so interested in McGruff's life story. Maybe her Hollywood studio pals could remake McGruff's life. Tell it on the big screen. Get DiCaprio to play him or something. He wasn't playing along with her. She eventually got up and said, "I heard the studio is re-releasing all of Sheila Evans's films."

"How thoughtful," Van Cleef said, studying his reports and comparing case notes. He didn't bother to look up once from his desk.

"I thought the film she did with Tom Selleck was her best work," Claudia said, fishing for information.

"She did several films with Selleck," Van Cleef said, organizing the strewn paperwork in front of him and trying hard not to break his concentration.

Claudia thought about it, "Yeah, you're right," she said. "The one I was thinking of was the western." Claudia was still hanging around, trying to elicit conversation that Van Cleef was not offering and seldom did on cases he was working on.

"I saw Tom Selleck was at her wake on the news," she said.

This broke Van Cleef's concentration. He said, "Yes, Claudia, he was there and so were a lot of people that she worked with. Industry people, Hollywood types, and people you probably know… look I have a lot of work here to finish, and I'd like to catch her killer if you don't mind… C'mon honey, you know I love you."

Claudia took the hint and left the room. Bacall stayed with Van Cleef since she knew she could get an extra walk out of him at night. Besides, he tended to talk less and just stare at papers and the computer, and sometimes she enjoyed the silence as opposed to Claudia always being on her cell phone.

Van Cleef heard his wife muttering something under her breath about him being a "crab ass" and "no fun anymore…" while she was banging dishes around in the cupboard.

She was still upset about him missing her holiday party at Spago, but understood this was part of being a detective's wife.

He dismissed her comments and opened the large FedEx box that contained the printed dog attack tome that Gordon Goldstone tried to give him the night Dr. Plotkin died. The paper even had Goldstone's stink on it, a combination of stale cigarette smoke and cheap old men's aftershave. Something putrid. Van Cleef was sensitive to smells and scents. He had to be careful being a migraineur that little things like odors didn't trigger one. He kept Goldstone's CDC report at arm's length on his desk.

He put on his reading glasses and referenced the CDC (Center for Disease Control) reports and his own stacks of crime scene photos and dogfighting magazines confiscated during the raids. All these items were strewn over Van Cleef's desk at home. Although the information in the CDC report was edifying, Van Cleef felt that Goldstone was just distracting him, like Van Cleef was doing to Overstreet.

He cross-referenced his hard copies with keywords on Google:

"Ancient Rome Coliseum" and "blood sports." "Michael Vick" and "Dogfighting" yielded pages and pages of dog-fighting and pit bull attacks.

"LeShon Johnson," another NFL football player busted for dogfighting. Michael Vick must've been a fan of his. Van Cleef never had any interest in sports. He was a rare breed himself. He thought for a moment. It wasn't a stretch to involve a has-been boxer in a dogfighting ring and illegal activity. The pieces fit. For some odd reason an abstract literary reference popped into his head. His mind drifted to Michael Crichton's classic book, *The Great Train Robbery*. In the book Mr. T would never be the sort of high-minded and proper model citizen one would suspect of engaging in ratting sports, but in that story Mr. T, a bank president of all things and a devout Christian, was mixing with the lowest common denominator throwing his own dog in the 'pit.' Van Cleef wondered, *could Dr. Plotkin be involved somehow?*

Van Cleef muttered to himself something he remembered from the book, "Every man has his fancy, baiting sports in reality."

His mind snapped back into the present and out of Victorian society and classic literature. He had set up Google Alerts for "pit bull attacks," and any breaking news or new information would be emailed to him. His inbox was getting barraged and cluttered with daily emails. News stories were cropping up all over Southern California like never before. He would scan comments on news sites and blogs on the internet and look for fanatics or hatred towards the pit bull breed. Then he'd subsequently contact his computer forensics division and have them trace the IP address if there was a reason to suspect the individual.

Pages and pages, he sifted through. It was overwhelming, like combing a beach with a metal detector hoping to find that one precious gem.

He felt Bacall staring off into space. Her eyes looked sad for some reason.

Van Cleef stopped what he was doing and reached over her to pet her head. He said softly, "I know… I miss him too." This case had strange timing and implications following the passing of his beloved family dog, Bogart. *Why now?* He felt himself doze off. His mind drifted back to the nightmare and the night he had to make that horrible decision to put his dog down.

1 MONTH EARLIER

All the lights were off that night at Van Cleef's house, which was atypical considering it was only 8 p.m. and Claudia always kept every light on. Her white BMW was parked in the driveway. Van Cleef could still remember the feeling in the air and the scent of vanilla candles burning when he entered their home. The first thing he noticed was Bacall was not there to greet him— Maybe she was outside or in the back of the house?

There was a candle flickering in the front room. Claudia's shadow animated the wall. She had her arms wrapped around Bogart, hugging him while he lay nearly lifeless in her lap when her husband entered the room. She did not even hear Van Cleef come in or see him standing in the doorway. She just stared ahead into the flickering flame. Grief-stricken. Rocking back and forth cradling Bogart. Her eyes swollen from crying. Van Cleef looked beyond Claudia and noticed Bacall sitting next to her. The world stopped spinning. Everything froze at that moment. It was so quiet he could hear her wristwatch ticking. They had decided that this was to be the day.

They had to make the dreaded decision to put Bogart down. He had been gradually declining for too long from Canine De-

generative Myelopathy, and it had gotten to the point where he could no longer eat or drink.

Van Cleef approached his wife lovingly and put his arm around her and gently petted Bogart.

The sound of other dogs in the neighborhood walking by his window got to him. He finally made a call to the veterinarian hospital and grabbed one of Bogart's favorite blankets that he used to like to curl up in— he petted his soft fur again and fixated on his dead eyes staring into space— that look that he had seen in victims hundreds of times. But this was different.

Claudia did not look up from the candle flame. She didn't say a word. They both knew this day was coming. This dreaded day. The day that every dog owner has to face. The death of their beloved pet... their family member. That was part of the deal. What you signed up for. So full of life, tricking you into thinking that they'd live forever. Always there to remind you that good things in life are temporary. A dog. A smile. Happiness.

Van Cleef imagined the same questions and conversation that would haunt him for a lifetime:

"Leo?"

"What honey?"

"Do you think we made the right decision..? Maybe we shouldn't have listened to the vet."

He went with the answer she needed to hear and said, "Absolutely. It was the only right thing to do at the time."

Van Cleef was angry. Angry that he didn't have more time with Bogart. Angry that dogs didn't live that long. Angry that it was over.

He said in a gentle, soothing tone, "We did everything we possibly could for him."

"I know we tried——"

Claudia started sobbing. Van Cleef got up from the couch and looked out the front window. Bacall did not move from Claudia's side. She just kept her head down.

Van Cleef remembered the smell of Jasmine in the night air outside. It was a peaceful night, and this was Bogart's last ride. He pulled over several blocks before the large Animal Hospital to speak his last thoughts to his loyal friend, but it was too late. His friend had passed away on his own. He put the car in park and cried like a baby.

Something his wife had never seen him do.

PRESENT

Van Cleef's thoughts were startled by Bacall's whimpering.

He rubbed his eyes, smiled, and said, "We'll go for a walk in a little bit, baby."

Bacall put her head down and let out a sigh. He muttered to himself, "I miss you, Bogie. Show me some love or some good luck from above, will you boy?"

He pulled the CDC Report and grabbed a ruler from his desk drawer. Van Cleef referenced the dog breeds and fatalities on the grid.

Doberman pinchers were on the usual suspects list. He said out loud to Bacall, "Did you know that your breed is on this list?"

Bacall was beginning to nod off. Spoiled mutt.

"You were real big in Nazi Germany... I'll bet you didn't know that."

Van Cleef went through the stacks of photos. He opened the photo of the metal fragment that Halliwell sent him earlier in an email. He enlarged the photo on his computer and noted a small series of numbers and letters impressed on the metal, possibly a partial serial number.

Van Cleef sat staring outside his empty backyard window, watching the wind animate the trees. It was almost hypnotizing him due to the lack of sleep. He stood up and startled Bacall, who also stood up from a deep sleep.

He grinned and caressed her head and gently said, "Pretty soon, girl, we'll go for a walk soon. Go lay back down."

Bacall did as she was told and laid back down.

Overstreet called with good news, "Get ready to be happy, boss," he said, his voice bursting with excitement on the other end of the phone.

"Lay it on me."

"Anthony, Tony "Killer" Manjaro. You ever heard of him?"

"You know I don't follow sports, Dennis. Fill me in."

"Well, that little shit, Sang, wasn't lying after all. He was famous for something 'likie' boxing," Overstreet said imitating Sang. He continued, "Manjaro exited around the time Manny Pacchio became a thing, but this guy was a heavyweight and apparently hit rock bottom after his career went south. I was watching his fights on YouTube. He wasn't bad at all. Brick shithouse, just probably got mixed up with a shitty promoter. Anyway, so he started driving for an independent limo company in L.A.— he would work infrequently and pick up a few odd shifts here and there for some extra cash. When he did work, he would shuttle high-profile guests around in town cars to and from LAX and take them back to their mansions or houses in the hills."

"So, you think Malibu was on our boy's schedule?" Van Cleef asked.

"Most definitely. I'm steps ahead of you on this one, brother. The owner of the limo company, a guy by the name of Lew Friedman, confirmed that Sheila Evans was a customer some time ago. He offered it up and beat me to the question. He also confirmed Manjaro was her driver or pickup."

"Which obviously connects this Manjaro creep to our victim, Sheila Evans," Van Cleef said.

"Yes," Overstreet said, talking louder on the other end

and getting even more excited than before. "It gets better. Lew had to fire Manjaro because he would show up late, take detours, and was difficult to work with, to the extent that Manjaro was drinking on the job. Manjaro also spent some time in one of those highfalutin celebrity rehab places out in Malibu. Apparently, he got addicted to painkillers, Oxy, and shit like that. I got that info off of TMZ, and it was all public in the news if you followed it."

"Dennis," Van Cleef said. "I'm afraid I underestimated you."

"Yeah, well screw you, Leo," Overstreet said, joking. "But wait, there's more…" He delivered this line in a tone of voice like it was an infomercial or something he was selling. "Guess who Manjaro had at one time representing him as an attorney?"

Van Cleef's brain was spent. He blurted out, "Gloria Allred?"

"Close," Overstreet said. "Gordon Goldstone."

Van Cleef fell silent and almost dropped the phone. Overstreet had to ask, "You still there boss?"

"Yeah, I'm still here."

Van Cleef had mixed emotions. He was happy with Overstreet's new developments, but angry that he missed something and that Gordon Goldstone was possibly lying to protect his one-time client, Manjaro. He would confront this omission soon with Goldstone.

"Great work, Overstreet. Really good work, thank you."

"Just doing my job. You should spend more time in the office or on the internet, Leo… nothing's private anymore—You can find most of this shit on the web. It's just a matter of connecting the dots, which is what we do."

"Yeah, it's what we do," Van Cleef repeated before he hung up with Overstreet, still troubled about Goldstone. He would have to put on his boxing gloves for the next round with this asshole.

Van Cleef continued to ruminate on the dogfighting connection. He added a visit to the LAPD's K9 Platoon division to his list of loose ends in the investigation.

37

VAN CLEEF STOOD admiring the canine tribute photos that hung on the wall of all the courageous police service dogs (PSDs) who lost their lives in the line of duty. A stern voice startled him from behind and said, "Handsome bunch, aren't they?"

Van Cleef turned around to face Winston King, the Chief Trainer of LAPD's K-9 Platoon. "They all look so proud and regal," Van Cleef said.

"And they all have pretty amazing stories," King said.

"I see that," Van Cleef said, turning back around as if he were at an art gallery or museum admiring the historic paintings and photos, hands clasped behind his back. Winston King stepped forward and stood at his side. Van Cleef extended his hand to shake and said, "Oh, ah... I'm Detective Leo Van Cleef from HSS, I was so engrossed—"

Chief Winston shook his hand and said, "I know. We were expecting you and you are early."

Van Cleef fixated on one particular photo of a German shepherd named Bullitt that kind of reminded him of his beloved dog, Bogart.

"What happened to Bullitt?" Van Cleef asked.

"Bullitt was one of our best K9s and died with the suspect," Winston King said. "He was one of our gun detection canines and was deployed in a dangerous situation in South Central involving gangbangers. Something set him off and his officer could not retrieve him. Bullitt went ballistic and disobeyed the commands and just kept attacking the suspect. He found the guns alright, but..."

Lieutenant Winston King paused. He became self-conscious of Van Cleef analyzing him, immersed in his story. He said, "Anyway, he was shot several times by another gangbanger, but he killed the first suspect. Went for his jugular. This was before we used E-Collars."

"E-Collars?"

"Sorry, electronic collars."

"Oh, you mean shock collars."

Winston corrected him, "We like to think of them as lifesavers. We don't misuse them for punishment. We use them properly for training and conditioning."

"I see," Van Cleef said. "Does the shock hurt them?"

"No," Winston said. "Try to think of it as an invisible leash. The E-Collar is beneficial on many levels. It also protects us legally with defense attorneys, the courts, and the suspect's families. If the K9 won't respond to a command, we can use the E-Collar and call off our partner back to our side. Again, it's a lifesaver."

Van Cleef was fascinated by the E-Collar and asked, "May I see a demonstration of the E-Collar today?"

"Absolutely," Winston said. "We've been using them over 25 years now and it's pretty straightforward."

Van Cleef turned his attention back to the tribute wall and focused on another Rottweiler lost in the line of duty by the name of Phantom. He asked, "What happened to Phantom?"

"Phantom was killed by a pack of wild dogs. He got

loose in a suspect's yard in San Bernardino. Idiot was running a Meth lab and had a damn kennel in his back yard for protection. Could've blown up the neighborhood with all those chemicals. Phantom did not survive the odds... it was four against one. I think they were pit mixes and a Preso. Phantom was outnumbered. The four dogs were like lions and overpowered him. It all ended very quickly, and the other dogs were shot by officers."

Van Cleef did not comment. His mind flashed to the murder victims and the focus of his case, which was the reason for meeting with the K9 unit. He said, "Well, I appreciate you taking the time today."

"Anytime. We don't get personal visits from HSS often, except when we work out in the field."

They walked out into the training yard where one of the K-9 officers was conducting exercises with another officer in a bite suit. Van Cleef and Winston King stood on the sidelines like coaches in a football game and watched the rehearsal exercises and drills.

"The K9 you see there is named Rilke," Winston King said.

"Like the poet." Van Cleef said.

Winston King nodded as they observed the female officer. She used the attack word "Creed" and the Belgian Malinois breed charged like a freight train at the officer in the bite suit who was just standing there bracing himself for impact, looking like a giant cloth cookie cutter puppet.

"Watch closely now," Winston King said.

Before Van Cleef could even ask 'watch what' the female officer yelled, "Courage" and Rilke stopped dead in his tracks and sat in front of the officer in the bite suit.

She then yelled, "Prometheus," and the dog went wild on the officer in the bite suit.

Van Cleef raised his eyebrows, leaned into Lieutenant Winston and said, "How does she make it stop?"

"Keep watching."

The female trainer yelled, "Tough."

Then something strange happened. The dog just stopped cold, cowered, and came running back.

Van Cleef, curious asked, "What just happened? Why did he just stop?"

Winston shouted to the female trainer to hold up her right arm for the detective.

The handler held up a transmitter in her right hand.

"Is that a radio transmitter?" Van Cleef asked.

"Sort of. It controls the E-Collar."

"The E-Collar," Van Cleef repeated, thinking to himself.

"Yes sir, as I mentioned earlier, the LAPD has been using them for about 25 years, and when the dogs don't listen to us and follow their own instinct, we get them back on track."

"And as you said, it doesn't hurt them?"

"No, on the contrary, it helps them and keeps us outta hot water, if you know what I mean."

"Yes, like you said earlier."

"Not being restricted by a leash gives us tactical control over the dog. When we can't recall our partner back, this does the trick. A long time ago we used to send a dog in and wait for him to come out of a building or house. Not anymore. These were originally used for hunting dogs."

"I appreciate the demonstration," Van Cleef said.

Van Cleef and Winston walked back toward the office. Winston took a seat behind his desk and said, "I've been meaning to ask you—"

Van Cleef smiled and said, "If I'm related to actor Lee Van Cleef?"

"No, never heard of him."

"Sure, go ahead."

"You worked Robbery-Homicide years ago with Ed Boots, right?"

Van Cleef reluctantly answered *yes*, since he never knew what Boots might have said to offend someone and wasn't here, or alive, to defend himself.

"You know, I never believed his dog killed him."

"Oh?" Van Cleef responded, surprised.

"Not for a minute," Winston said. "I met his dog, Figaro, a couple of times. Sweet animal."

"Did Boots want you to help train Figaro or something?"

"Well, let's put it this way… Figaro would've never made it on our K-9 Team."

"Too wild?"

"Too wild?'" Winston laughed. "Hell no, too meek. That dog was one Poodle of a pit bull, a real powder puff."

Van Cleef smiled and nodded, "I know what you mean. I met the dog a few times— Boots used to joke about how he had to go out and buy a real home security system since his dog would sleep through a robbery. I have a dog like Figaro."

They both stopped laughing and reflecting on Boots and his lazy pit bull Figaro.

"I mailed him one of our E-Collars once as a joke."

"Really," Van Cleef said. "How long ago was that?"

Winston thought about it for a moment. "About six months before he died."

Van Cleef's mind raced back to the photos of Figaro on the refrigerator. The strange collar he noticed in the photo must have been the shock collar. Van Cleef also recalled that the E-collar was missing and not mentioned in any of the detective's notes from the night of the murder or in the Animal Control's report.

Van Cleef shook hands with Winston and thanked him.

38

THE CENTURY TOWERS were located in Century City on Avenue of the Stars. The unmistakable, miniature World Trade Center architecture gleamed in the sunlight. Lawyers were a dime a dozen here. Gordon Goldstone was one of those dozens.

Van Cleef pulled into the subterranean garage from Olympic Boulevard and circled his way down to the bottom of the structure and located one of the remaining visitor parking spots available. He referenced Goldstone's suite number and headed up to the lobby.

The shiny marble floors reflected Van Cleef's shadow as he approached the female Asian desk clerk. She walked around from behind the desk and gave Van Cleef a personal escort to the inside elevators after he showed her his ID. They wished each other a good day and a genuine smile.

15th Floor. Suite 1550.

Goldstone's legal secretary greeted him and ushered him into Goldstone's brass and mahogany office.

Van Cleef took a seat, gazing out at the mountains in the distance. He noticed the family photos and various celebrity photos not dissimilar to Dr. Plotkin's office.

"Listen, I gotta go," Goldstone said to the person on the phone, perturbed at Van Cleef.

He hung up and his demeanor changed.

"You've got a lot of nerve, Detective," Goldstone said, pushing back from his desk.

"So, I've been told," Van Cleef said, sitting down.

"You've done enough damage, Detective Van Cleef. I'd start considering a new career if I were you."

Van Cleef dropped the large rubber-banded stack of papers in the middle of his desk, making a loud thud. The dog attack reports from the CDC that Goldstone printed out for him were staring him back in the face.

"I'm returning this waste of paper to you because you left out one killer breed," Van Cleef said.

"Pardon me?" Goldstone asked.

"You forgot to include a boxer."

Goldstone was confused and reached for the stack of papers in the middle of his desk. Van Cleef stopped him. It was all an act, anyway.

"Save it, Goldstone. The boxer I'm looking for is not in that dog pile of crap. I'm looking for a killer boxer you used to represent."

"I'm afraid I don't understand, Detective, and I'm late for a meeting." Goldstone walked around his desk and headed for the door. Van Cleef stepped in front of him.

"I didn't come here for career counseling, Gordon, just some straight answers once and for all."

Goldstone laughed in disbelieve. He was a quick study. He stepped over to the floor-to-ceiling window overlooking Los Angeles. The ocean was visible today in absence of smog.

"Let's cut the shit, Detective Van Cleef. I'll take a wild guess and assume you've got another one of my clients in your gun sights, is that correct? Is that what you came sniffing around for?"

"You represent Tony Manjaro?"

"Used to."

"Used to recently?"

"As recently as two years ago."

Goldstone checked his calendar on his phone as he moved away from the window, while putting on his suit coat and straightening his tie. "I am due in court at 11 a.m. in Santa Monica," he said, checking his watch. "I am preparing for a high-profile case and cannot be late, so in short summary, why would Mr. Manjaro be on your list of suspects?"

"His name was recently brought up in connection with the San Bernardino dogfighting ring and we're having some difficulty tracking him down."

Goldstone excused himself as he dialed his legal secretary while opening several nearby file cabinets. Van Cleef heard him bark at her, something about TMZ and Robbins.

The legal secretary burst through the door moments later with the file that Goldstone was rummaging around for. He said, "Well, Detective Van Cleef, I suggest you get a better GPS system and get busy locating him. I am not responsible for my client's actions after they sever their ties or their cases are closed. You should know that Mr. Manjaro closed out his bill with me several years ago, and I have not spoken with him since."

Gordon Goldstone walked around Van Cleef and muttered something about showing himself out and not validating for parking.

His legal secretary emerged moments later from outside the door and opened Goldstone's door wider for Van Cleef to leave. She also reiterated that their law office would not validate for parking.

Van Cleef figured Goldstone wasn't the type to pay for parking, the cheap son-of-a-bitch.

He placed a call to Overstreet and asked for the name of

the Malibu celebrity rehab center that Manjaro had dried out at. He then placed a call to the rehab facility and got directions and some attitude from a receptionist named Dory that sounded like she was fresh out of high school, but was willing to book a same day "free" consultation with their prestigious addiction guru, Dr. Trent Thompson. He then pulled out of the parking lot of the Century Towers and headed towards Malibu.

He wasn't happy that parking cost him sixteen dollars for his half-hour visit to Goldstone.

"Lawyers..." Van Cleef said in a cynical tone to himself on his way out.

39

VAN CLEEF DROVE UP the rolling Pacific Coast Highway back to Malibu. He had been spending more time on the road than he hoped to, but there were worse places in Los Angeles to be than Malibu. His instinct told him that he was getting close to solving the Evans-Plotkin murders. He referenced the rehab center address in his notes and made a sharp turn up the vertiginous road near Point Dume where the canine homicide murder of Sheila Evans-Plotkin occurred.

He parked his black Dodge Challenger at the top near the entrance gates of a palatial mansion that had been converted into a rehab center for recovering drug and alcohol addiction patients. He knew that Hollywood celebrities paid top dollar, sometimes near $100K for a month at these recovery centers. Most people didn't know that the poor, addicted celebrity's union health insurance plan paid for a good portion of their time drying out in these facilities. The rehab center's simple name, "The Cove," was in sharp contrast to its immense Mediterranean structure which stood overlooking Malibu at the top of the mountain. Van Cleef heard that the mansion belonged to some wild music mogul, a Phil Spector type, who converted the monstrosity into a high-priced rehab center.

Before he exited his vehicle, he enjoyed the view and the silence. It was still and quiet with a slight breeze of ocean air. He took a moment to enjoy a beautiful hummingbird in the distinctive purple flowered Jacaranda tree nearby. He downloaded a copy of the Founder and Author Dr. Trent Thompson's book from Amazon entitled C.O.R.E. Formula for a Healthier Life Forevermore onto his iPad before he headed in. The acronym stood for Completion. Oneness. Resilience. Equanimity.

Van Cleef wondered how much the "C.O.R.E. Formula" cost on an ongoing basis. He was skeptical of anything or anyone that claimed to find the Holy Grail or formula to such a complex problem as addiction. Trent's author photo on the back of the book conveyed the Freudian white-haired, bearded, professorial psychologist one would expect to see and trust. It was the Hawaiian shirt, George Hamilton tan, and Tiki lamps in the picture that bothered Van Cleef. Also, the hard selling 20% off promotional offers throughout his book that promoted additional pills, powders, and potions to get the addicted back on their feet. He thought about how much money Dr. Thompson probably spent on exotic island vacations in the South Pacific while he swung on a hammock counting his profits.

Van Cleef walked up to the black guard sitting inside the stone gatehouse. He was listening to something more important, like a sports podcast on his iPod, bored out of his mind and inattentive to the detective standing in front of him. Van Cleef cleared his throat and the guard looked up with an attitude, pulling out his iPhone earbuds as if to say, "You want something?"

When Van Cleef told him that he had a meeting with

Dr. Thompson, the guard straightened up and changed his apathetic demeanor. He politely handed him the clipboard and a little foldout, handout map to find his way to the doctor's office.

After a steep climb up a winding wooden staircase, Van Cleef found himself at the doorstep of Dr. Thompson's office, slightly out of breath.

A tattooed, young redhead greeted Van Cleef to his surprise. "I called earlier," Van Cleef said to the redhead who was snapping her gum and blocking the doorway. "I'm Detective Leo Van Cleef. Are you Dory?" he asked. Van Cleef handed her his business card.

The girl said, "No, I'm Iris. Dory left an hour ago. Do you have an appointment?"

"Yes, I do. I made it with Dory."

Iris inspected his card and his attire and then opened the door wider to reveal an opulent and empty office. "The doctor is running late, so make yourself comfortable," Iris said.

Van Cleef stepped in and stood admiring the various signed celebrity photos, each of them thanking the doctor. There were more photos of exotic trips of Dr. Thompson fire walking in Tahiti with volcanoes erupting in the background and the doctor mugging in the foreground. His desk was cluttered with Zen-like artifacts and more photos of himself with what appeared to be family members. Stacks of his C.O.R.E. book surrounded his desk. Van Cleef noticed the publishing company was Core Principles LLC, which meant the doctor self-published his book.

Van Cleef sat down in front of the desk and reviewed his questions for the doctor. He also took the time to speed read Dr. Thompson's book and Google him and his LLC while he was waiting.

There was a commotion in an adjacent room. Van Cleef recognized the female voice as Iris, whom he just met, and guessed the male voice to belong to the doctor based on the questions: "How long has he been waiting?" "Van who again?" "Where's Dory?" and "What does he want?"

There was a moment of silence and then Dr. Thompson entered with an armload of files which he set down on his desk.

Van Cleef sat for a moment waiting for the doctor to start asking questions, however, the doctor just kept methodically organizing files and filing them away, ignoring Van Cleef.

"Dr. Thompson," Van Cleef said. "I'm Detective Leo Van Cleef from Homicide Special. I came out today to speak with you about a patient by the name of Anthony Manjaro."

"You know better than that, Detective, really," Dr. Thompson said, looking down the nose of his glasses. "I can't disclose confidential information about our patients."

"It's not confidential if it's all over the internet and TMZ got a hold of the story, Dr. Thompson," Van Cleef said.

"Well, you know what I mean, and I can't help that or what gets reported on the web."

"No, I don't know what you 'really' mean," Van Cleef said. "Explain."

"I mean, Anthony is no longer my patient," Dr. Thompson said, continuing to sort and file, occasionally peering over his trendy Kenneth Cole eyeglasses.

"When did you last treat Mr. Manjaro?"

"It's been a while."

"How long ago."

"I'd have to check."

Dr. Thompson glanced out the large bay window behind his desk as if for inspiration and then began writing copious notes on a legal pad. Van Cleef waited, patiently watching the doctor and then said, "Could you check now?"

"Check what now?"

"Anthony Manjaro."

"How 'bout I get my legal department in on this meeting right now," Dr. Thompson said, attempting to dial his desk phone.

"Sure, and I can get a subpoena for your legal team right now, too, if you'd like," Van Cleef said.

Dr. Thompson slammed down the desk phone, tossed his pen across the desk, and then pressed the speakerphone on his desk once again. He let the distorted, irritating dial tone sound reverberate throughout the room for about 30 seconds and then punched in Iris's extension.

"Iris?" he asked, annoyed. "Please bring me everything you have on an Anthony Manjaro."

Van Cleef said "thank you" as they both sat patiently observing each other.

"Did you get a copy of my book, Detective?"

Van Cleef pulled out his iPad from his briefcase and held it up for Dr. Thompson to see.

The doctor smiled and then said, "I'm afraid I can't autograph that for you. Would you like a hardcover autographed from yours truly?"

Van Cleef politely said "sure" since the doctor seemed to have ample books collecting dust in his office. He watched Dr. Thompson autograph his copy and pass it across the desk to him.

"So, tell me Detective, what's special about your homicide unit?"

"We handle high-profile cases that tend to attract a lot of media."

"Is that why you are investigating Manjaro?"

"You could say so," Van Cleef said, "What was Tony in for?"

"What else, addiction."

"I figured that much. But what kind of addiction."

"Mostly alcohol."

"Mostly?"

"I'd have to review his file, but it is not uncommon for professional athletes like Tony to get addicted to painkillers like Oxycontin and Percocet, then wash it down with some hard stuff and eventually one day wake up here."

Iris returned with Manjaro's patient file and handed it over to Dr. Thompson. She did not make eye contact with Van Cleef and left the office abruptly. She looked like she might have been a patient at one time herself.

Dr. Thompson leaned back in his large, leather seat behind his desk and studied his notes, occasionally flipping through additional pages. Several minutes passed until he revealed, or censored, what he read and summarized the contents of Manjaro's file for Van Cleef.

"Anthony Manjaro left our facility completely healed," Dr. Thompson said, proud of himself. "He went through a complete detox and finished our C.O.R.E. certification program. His life should be back on track along with his career."

"Would you have his labs?"

"Is my patient a suspect?"

"He's a person of interest."

"Come now, Detective. I can assure you Mr. Manjaro contained his violence to the ring. He exhibited no violent tendencies while under our supervision."

"Look, Dr. Thompson, I'm not here to investigate your rehab facility and I certainly don't care what the FDA thinks about your C.O.R.E. Formula 1 product that you promote on every other page of your book, or even an ostensible MLM company masked as a pyramid scheme that the FTC might have significant interest in. No, sir. I'm simply here to ask for your help with a patient that our department has interest in and is a person of interest in the case I'm working on."

"Then why aren't you speaking with him?"

"You see," Van Cleef said, "That's the problem. We can't seem to locate him these days."

Dr. Thompson cooperated with Van Cleef and referenced Manjaro's last known address on file. He said defensively, "My products are not some cheap pyramid scheme. It's legitimate multi-level marketing, and this is not the first time we've had detectives out here. We're in the celebrity rehab business and I'm used to the drill. We've treated some pretty prominent celebrities here, I'll have you know— I even cured that poor woman that was mauled by the pit bull recently in our community."

"Could you repeat what I thought you just said, Doctor?" Van Cleef asked.

"I said, we've treated some pretty prominent—"

"No, not that— Sheila Evans... did you say she was a patient of yours?"

"Did I say that?"

"No, you said that 'poor woman that was mauled by the pit bull.' That was Sheila Evans."

"Oh, I can't comment on that, Detective."

"You just did."

"I guess I was thinking out loud."

"I'd also like a list of patients that were being treated at the time of Manjaro's stay," Van Cleef said as he stood up and walked around the office.

Dr. Thompson studied his every move, no matter how subtle.

"You know, Detective, when Anthony Manjaro came to me, his supplier was not some garden variety pusher or dealer. I'm sure you know as a detective that the trail usually leads back to a doctor."

Van Cleef said, "We call it 'Iatrogenesis' back at the shop." He got up to admire one of the paintings on the wall.

"Exactly," Dr. Thompson said, emerging from his desk,

clasping his hands as he joined Van Cleef at the painting he was admiring. It was surrealist Rene Magritte's painting of "Le Seducteur" which featured a ship reflecting the sea— a brilliant blue and white illusion that would play games with your perception.

"Our work here, unfortunately, is to correct the habits and addiction that some of my professional colleagues have created. Doctors like myself. One doctor prescribes Xanax and the next thing he knows the patient is addicted. Prescription drug addiction is an epidemic in our country right now and I don't condone it, I treat it."

"Did you happen to know Dr. Jordan Plotkin by any chance?"

"The Beverly Hills plastic surgeon?"

"Yes."

"I probably talked to him once or twice on the phone when his wife was a patient, why?"

"But you didn't know Dr. Jordan Plotkin?"

"No, I can't say that I did. Never met him, only his wife."

"You know he died recently, didn't you?"

"Yes, of course, everyone in our community knows about it. It was big news. Suicide or something of that nature, wasn't it?"

"Something of that nature."

Van Cleef's mind was reeling with speculation and scenarios. His read on the doctor was that he seemed to be telling the truth, but some people, or suspects, were good actors. He liked to reserve judgment. He turned his back on the doctor as he continued to admire the Magritte painting on the wall.

"I caught the Magritte exhibit at LACMA in Los Angeles back in 2007." Van Cleef said. 'Le Seducteur' was not part of the exhibit to my recollection."

"Is that a Magritte?" the doctor asked, which surprised

Van Cleef. "A patient of mine gave that to me years ago."

"Yes," Van Cleef said. "I'm a fan of illusions, Doctor. I deal with it every day. Things made to look another way, sort of like this painting. Detective work requires perception. When you uncover the illusion, you get the truth. I'll look forward to receiving all the information I asked for today."

Van Cleef handed him his card on the way out.

Dr. Thompson examined the card and said, "I have to say, I like your pleasant demeanor and style better than the other detective that was here."

"What other detective?"

"The one that was here before."

"How long before?" Van Cleef asked.

Dr. Thompson thought about it and said, "Oh, I'd say about a month ago."

Van Cleef was confused since he was not working on the Evans-Plotkin murder case a month ago. He asked, "From my department… LAPD, Homicide?"

"I don't know, he didn't have a card like you, but he did have an LAPD detective badge like you."

Van Cleef's mind was racing.

"Older or younger guy?"

"Certainly, older than you and meaner."

"What was he investigating?"

"Dr. Plotkin."

Van Cleef stepped back, thinking. "Did he have an appointment?" he asked.

"No, he just barged in like gangbusters or something you'd see on a crime show. Very rude."

Van Cleef turned away from Dr. Thompson and said under his breath, "Boots."

"Did he ask or know about Manjaro?" Van Cleef asked.

Dr. Thompson thought for a moment and then said, "No, his name never came up."

"Well then, what in the hell was so important that he barged into your office like that?"

Dr. Thompson was losing his composure and getting confused. He said, "It was about the doctor's wife."

"What about her?"

"I don't know, it was more about her visitors, or who came to visit her, if I recall."

"Did Sheila Evans have visitors?"

"Not a one."

Van Cleef did not believe Dr. Thompson and it showed on his face. Dr. Thompson could read his expression and said, "Detective, I am leveling with you. We are bound by strict ethics at our facility and we treat our patient's privacy like a trade secret."

"Is that why TMZ has her stint in your facility on their website?"

"I can't help that. We do our best."

Van Cleef's thoughts drifted back to Ed Boots and what he might have been investigating.

Dr. Thompson interrupted Van Cleef's thoughts and said, "I'm afraid I neglected to mention one item. I'm sure it will come out sooner or later, or in the wash, as they say."

Van Cleef turned back around and asked, "Oh, and what's that?"

"Dr. Plotkin was the doctor that was writing the prescriptions for Anthony Manjaro."

While Van Cleef walked back to his car, he thought about what a blowhard and bullshit artist Dr. Thompson was and he figured the doctor, or someone in his office, probably tipped off TMZ that Manjaro was in rehab. It was good PR for Dr. Thompson, but it was also even better news for Van Cleef because now he could place the suspect in the victim's life. There was a connection.

40

TONY "KILLER" MANJARO stood at the urinal with one hand on his prick and the other clutching his cell phone. He retrieved a message from Gordon Goldstone about Detective Van Cleef paying him a visit. He advised Tony not to talk to anyone in law enforcement, namely Detective Van Cleef, regarding the alleged connection to a dogfighting ring.

Manjaro knew to keep his mouth shut as a general rule, especially when it came to law enforcement... he was a man of few words, generally speaking.

He was about to exit the men's restroom when two run-of-the-mill gangbangers flanked him at the urinal and stared him up and down. He simply smiled, zipped up his prick, stared at the polished tile in the men's room at the Commerce Casino, and ignored them.

They weren't there to be ignored.

They weren't there to gamble either.

"Gator wanna speak wit 'chu," the taller and meatier of the two gangbangers said, breaking the silence. His low voice reverberated in the restroom.

Manjaro figured he'd lay this joker out first and then bitch slap the bald squirt sidekick next and use him as a punching bag. The squirt reeked of marijuana and cheap aftershave. Manjaro made his way to the sink, lathered his hands, and turned on the hot water to rinse them. He proceeded to hit the hand dryer and continued to ignore them, pretending they did not exist.

The taller gangbanger put his back against the wall next to the hand dryer and faced him. He repeated himself louder this time, "I said, Gator wanna speak wit 'chu."

The hand dryer automatically shut off and Manjaro caught a glimpse of the squirt behind him in the mirror.

"Tell Gator to go fuck one of his mutts," Manjaro said.

The two gangbangers looked at each other and started to laugh. They seemed high and glassy-eyed.

"You hear dat shit, Ziggy?"

The squirt has a name. Isn't that cute, Manjaro thought.

"Hey man, I heard it," Ziggy said. "I just can't understand why he say it." The little squirt shook his head.

"Maybe, he punch drunk or somethin'... Let me put in another request at the front desk... I said, Gator—"

"I heard you the first time," Manjaro said, grabbing the door handle to exit.

Ziggy the squirt spoke again and said, "Hey man, did ya' also hear Kim Sang got popped? Don't ya' even know dat?"

Manjaro opened the door slightly and said, "That's his dumb luck. Get the fuck out of my face. I can't be seen associating with shit stains like you two."

The squirt had guts. He got between Manjaro and the door and closed it. He was stronger than he looked.

"Let me spell it out. Gator-is-in-town-now and wants to pay 'chu... you know what I'm saying? Now you should try a 'lil tenderness when someone wants to give 'chu some money, 'Killa'."

"Let me spell it out," Manjaro said. "Maybe you two brothers didn't hear me the first time when I said—"

The taller gangbanger kept his hands visible and did not make any sudden moves. He knew Manjaro would deck him with those huge mitts for hands.

"Gator sent us to square up wit 'chu and get outta town."

Manjaro asked, "How much? We talkin' the full $30K from the last show?"

"Every penny."

"Hand it over," Manjaro said, then deciding it was his turn to block the door with his large open palm outstretched.

The gangbanger slapped a thick rubber-banded wad of one-hundred-dollar bills in Manjaro's hand.

Manjaro snatched the wad and counted it quicker than a bank teller. "Your mama teach you how to count money, boy?" Manjaro asked, towering over the two of them at 6'3, 260 lbs. "You're twenty-five thousand shy, boy. Where's the rest of it?"

"C'mon man… Five-thousand is all he trusted us to deliver to you and he ain't even said shit about you rippin' him off with his prizefighter, Kali… I think he just plannin' on writtin' that shit off…"

"I think the front desk is finally gettin' through to the guest," Ziggy said to his sidekick with a stupid grin on his face. He was definitely high on grass. "We can leave if 'Killa' don't wanna play with us… thing is, if those pigs start askin' us 'bout a killer dog that likes to eat up Malibu actresses, I dunno what I'd say—"

Manjaro slammed the squirt up against the wall by his throat and lifted him off his feet. He looked to his left in the mirror and yelled at the other gangbanger, "Hey… keep your hands out of your pockets and back off. Do it!"

The squirt's feet were dangling and his eyes were bulging out of his head. Manjaro's massive grip was like a python.

Manjaro yelled at the gangbanger in the mirror. "He's got about two minutes before I snap his neck or I drop him, it's your call."

The gangbanger raised his hands in the air. Manjaro dropped the squirt.

He slid down to his rear gasping for air.

A hammered gambler tried to push the door open and started yelling at the door on the other side. His speech was slurred as he shouted at the closed door, "What are you doing in there, jackin' off or something? Open up in there. This is a public restroom. Open up."

Manjaro did not want to draw attention to their tiff or their bathroom transaction or have casino security nosing around, so he let the hammered gambler in. The mid-six-ties looking black man stumbled right into Manjaro, nearly spilling his free cocktail on him. He looked up at him ter-rified as if he were the Jolly Green Giant. Manjaro scowled back at the drunken gambler, who kept looking over his shoulder while he tripped into the stall with an unsteady gait.

Manjaro lowered his voice and said, "Look assholes... I was tailed here and I'm sure I am being watched. Have Gator meet me in the casino parking lot."

"C'mon 'killa," said the squirt gangbanger, "You know he don't work dat way. He never meets anyone in public. 'Cus his disfigurement—"

"Come again?" Manjaro asked.

"You know he ain't a pretty sight, right?"

"So, I heard."

"Well seein' that shit is somethin' else… let's just say he got ta face only a mutha could luv."

Manjaro heard the rumors that Gator was a ghastly sight. They weren't bullshitting. He also thought these two fools might be a way to lose the trail of this detective that Gold-stone warned him about in the message.

Maybe these two badasses could be his ticket out. Manjaro was street smart and grew up in Brooklyn. He knew the hustles, the cons, and the way police operated. He kept the $5K wad and said, "Meet me across the street… there's a 76 Station. Be there in 10 minutes."

"Now wait a minute," the squirt spoke again, "How we know you gonna meet us and not take off wit da Gator's money?"

Manjaro said, "Cuz 5K ain't worth the trouble. I can burn through that in two hours. I want the full amount that I was ripped off, and he's going to pay up or he'll be more than disfigured… he'll be crippled to boot. You got that?"

The taller gangbanger raised his fist to bump it with Manjaro and said, "Hey, 'Killa, why we wastin' time for, s'what I'm sayin'."

"Good, now what kinda car you drive?"

"'72 black Chevy Chevelle. Mint."

"10 minutes," Manjaro said. "Now get outta here before I change my mind."

Manjaro waited behind for a few more minutes and checked his cell phone messages while he watched for the drunk to emerge from the bathroom stall. The drunk was so loaded, his slurred speech reminded Manjaro of the Damon Wayans homeless drunk character from the "In Living Color" sketch comedy bit.

He kept staring at Manjaro and asked, "Hey, aren't you famous for something?"

Manjaro lied and said, "Yeah, I do mattress commercials."

He exited the men's restroom with the drunk.

41

MANJARO SCANNED THE CASINO floor outside
the bathroom and watched the drunk from the bathroom
collapse at a nearby slot machine, nearly missing the seat
and doing a pratfall. The tables were full at the Commerce
Casino. Fairly crowded for a weekday.

Manjaro went for it and walked briskly in the opposite
direction of the slot machines. He made a sharp turn into
the crowd and then zigzagged his way past the first undercover cop disguised as a casino worker. Manjaro could
pick him out from the other casino workers just by his
eyes— too vigilant. His stance— like he was still 'at ease'
in the military or academy. His build— most of the Commerce Casino security guards had a street seediness about
them. Not this guy. He was too clean. Manjaro picked up
his reflection in the gift shop window near the craps table.

The undercover cop spoke into the small microphone
headset and alerted the other undercover casino workers
that Manjaro was on the move.

The undercover detectives took their positions, caging

Manjaro in.

Manjaro headed into the gift shop for a pack of Big Red chewing gum. He watched the second undercover cop pull the tarp off a blackjack table and pretend to set up shop, shuffling cards and stacking chips.

Manjaro thought he looked like the other guy; cookie- cutter undercover guys tasked to tackle a big hard-ass like himself. This one had a crew cut. The other guy was bald and shiny. Manjaro was fearless. He once fought Mike Tyson and almost won. *Get in the ring pals*, he thought to himself.

He left the gift shop and let baldy follow him to the roulette table. He made himself comfortable like he planned on staying a while. He deliberately laid down two c-notes on red making sure he was seen. He also ordered a drink. Jack and Coke. *That's right cue ball and crew cut. Keep an eye on me*, he thought to himself. The dealers were switched and a third undercover casino worker took his post. This guy was Hispanic and had a middle-aged beer gut. He wasn't going to do any chasing other than a few skirts. Manjaro pegged him to also be working or cooperating with the others. Why? Because he tried to talk him up. Saying shit like: "Don't I know you from somewhere?" "You're a famous athlete..." The let's try and relate bullshit that detectives try to do.

Manjaro smiled and said, "Yeah, Chico, you've seen my underarm deodorant commercials. I used to play for the NFL." He swiped his money from the table before the ball was in play and left his drink without touching it. He zigzagged back through the crowd, slouching as he picked up the pace to not draw attention to his height.

Chico nodded to baldy and crew cut to head off Manjaro.

Manjaro took a hard right into the hotel kitchen and turned the heads of all the Mexican cooks. He asked where the bathroom was. They looked at each other to comprehend his question and then one of them pointed back to where he entered. He said "gracias" and plucked one of the pieces of shrimp off a serving tray and popped it into his mouth, then went out the opposite door which led to outside. The Mexican cook who pointed was equally confused, but shrugged it off and returned to making the shrimp cocktail.

The three undercover cops were now in the kitchen with the Mexican cooks and servers. The Mexican cook who pointed Manjaro to the exit, now pointed them to the other door Manjaro escaped through.

They rushed out single file to the empty street outside the casino.

Manjaro had managed to duck into a nearby restaurant named Stakes Supper Club. He stood at the front, chatting it up with the hostess who seemed sweet on him. He kept a lookout for the 3 undercover stooges, and when he felt the coast was clear, he told the hostess he made a mistake and was meeting his friends at another restaurant.

The 76 Gas Station was across the street on Telegraph Road, a major intersection.

Traffic was heavy, but his options were limited.

Manjaro took his shot.

Cars were like punches. He could dodge them. He played chicken on Telegraph Road running between speeding cars. Vehicles swerved and honked. Drivers yelled obscenities and skidded to a stop.

He came close to getting smashed by a pest control truck. He saw a flash of a yellow streak as he shoulder rolled on the sidewalk. He got up and looked back across Telegraph Road. He was in the clear. By the time the undercover creeps got to him, he would be on his way to collect the other $25K from that disfigured freak Gator.

"Where is the fucking Chevy Chevelle?" he blurted out loud. Manjaro circled the gas pumps at the station. There were several cars and people at the pump, but no sign of the Chevy Chevelle and the two gangbangers from the bathroom.

Manjaro stood behind the pump on the far end and stepped up on the concrete platform the pumps were mounted on to get a better vantage point.

He checked his watch momentarily: 2:35 pm.

He could see the three undercover cops halting traffic and making their way across Telegraph Road and people pointing in his direction. They were closing in on him.

Then three short horn blasts and headlights from behind the nearby convenience store startled him. It was the two punks sitting in the black Chevy Chevelle.

Manjaro grabbed the windshield squeegee from between the pumps, shook off the soapy water, and walked to their car. The two gangbanger punks had dumbass grins on their face. The tall one behind the wheel said, "Shit man... what took you so long? Been waitin' here f'ever."

Manjaro ordered him out of the front seat so that he could squeeze in behind him in the back. He kept the squeegee at his side when he wedged himself into the back seat.

When the driver got behind the wheel, Manjaro grasped each end of the squeegee and pulled it down over the driver's neck like a safety bar locking down on a roller coaster patron. He tugged the squeegee back hard toward him and the headrest and said, "I asked you to meet me at the pump, you dumb son-of-a-bitch. Don't you listen?"

The driver was gasping for air, his voice high-pitched and cutting in and out like a static radio.

Manjaro watched Ziggy the squirt gangbanger attempt to reach for a gun in the glove box. Manjaro said, "You fucking grab that piece and you'll be choking on this next, you got that? I will shove this squeegee down your motherfucking throat followed by my fist. You got that, squirt?"

The shorter gangbanger got it and slowly put his hand

back onto his lap where Manjaro could see it. Manjaro whispered into the driver gangbanger's ear as he pulled the squeegee tighter on his neck and said, "Listen, sweetheart, if you two are fucking lying and I don't get paid in full... I will feed all three of you, including Gator, to the dogs. You hear me, boy?" He emphasized the "boy" like a Southerner.

The driver gangbanger nodded as he choked.

Manjaro released the squeegee. The driver gasped for air and rubbed his neck, looking in the rearview mirror at Manjaro like he was out of his mind. His eyes were tearing from near-strangulation.

Manjaro leaned back and smiled at the reflection of the driver's frightened face in the rearview mirror. Manjaro laughed and said, "Gimmie one of those cigarettes, boy."

The black Chevy Chevelle squealed out from behind the convenience store and hit the 5 Freeway to Calabasas.

The three undercover cops canvassed the 76 Station. They checked every square inch. They interviewed customers and no one had seen anything, which wasn't unusual in Los Angeles.

Manjaro and the gangbangers were miles ahead of them.

42

THE SECURITY TEAM at the Commerce Casino sat with Van Cleef and Overstreet reviewing the soundless and slow-motion video surveillance featuring Tony "Killer" Manjaro. Overstreet leaned over to Van Cleef and commented, "Is there a Director's Cut? I feel like we could be here all night."

"This is nothing, Overstreet," Van Cleef said, slapping him on the back. "Back in the day before the world went digital, we'd be here two days reviewing video footage."

Something caught Van Cleef's attention. He asked the casino security guy working the cameras to back it up a few frames. The rewind revealed two gangbangers. The shorter one stumbled out of the men's room rubbing his neck. "He looks worked over if you ask me," Van Cleef said.

Manjaro was seen walking out of the Men's room moments later, followed by a casino drunk.

"Did you interview him, Overstreet?" Van Cleef asked.

"Yeah," Overstreet said. "He ID'd Manjaro, all right. Manjaro told him he did mattress commercials on TV, and the drunk believed him."

Van Cleef smiled and said, "I like it when our murder

suspects have a sense of humor… they're going to need it when we put them away. Do me a favor and get the Gang Unit's eyeballs on these two jokers. See if they have a history or if we can pick them up."

Overstreet flipped open his gaudy silver notebook and wrote down some notes. Van Cleef tried to ignore the notebook and decided to address the issue later in private.

"Stay here and let me know if you see anything else unusual on the cameras. I'm going to interview the undercover cops that tailed Manjaro and see what they have to offer."

Overstreet continued to watch the footage with the casino security and video surveillance team and take notes. Van Cleef met up with the undercover cops, and all four of them walked across the street to the Union 76 Gas Station.

The Persian owner of the 76 Station was upset about another stolen squeegee from the self-service island. He told the police that the big ape took it with him and did not even buy any gas.

The 'big ape' was positively identified as Tony Manjaro.

The owner also offered the detectives access to his video footage which showed Manjaro getting into a black Chevy Chevelle. Van Cleef would be able to get a plate number off the Chevy Chevelle when forensics enlarged the footage. He also noticed a Dodge Caravan pulling out of the parking lot following the Chevy Chevelle.

"Anyone locate the suspect's vehicle yet?" Van Cleef asked one of the Rampart divisional detectives.

"Sorry, Leo," the detective said. "No sign of the black SUV that matches the plate you gave us. We've been all over nearby parking lots, structures, streets, and the customer lot. Nothing."

"Thanks," Van Cleef said. "I didn't think so. He might have been dropped off or took another means here. I'm sure he knows we're hot on his heels."

Van Cleef walked around the service station to the unlit area where the Chevy Chevelle was parked and then drove out of. He knelt and noticed a Big Red gum wrapper balled up on the ground. He pulled a pair of latex gloves from his pocket, put them on, and placed the gum wrapper in a baggy.

His cell phone rang. He did not recognize the number.

"Is this Detective Van Cleef," the voice on the other end asked.

"This is he," Van Cleef said, recognizing the voice of Sheriff Mohan.

"It's Sheriff Mohan from Malibu. We met at the Evans murder—"

"Yeah, yeah," Van Cleef said. "I recognize your voice. What's up?"

"Can you make it down to Malibu in the next hour?"

Van Cleef checked his watch and was not ready to wrap up the Commerce Casino investigation just yet. "I'm in the City of Commerce. What'd you have?"

"Tad Keller was killed this evening out here on PCH, or Blood Alley, as some of us locals like to call it."

Van Cleef stood up slowly and asked, "Traffic accident?"

"No, pedestrian."

"Hit and run?"

"No, nothing like that. Just an unfortunate accident. We got the driver. The young woman stopped and called the police… It was an accident. She was not drunk or anything like that… which is more than I can say for the Keller kid. She said he came out of nowhere, just walked right in front of her and… well—"

Van Cleef tuned out the rest and wrapped up the Commerce Casino investigation. He convinced himself he would make the drive back out to Malibu in a record 45 minutes. He made it in 43 minutes.

43

"**WELCOME TO BLOOD ALLEY**," Chief Mohan said to Van Cleef as he emerged from the coastal fog darkness.

Van Cleef exited his vehicle and nodded to Malibu Chief, Mike Mohan, along with two other CHP officers. Mohan continued talking and ranting as they approached the covered dead body of Tad Keller. "Well, this is another one for Malibu City Council to prove once again why our community needs better safety— all the California Coastal Commission and Mountains Recreation & Conservation Authority cares about is saving the 675 parking spots along these 21 miles instead of saving lives.

"Did you interview the driver?" Van Cleef asked.

Sheriff Mohan said, "Like I said on the phone—"

A CHP officer interjected and said, "Yes, I did. Wasn't her fault. No alcohol involved. She checked out. Her son was in the car with her."

The Medical Examiner joined the conversation. Van Cleef asked, "Tad Keller?"

"His BAC was around 0.30 percent," the M.E. said.

Van Cleef whistled and rolled his eyes.

The Medical Examiner cleared his throat and continued,

"It looks like Tad Keller consumed a lot of Jack Daniels, snorted a few lines of coke, and smoked some hash alone in his car parked along the Pacific Coast Highway, then, for some reason, he got out of his car... but I'll confirm all the obvious when I get the toxicology report back."

"Anything else remarkable about the driver that hit him?" Van Cleef asked the CHP Officer.

"Not at all. No hit and run. No reckless driving. Apparently she was on her way home from her kid's bar mitzvah. She had her teenager in the car and they both said and saw the same thing. She called us immediately and reported it. Did the right thing."

"Speeding?" Van Cleef asked.

"Five-ten over, if that, based on what I can tell. We're checking everything out. Seems to gel. She's hysterical."

"She say anything else that was useful?"

"Only that Mr. Keller came out of nowhere between two cars, almost leapt out at her like a deer running across the road. Her son said the same thing."

"—Like a deer, huh?" Van Cleef repeated the phrase.

Van Cleef, Chief Mohan, and the CHP officers walked over to Tad Keller's body. Van Cleef pulled back the sheet at the bottom where Tad's feet were. Mohan and the CHP officers exchanged puzzled looks. Tad's legs were broken, bruised, and twisted like pretzels. Van Cleef examined his one remaining shoe on his left foot. An average run-of-the-mill, worn Skechers style, store-bought shoe. Van Cleef turned his attention to the M.E. and asked, "Died on impact?"

"Instantly," the M.E. said. "Massive head trauma. Internal bleeding. His body got thrown a good thirty feet where it came to rest on the other side of the road."

Van Cleef turned away from the mangled body of Tad Keller and faced the dark side of the Pacific Coast bluff, his back to the ocean. He turned back around facing the ocean, the waves crashing below intermittently illuminated by the passing headlights of oncoming traffic.

"So, Mr. Keller was walking away from the ocean and in the direction of the mountains across PCH?" Van Cleef asked.

"Looks to be the case," Chief Mohan said.

"Anything within walking distance on that side?" Van Cleef asked.

Mohan shook his head.

Van Cleef fixated on the other side of the surrounding area, his hands on his hips, looking up into the night and the faint outline of the mountain tops.

"Where's his car?" Van Cleef asked.

"It's parked up about ten spaces on the right here along the shoulder," the second CHP officer replied.

"I'll want to have a look through the car if you don't mind." Van Cleef directed his request at Chief Mohan.

"Be my guest," Chief Mohan said. "I know you had interviewed him recently and the day of the Evans mauling, so that's why I contacted you."

"Appreciate it, Chief."

Van Cleef could see no logical reason why Tad Keller was walking in the direction of the mountainside. PCH runs north and south. There was nothing over there on that side of the stretch of PCH. No restaurants. No other parking. Not even a roadside vendor selling fruit… and he wasn't there to rock climb. Unless someone was chasing Tad, it was clear to Van Cleef that Tad Keller committed suicide, or was just so drunk and drugged out that he didn't know where he was or what he was doing.

He pulled a pair of latex gloves from his pocket and walked up to Tad Keller's beat-out, silver '98 Nissan Altima. Van Cleef noticed the keys still in the ignition with the door unlocked, and he put on his latex gloves to search the car.

He shouted back to the CHP officer that was taking a statement from another witness along the highway. "Were the keys left in the ignition?"

The CHP officer gave him a thumbs up to indicate 'yes' over the rush of traffic. Highway beams of lights occasionally cut through the fog from passing cars driving way too fast in these conditions.

Van Cleef found some overt drug substances that the M.E. had mentioned and a small hash pipe sticking out of the car's console like a straw in a drink. Van Cleef sniffed and examined the pipe. It was recently used. There was also that overwhelming scent again... the whole vehicle reeked of Patchouli. Van Cleef tried to hold his breath while he searched. He then reached across the passenger side and pulled down the visor, which was empty. He reached under the seats and pulled out various fast food wrappers and other garbage people have in their cars that don't clean them regularly. Tad's cheap liquor store sunglasses were sitting on the dusty dashboard of the car. Van Cleef reached under the steering column and popped the trunk. He exited the Altima and began carefully inspecting the trunk contents. Van Cleef found a laptop, a disposable cell phone, and two shoe boxes that caught his attention right away; the Sportia rock climbing pair he had on the day of Sheila Evans's murder and the other large box of Evolv Kaos II brand. Van Cleef opened both boxes. Tad's worn-out pair was still inside the Sportia box. However, the Evolv box was empty. He inspected the side of the box and found something interesting. He placed both boxes side by side and noticed that the Evolv brand was six sizes larger than his Sportia. A size 9 versus size 15.

Van Cleef pulled out his cell phone and placed a call to Overstreet.

"Dennis," Van Cleef said, closely examining the Evolv shoebox. "I need you to do some footwork for me." He also noticed a worn REI sticker on the side.

"Ah, man, my feet are tired... been on them all—" Overstreet said.

"Not that kind of footwork, Dennis. Footwear work."

Overstreet knew exactly what Van Cleef meant and took down the brand, size, and store chain they were purchased from. He also informed him that Tad Keller would not be seeing a courtroom, just a morgue.

PART THREE:

THE SHOW

44

THE FARM RANCH IN CALABASAS was remote and abandoned. The black Chevy Chevelle drove down a winding dirt and gravel road to get there.

Manjaro was not thrilled with the long haul. His legs were cramped and his linebacker body was stiff from being wedged in, but this was the best way to keep an eye on both gangbangers in case either one made a false move. He felt that the trunk would have been just as comfortable.

The Chevy Chevelle came to a stop. He watched a large shadow pull back the curtain for a moment and emit light from the house, which was boarded up. He figured the blob of a shadow was Gator.

The squirt's cell phone rang. He said, "Yeah, bringin' him in now."

Barking dogs were heard when the Chevy Chevelle cut the engine. Manjaro climbed out of the car.

He stretched his long legs and swiped the taller gangbanger's cigarette out of his hand.

"Get movin'," Manjaro said to the two gangbangers as he extended his hand toward the porch of the farmhouse.

"And give me a light."

The two gangbangers walked ahead. Manjaro grabbed the squirt by the scruff of the neck and said, "Hand it over."

"Hand what over, man?"

"The piece you grabbed from under the seat."

"Whatchu you talkin' —"

Manjaro snatched a police Beretta from the gangbanger's baggy jeans and raised the firearm to his head. He quickly trained it on both of them, stepping backward. "This one, jackass. You two will be the first ones I aim for if any shit goes down in that house."

"Hey man," the taller one said. "Ain't nothin' goin' down. Jus' squaring up... like we said."

The squirt lit Manjaro's cigarette for him before they entered the farmhouse.

At first the taller one hesitated, and then he twisted the knob and creaked open the door.

The place looked haunted. Cobwebs. Black drapes. Covered furniture. Like something out of a Roger Corman film.

Manjaro could see candlelight from the next room. He kept the Beretta on the two of them as they all entered the room to their right. The floors creaked. The wood was old and rotten beneath their feet.

There was Gator. His hooded head was down. Candlelight flickered in his face, or what part of it was visible. Manjaro didn't allow the theatrics to spook him. He asked, "Did you convert to Buddhism or what?"

Gator lifted his head slowly. He was almost tranced. "Come in, Killer," he said in a monotone voice. This was his style of speaking. Manjaro figured that the dog that took a chunk out of his skull also took a part of his brain. If you got to know Gator, you knew you had to wait in uncomfortable silence while he chose his words. This time was no different.

Gator motioned for Manjaro to take a seat on one of the dust covered easy chairs across from him. Gator tossed a heavy brown grocery bag on the table between the two of them.

"Go on... open it," Gator said.

Manjaro looked at him for a moment in the flickering light, keeping his right hand on the Beretta and the gang-bangers in his peripheral.

He ripped open the brown bag and saw stacks of one-hundred dollar bills.

"You didn't think I'd pay up for 'The Show' did you?" Gator said in an almost robotic voice.

Manjaro, pleased with himself and the wad of cash, sniffed the money as he fanned it and said, "No. I knew you'd eventually pay up. You can only run for so long. This includes interest and waiting time penalties for all my troubles?"

"Hell yes," Gator said. "I threw in an extra twenty percent 'for your troubles.'"

Manjaro got the creeps from Gator, not physically but emotionally. He'd been in the ring with some ruthless, cold-blooded motherfuckers and been on the street with down and dirty, dangerous types, but Gator had a certain patient vibe about him that he didn't trust. That vibe had nothing to do with his disfigurement. Even his stature, which was imposing like his own, was not what creeped him out. Something about him. He just exuded an evil mind. Capable of anything. He recalled the one time he saw Gator electrocute a pit that lost a fight. He would never forget that look.

Gator placed two shot glasses on the table and pulled out a new box of Patrón Silver. Manjaro took a long drag off his cigarette, tossed it on the floor, and stomped it out with his boot. He examined the bottle. He would not have taken a shot if the bottle had not been sealed. He could see that it had not been tampered with.

He took a close look at the shot glasses that were empty and did the honors.

They toasted.

Manjaro knocked back two shots and said, "Man, that's good."

Gator downed another shot and said, "Did those two knuckleheads tell you about Kim Sang?"

Manjaro leaned back and said, "Yeah, well you don't have to worry about me. I've got one of the best attorneys in Los Angeles and the best part is... he's well-versed in dog law too. I guess that's what you call irony." Manjaro seemed amused by his wisecrack.

"So, why'd you think I'd come all the way out to L.A. for anyway?" Gator asked.

Manjaro studied Gator's body language. The shadow of his face. He said, "I thought maybe to catch a Laker's game."

Gator said, "No, you see I had a visit recently from the Feds."

"They peg you for a terrorist?" Manjaro asked, not taking the conversation seriously.

"Hardly," Gator said. "It was more like a raid. They had warrants and tossed my place pretty good."

"Fuck 'em. You're just a breeder," Manjaro said.

"A breeder on an FBI watch list now."

"Let 'em watch."

"You don't understand," Gator said, getting perturbed. "I don't like being watched. I'm paranoid that way. Keeps me outta jail, you know what I'm sayin'?"

"Fuck 'em."

"Where is the dog, Manjaro?"

"Kali?"

"Yeah, Kali. Stop playing stupid."

"How the hell should I know, and don't ever call me stupid. Maybe it got loose and ran away."

"You're lying," Gator said. "Where is Hamid?"

"Who the hell is Hamid?"

"The guy that delivered Kali to you on credit."

Manjaro thought about the Arab man he shot and killed after he delivered Kali to him. He laughed and said, "You mean that towel head?"

Gator was growing impatient with Manjaro's games. He said, "I didn't sell it to you for a murder weapon. I don't operate that way, and I'm trying to keep my nose clean. So, I got a missing dog, a missing driver, and missing money. What am I supposed to do with that?"

"You'd have to take that up with that towel head that ripped you off, man. I paid 'em."

"Nah man, you didn't. You killed 'em."

"C'mon Gator, you know that's bullshit. Hussein made off with the cash, pal. Talk to him."

"His name is Hamid, and he seems to have vanished, along with my dog."

"Sounds like a mystery to me," Manjaro said. "City's filled with 'em."

"The way I see it is like this," Gator said. "You killed him, kept the cash, and then killed Kali after you used her to kill that woman out in Malibu.

"Says you," Manjaro said, standing up for a moment, feeling off-balance. "Wrong dog, man. That woman was killed by a pit bull, not your precious Bully Kutta. Like I said, you better talk to the Iranian. They're always rippin' people off."

"Is that so?" Gator said. "So you're tryin' to tell me that you never got Kali and a guy I trusted to deliver her to you just fell off the face of the fuckin' earth? Naw man, you give me my dog back and you can walk outta here with that bag of cash."

Gator didn't say anything for what seemed like a long time. Manjaro eventually broke the silence between them and said, "You're crazy man if you think I give a flying fuck about some rich bitch out in Malibu that was killed by some stray pit bulls. Shit, those… things… killing people are as common as—"

Manjaro's mind went blank and his words stopped making sense. He started talking gibberish and then the room started spinning. He heard himself repeat "as common as…" several times in a disembodied voice, like he was talking outside of himself. He was hallucinating like he was on acid or some other psychedelic drug. His massive arms were tingling and getting weak and numb. His speech was slurred as he spit out each word, "Well- they- can- look- all- they- want. They- ain't- gonna- find- shit- 'cause- that-dog's- been-disposed -of."

"What did you do with it?"

"Put-it-out… put-it-down… p-p-p-p-put zat damn thing out of zits mizzz… surrey," Manjaro slurred his words. His speech was incoherent.

"Where did you bury it?" Gator asked.

Manjaro didn't answer and didn't know what he was saying. He just stared into space.

"Where is the dog?" Gator asked again.

Manjaro tried to swing his fist into the air, but his arm collapsed at his side. He slurred, "Malibu 'shwere she's buried. Out witsh' that lady."

Gator knew their conversation was over. He said, "I don't breed my dogs to kill people. I got people to handle that. We got a real problem on our hands with this detective."

Manjaro felt his tongue go numb. Two shots shouldn't have phased him. *C'mon, get a hold of yourself…* He told himself. *Food, that was it…* He needed to eat and get the hell out of there.

He noticed the two gangbangers left the room. A quietness and warm rush passed over him. At first, he felt a bit of vertigo and averted his attention to Gator who was still sitting like a Buddhist monk over the flickering candle. Arif, the thin Pakistani man, now entered the room with a sawed-off shotgun pointed at Manjaro's head. Manjaro thought he was hallucinating and that Arif was Hamid, the other brother that he killed that tried to sell him Kali the Bully Kutta. They did resemble each other. Manjaro laughed, thinking maybe it was a zombie.

Gator stood up, blocking the barrels of the shotgun.

"We do it my way," he said, towering over Arif.

"He killed my brother. Where is my brother?" Arif said.

"Calm down man, we'll find him," Gator said.

"You're lying like him," Arif said, raising the shotgun at Gator and pointing it at his face.

"Look man, I didn't want any part of this. Our whole world has turned to shit because of this asshole. So don't blame me, I'm on your side."

Arif stood frozen in place with this shotgun pointed at Gator's face. After several minutes, he lowered the shotgun and walked out of the room.

Manjaro's speech was slower, like an old record on 16 rpm. It echoed throughout the room. Manjaro felt his legs go stiff first, then his right arm. He no longer could grasp the shot glass. He dropped the glass on the floor and watched it skip and bounce like a stone bouncing along the riverbed.

His body went limp, and he fell hard on the wood floor. He could see the gangbangers carrying plywood up the stairs.

He could hear Gator say, "The Diazepam is kicking in. Works like a charm. Had no idea, I palmed it and slipped it in his drink." He could feel him standing over him. Manjaro struggled to mouth the words, "Why?"

Gator said, "It's a muscle relaxer, champ. We use it on

the dogs. I imagine when you mix it with Tequila... "

The last thing Manjaro heard was hammers pounding from upstairs.

He blacked out.

The two gangbangers entered the room and stood over Manjaro's body.

Gator grabbed the brown shopping bag of money and said, "Drag his ass upstairs. He paid for a good fight, let's give him one."

The two gangbangers struggled to manhandle Manjaro's dead-weight body off the floor. He felt like solid bags of cement as they transported his body upstairs.

Headlights passed through the drapes, and the sound of crunching gravel and barking dogs alerted Gator to grab his semi-automatic stuffed in the couch.

He parted the drapes and saw two cars pull up: a black SUV and another Chevy low rider.

Gator opened the front door, stepped outside, and signaled the drivers to park alongside the blue Dodge Caravan. He asked the driver of the black SUV, "Any trouble?"

The gangbanger shook his head with a wise smirk and said, "Shit man, I gave the casino valet some bullshit about losing my keys and when I threw in the C-note, the dude just gave me Manjaro's keys like you said he would. I coulda left that place with someone's Bugatti. Motherfucker didn't even care, just like you say."

"Yeah," Gator said. "Just like I say."

The driver tossed Gator the keys to Manjaro's SUV. Gator peeled off some cash, and they both got back into their Chevy low rider and left the farmhouse.

45

WHEN TONY "KILLER" MANJARO WOKE up on his side, he found himself surrounded by plywood. Blood-stained plywood. He felt his arms and legs restricted, which sent him into a full-blown panic. He began flailing like a fish on a hook. Was he injured, shot, knifed? At first he thought they buried him alive, but then he calmed down realizing he could see light. The top was open and he could breathe, but only through his nose because there was duct tape on his mouth. He tried to scream for help, but the tape gagged him. The carpet reeked of urine and feces.

He turned over on his back and stared at the light bulb above him in the ceiling. He was sweating profusely and feeling nauseous now.

Manjaro cocked his head to the side and could see the red scratch lines on the carpet as his vision began to focus.

They had put him in the dogfighting pit.

He could hear heavy footsteps creaking up the stairs along with the tap of dog nails and heavy panting.

He closed his eyes and prayed to God like he used to do before each fight in the boxing ring, even though he never really believed in God.

The panting and scratching of nails on the wood floor became louder and more intense, along with his breathing. His hands were bound too tight to break free. He panicked again as he saw the side of the pit open.

The plywood separated and two vicious pit bulls entered the pit. It was too crowded for all three of them. The gang-bangers struggled to keep the dogs on the heavy chains. They were overpowering them.

Manjaro could see them salivating. Clawing and drooling. Blood-thirsty creatures. One of the pits snapped his powerful jaws close to his face. Manjaro caught a whiff of his hot breath.

He asked God, the God he didn't believe in until this moment, to forgive him for the murder of that woman in Malibu. "That woman in Malibu" whose name he didn't even care to remember.

The pit bulls were on their hind legs now.

The heavy chains holding them seemed to fall in slow motion.

He squeezed his eyes shut as the pit bulls lunged and leapt onto him. He tucked in his chin knowing they would go for his throat, but that didn't help. They tore his flesh apart. He could hear his bones crack and snap.

This is what that woman felt. That poor woman. Not even half his size.

Again, he asked for forgiveness as he screamed bloody murder through the duct tape. The last image Manjaro had seen before he died was even more frightening than the dogs that were ripping him apart. Jerome Tyler aka "Gator" removed his hoodie as he stood looking over him in the wooden pit. Half of his face and head were indented, missing, and disfigured like something you would see in an old circus freak show. This was the first and last time Manjaro ever got a good look at Gator. This was the last image Manjaro was taking to hell with him. This was the last sight he saw before one of the pit bulls ripped his face off and tore his throat out.

It was all over in a matter of minutes before he faded into darkness.

The tall, unphased, and homicidal gangbanger pulled out his stun gun that he routinely used on the pit bulls to control them.

After several minutes of watching the bloodbath, Gator stepped in, put his hoodie back over his head, pushed the gangbanger with the stun gun aside, and shot two precise tranquilizer darts from a tranquilizer gun into the rabid pit bulls.

Both canine bodies thudded on the floor of the pit.

Lights out.

Gator said, "Clean this shit up right quick. Understand?"

The bald squirt gangbanger spit on Manjaro's corpse inside the pit and said, "TKO Muthafucka."

They both followed Gator's orders and began rolling up the carpet with Manjaro in it and breaking down the plywood pit.

"I'll dispose of the car," Gator said. "You remember the propane tank and gas can?" Gator asked.

The bald gangbanger nodded. He had stolen the tank from the back of an RV parked at a local Home Depot parking lot the day before and the gas was siphoned from another vehicle nearby.

Gator slipped on a pair of leather gloves from his pocket and pulled out a flashlight from inside his jacket. He headed downstairs, hurried outside, and rummaged through Manjaro's black SUV. He searched for any shred of evidence that Manjaro might have left behind or that he could ultimately tie to him. He reached under the seats and then ripped them apart. He emptied the glove box and then popped open the back hatch. He threw everything he could find, which wasn't much, on the side of the vehicle. The dog cage that Kali had been transported in was folded down. Gator tossed it to the side on the gravel road. After he cleaned out the vehicle, he doused the interior with gas and threw the propane tank in the back hatch.

***

Arif entered the main room with a sawed off shotgun. He thanked the gang members politely for bringing Manjaro back to the ranch, and then he murdered both of them with the shotgun. The two blasts kicked both of them back against the farmhouse wall. One in the head, the other in the chest.

Gator heard the gunshots and headed back towards the house when he ran right into Arif and his shotgun standing in the front door. Gator slowly lowered the Zippo lighter in his right hand and the can of gasoline in his left. Arif kept the shotgun on him and did not lower it this time, commanding him to go back over to the SUV and finish the job.

Gator did what he was told which was his last mistake.

46

"DID YOU GET A MATCH on the SUV?" Van Cleef asked.

"That's going to be a problem," Detective Tanaka said, speaking over his cell phone. Van Cleef could hear several voices, sirens, and what sounded like water running nearby in the background.

"How so?" Van Cleef asked.

"The killers torched it," Tanaka said, matter-of-fact.

"Torched it?"

Van Cleef was sitting in his parked car watching the only entrance and exit next to the management office of the Super 8 Hotel. His visor was down and his car was reared in against the brick wall.

"Yeah, car fire," Tanaka confirmed. "Fire Chief is pretty sure it's arson. At least that's what they're saying. So, we got a bloodbath upstairs and downstairs, and a car fire out here with suspects on the run."

"Was Manjaro killed in the car fire?"

"No man, worse."

"Shot?"

"Eaten alive," Tanaka said. "Our 'boxer man' didn't die in the ring... more like the pit. Detectives and police in Calabasas just found "Killer," or what's left of him, anyway."

"Where are the dogs?"

"No sign of the dogs anywhere, just a lot of blood—"

"It gets worse," Tanaka said. "You're also looking at the distinct possibility of the two dead gangbangers from the Commerce casino." Tanaka lowered his tone and could be heard walking inside then into another room and closing a door behind him. "Shotgun style. Oh, and there is something else you should be aware of... Slezick and the Feds are on the scene."

"You're shittin' me?"

"I shit you not."

Van Cleef was silent a moment on the other end, thinking. He asked, "How long?"

"'bout the same time we arrived," Tanaka said.

"Manjaro belongs to us... Don't say anything about where we're at in our investigation, understood? Especially that Gator creep."

"Understood."

"I'm guessing they were shadowing them at the Commerce Casino and they might have put a GPS tracking device on the gangbanger's car. They could've also tapped their phones."

"Which means we're running out of time," Tanaka said.

"Yep, they could beat me to Gator before I get a chance—"

"Hold on Leo—"

There was a knock at the door. Van Cleef could overhear another officer talking to Tanaka on the other end of the phone and then some commotion. Tanaka returned on the line after several minutes. "I think we just found Gator."

"Slezick got to him?" Van Cleef said, pissed off.

Detective Tanaka was outside now. He said,"Too late, Leo... looks like he was fried in the SUV. I was just informed that police found what appears to be a large, charred man in the backseat, facedown with a hole in his back. You can smell the flesh, gas, and propane. Agent Slezak and his team are nodding, and judging by their body language and what I overheard, they think it's Gator. We'll need a positive ID still to be one-hundred percent certain. The M.E. is on the way."

"I think I just found the cargo van...." Van Cleef said. His voice trailed off.

Van Cleef heard FBI Agent Slezak shouting that he needed to speak with him and don't hang up, before he hung up on him.

Van Cleef texted Tanaka his location:

"Super 8 Motel in Culver City, Washington Blvd. Suspect just pulled into lot in blue Dodge Grand Caravan."

47

ARIF PULLED UP ALONGSIDE the gated pool area of the hotel. Van Cleef watched him from the back of the dark parking lot as Arif entered one of the lower rooms underneath the staircase. A white light went on in the room behind the drapes. An occasional shadow was seen moving back and forth in the room. Arif came out several minutes later. He tossed a couple of bags across the driver's side and did a quick u-turn back out of the Motel 8. Van Cleef called in the plate to the traffic division, and the officer confirmed the registration of the vehicle belonged to Arif Nizamani, a resident of Highland Park, Michigan. Van Cleef tailed him to the I-405 Freeway where he traveled south towards LAX airport. He almost lost him as the blue Caravan picked up speed after merging onto the I-10 freeway heading into downtown Los Angeles. He was unsure if Arif was just driving like a maniac to go with the flow of traffic, or was aware that he was being tailed.

Van Cleef requested a helicopter from LAPD's Air Support Division as a backup.

The L.A. skyline and Library Tower were lit up like a

perennial Christmas tree. He reached over into his glove box for the .38 Special Caliber 5 Shot revolver and placed it into his shoulder holster.

The blue Caravan exited the freeway on North Grand Avenue and hit the first red light on the city street.

Van Cleef's Dodge Challenger crept far behind, timing the red light.

The traffic light on North Grand Avenue turned solid green, and Van Cleef's vehicle accelerated behind the blue Caravan, tailing Arif.

He called in his location as he turned onto the Figueroa Corridor and turned his headlights off. The alley was gravel and filled with potholes, and it felt like the moderate chop of turbulence in an airplane as he drove on it.

He reached for several rounds of wrapped ammo on the passenger side and stuffed them into his pocket.

The blue Caravan turned on Vernon Street.

He was headed in the direction of the Vernon Power Plant. Van Cleef had to be careful now, because the large industrial-sized buildings and iconic old water tower illuminated the area and he did not want his vehicle to be seen. He drove slowly over old railway tracks and through train yards. The brief thought occurred to him that the white service truck that Earl, the store manager from Earl & Pearl's shop in Lancaster, mentioned could have belonged to one of the industrial businesses or warehouses in this area. Arif seemed to know his way around and where he was going.

Smoke from the power plant billowed into the black night.

Van Cleef's Dodge Challenger came to a stop about 100 yards from a rusted and abandoned warehouse. He parked near the tracks. Observing. Hanging back. Unseen.

Van Cleef slowly unbuckled his seatbelt and looked around. The last thing he wanted was some gangbanger blowing his head off, or a homeless person blowing his cover. The area was sketchy.

Arif got out of the blue Caravan. He was hooded and hard to see from Van Cleef's perspective.

Van Cleef located a pair of binoculars in his driver's console and raised them to his eyes. He watched Arif look around and then unlock the side door to the warehouse. He saw him squeeze between the side of the van and the building, and he watched him disappear inside the warehouse, leaving the side door of the warehouse open.

Van Cleef was not entering in that way unless he had a death wish.

His instinct and experience clicked in. He thought this could be a possible set-up. He assumed Arif might have led him there and was armed and dangerous.

He sent Overstreet and Tanaka another text on his phone:

"I'm located down by the Vernon Power Plant. The suspect just entered the building. Send the LAPD and some backup now. My car is parked across from the Old Water Tower by the train tracks."

Van Cleef turned off his cell phone. He emerged from the car and loaded his .38. He also grabbed a small pocket flashlight from his backseat. He was not going to let Arif slip through his hands.

As Van Cleef moved closer, he noticed the warehouse Arif entered was up for sale and unoccupied, empty of any commercial tenants. He crept along the far right side of the warehouse next door and noticed sparks flying in the windows. A welding shop. Employees working the midnight shift. Loud machine noise and hammering obscured his footsteps and echoed in the night.

He moved slowly along the side of the warehouse and occasionally glanced up at the excessive amounts of gang graffiti emblazoned on the metal exterior and busted out windows. He kept his focus on the warehouse Arif entered and moved closer to the blue Dodge Caravan. Van Cleef raised his .38 to the tinted windows, slowly stepping to the front of the vehicle. He could see there was a back alley but it didn't seem like there was an alternative entrance to the warehouse.

He was just about to move past the front of the Caravan when loud, vicious, staccato barking came from inside the car, scaring the living shit out of Van Cleef. He caught a quick glimpse through the window of the two frothing pit bulls' massive heads and teeth ready to rip his throat out, their hot breath fogging up the glass in the cool air. He now had an instant answer as to where the two missing killer pits were that devoured Manjaro.

Van Cleef dove in front of the van and crawled like a sniper to the side of the building where he noticed the alley. His heart was in his throat and pumping a mile a minute. The pit bulls were violently rocking the van trying to get at him.

Van Cleef scrambled fast to the back of the warehouse and ducked behind it. His pulse was racing. He figured the rabid dogs were left outside to alert Arif if someone was nearby. It worked. There was enough of a disturbance to signal Arif that his victim was nearby.

Van Cleef knew he had to move fast because he didn't know who or what else was waiting for him inside. The police and detectives were on the way, but he needed to stay on him.

Van Cleef spotted large rolls of steel and scrap metal stacked on racks along the backside of the warehouse. He glanced above the stacks and noticed an entry point. The warehouse was three stories high with open and half-cracked windows above the stacks on the 2nd floor where he could see some fluorescent lights were still on.

He looked back over his shoulder. He could hear the dogs still barking at him.

He made his move and scaled the stacks of steel. He crouched down under the windows and looked down from the stack. He was a good eight or 9 feet above the ground and 2 feet from the windows. He kept down and waited. Motionless. Perfectly still. He just waited for the damn dogs to stop barking. No one was coming for him.

No doors opened. No one came out the back.

Then the lights on the 2nd floor went dark.

Van Cleef poked his head up from the rack of steel and reached for his pocket flashlight. He braced himself by the window ledge and scanned the flashlight's small beam of light across the warehouse. He shined the light inside below the window to see the length of the drop. There was nothing to break his fall below, just garbage.

He thought for a moment and then decided this was his only option. The van with the vicious pits was blocking the only way in. He carefully cracked the window open, clicked off the flashlight and secured it in his pocket, and grabbed the edges to hang from the ledge.

He passed through the dark window and hung from the inside, controlling his breathing. He told himself he was alone now and to remain calm. He thought of Claudia and how much he loved her and hoped he would make it out alive.

Now let go...

Fall...

You've done this before.

He hit the cement floor and rolled. The smell of rotten garbage, sour old wine, and piss hit his nostrils.

The place was gutted. Shut down. Probably closed since the recession. He sat with his back to the wall a moment and just listened. He thought he heard papers rustling and an old voice grumbling.

Van Cleef removed his .38 revolver and stood up, his small flashlight in his left hand.

He clicked it on.

The pit bulls outside seemed to settle back down and stopped barking. It was quiet again. Maybe it stopped before he landed inside. He was concentrating on his environment. He heard a small scamper across the warehouse, maybe a rat rustling papers. Sure enough, his flashlight beam caught a king-sized black rat running along the wall away from the door.

Van Cleef exhaled and stopped dead in his tracks. He thought he heard a strange sound.

Was another dog inside the warehouse with him? Did the rat sense the dog? Was it running away from him?

He froze. If another dog was inside, it would sense and smell him.

He clicked on the flashlight in the direction of a metal door that looked like a stairwell. He noticed a clump of clothing and old blankets near the door. He looked up at the ceiling and figured Arif was waiting to ambush him on one of the upper levels.

Van Cleef kept his back to the wall and crept along to the other side. His shoes crunched broken bottles and glass as he moved through the warehouse closer to the stairwell door.

He waited.

The movement was coming from above.

A strange sound emanated from the stairwell.

He was closer now to the clump of clothing and blankets.

He stopped and listened. Clicked on the flashlight.

The blankets moved.

Van Cleef raised his .38.

The light beam caught a crusty old homeless person shielding his eyes, grumbling.

He exhaled and lowered the flashlight, the beam of light hitting the ground. He continued to move forward toward the stairwell door.

The squelching sound of a car locking or unlocking made Van Cleef freeze in his tracks once again. He clicked off his flashlight and stood motionless in the darkness for a moment and told the grumbling, cussing homeless person to be quiet.

The subsequent sound he heard was an electric van door sliding open.

He could hear the heavy weight of the two pit bulls hit the cement floor of the warehouse as they shot out from the open door of the van. The sound of their claws echoed in the large warehouse and was headed in his direction.

He heard footsteps coming toward him from the stairwell.

If it was Arif, he was approaching him fast. He was light on his feet. Van Cleef heard metal clanging and reverberating down the stairs as if from a firearm hitting a railing in the dark.

The growling and stampeding were only several yards away. That's when the beam of the flashlight caught the rabid pits charging directly in front of Van Cleef.

He grabbed a large steel pipe that was laying on the floor and batted the first pit bull in the mouth. He could feel the dog's jaws clamp down on the steel.

Van Cleef lost his grip on the pipe and was thrown aside as the pit thrashed the steel bar side to side as if it were a wooden stick to fetch.

He went for his gun as he felt immense pressure clamp down on his left leg that felt like he was caught in a bear trap. His gun went off and he heard a deep guttural yelp. He buckled in agony and felt the warm rush of blood pass over his calf.

The ferocious pit bull still wouldn't let go and had his leg in his mouth and was thrashing it back and forth like a shark. Van Cleef let out a blood-curdling scream. He felt immense pressure on his bone.

He dropped his .38 and flashlight in the darkness.

He kicked and punched the pit in the skull as hard as he could.

Where did he drop the gun?

He desperately fished for his weapon, sweeping his hand back and forth, pulling away from the beast.

The homeless person then retrieved Van Cleef's flashlight from the ground and shined it on the attacking pit bull. He then started beating the pit with a large piece of wood which was a mistake, because the pit bull that was attacking Van Cleef violently turned on the homeless person and was now joined by the other vicious pit bull.

Van Cleef sliced his hand on a broken piece of fluorescent lighting, but found his .38. He squeezed off several rounds into the pit bulls who were mauling the homeless person who tried to help him.

He could also hear a police chopper drawing near outside over the loud screaming from the dog attack.

He needed to stop the bleeding. He was feeling dizzy, nauseous now. Ready to pass out. He reached down in the darkness to feel his leg, hoping it was still attached.

He could feel the flesh hanging off his leg.

He squeezed his eyes shut and ripped off his dress shirt to create a tourniquet. He wrapped the tourniquet above his thigh, just below his groin. His breathing labored now. Ready to faint.

A large searchlight briefly illuminated Arif's thin frame.

Van Cleef could feel himself fading fast. His thoughts were incoherent. He could hear louder sounds of police choppers outside the windows now. He could also see intermittent search lights pass through the windows above his head.

Van Cleef tried to prop himself up and yell over the deafening chopper blades not to shoot, but it was too late.

Three precise shots fired in unison hit Arif and killed him.

Van Cleef got out the words, "No, don't shoot..." before he blacked out.

Police and sheriffs burst into the warehouse immediately following the shots and flooded the darkness with light.

Van Cleef woke up on the roof of the warehouse as he was being strapped into a gurney and airlifted to the medical center. He felt the lift of the gurney and closed his eyes.

48

VAN CLEEF WOKE UP IN the L.A. Downtown Medical Center located on 1711 Temple Street. A young ER doctor entered the room and introduced himself. He said, "Detective Leo Van Cleef, my name is Dr. Bernard. How do you feel?"

"If my leg is still attached, like a million bucks," he said. Actually Van Cleef's head felt heavy when he lifted it and his leg was throbbing. That was a good sign. It meant it was still there. He peeked under the sheets for confirmation. He could also feel and move his toes on his left leg.

Claudia woke up instantly when the doctor entered the room. She had dozed off in the chair next to Van Cleef's bed with a film script resting in her lap which was now on the floor.

Dr Bernard studied Van Cleef's patient chart. "You got lucky tonight," Dr. Bernard said, smiling. "A thick steel pipe and heroic homeless person saved your leg and life this evening. It could have gone the other way and had been a whole lot worse."

Van Cleef was disoriented and did not recall anything

about a pipe. He barely remembered the homeless man.

"I'd like to thank that homeless person—"

"He didn't make it like you, I'm sorry to say," Dr. Bernard continued and said, "We cleaned, debrided, and stitched the wound— it was pretty bad... down to the bone."

Van Cleef recalled the homeless person who tried to save him. He was saddened and then repeated, "Debrided?"

"Sorry, removed any damaged tissue."

"How much?"

"You'll live."

"How long will it take before I can walk on it?"

"I'd like to keep you here a couple of days just to keep an eye out for infection. We always have to worry about Rabies since we don't know where these dogs came from."

Van Cleef thought he had a good idea of where they came from. He was also still troubled about the homeless person.

"You're going to have some heavy bruising, and we stitched you up pretty good," Dr. Bernard said. "But I think you'll have a fast recovery in my estimation and experience. I'll give you something for the pain and we'll keep you on antibiotics for a couple of weeks to be on the safe side. I'd like for you to use a cane to keep the pressure off the leg for several weeks as you get back on your feet."

"A cane?"

"You still have your leg, Detective Van Cleef."

Dr. Bernard left the room.

Claudia squeezed Van Cleef's hand tight at his bedside and began sobbing, She said, "Leo, thank God you're still alive."

He lifted his heavy head from the pillow and peeked under the bed sheet examining both of his legs and tried to lighten the situation. He said, "You think Animal Planet will want to buy my story?"

She picked up the script that fell on the floor and swatted him with it. They both laughed. Van Cleef fell back asleep.

49

VAN CLEEF AND OVERSTREET entered the Law Offices of Gordon Goldstone. His receptionist attempted to shut the door on them, but Van Cleef inserted his cane as a doorstop.

Overstreet barged in and ignored the receptionist, and Van Cleef hobbled in behind him.

They startled Goldstone who was sitting behind his desk on speaker phone in an intense meeting with a client. Goldstone muted the call and told them to get out of his office, fixating on Van Cleef's cane.

Van Cleef said they would wait. The client on the other end of the phone kept talking.

"You'll be waiting a long time," Goldstone said.

Goldstone unmuted the call and attempted to answer the client's question and keep his composure with the detectives sitting in front of him. He muted the call again and said, "This is a private call and private property. I will call security… and have you both removed." He unmuted the call again and answered another one of the client's questions while splitting his concentration.

The detectives waited patiently, and both listened to talk of "continuances," "Master Calendar," "Judge Fogel being dismissed," and "orders," "motions," and "interrogatories."

Gordon Goldstone had lost his composure by the time he hung up with his client. "This intrusion is most un—" Goldstone said.

Van Cleef cut him off and said, "Your client was eaten alive a couple of nights ago."

Overstreet chimed in and said, "Fed to the dogs."

"I have many clients."

"Well, you have one less today," Van Cleef said. "In fact, that's three less counting Dr. Plotkin and his wife."

"Detective Van Cleef, I told you in no uncertain terms that Anthony Manjaro was an ex-client."

Van Cleef interjected again and said, "An ex-client you still kept in touch with. I'd be real careful, Gordon, how you answer my questions."

Goldstone began violently stuffing files and court documents into his briefcase.

Van Cleef continued, "You withheld information and obstructed our investigation, and you knew all along that Manjaro was involved in this dogfighting ring."

Goldstone had that stupid smirk on his face again, like a simpering idiot and said, "Lieutenant, I will pretend you did not say that… and you are right, I will be careful and not even dignify a response to such an ignorant and ill-informed question."

"So, you deny having any communication with Anthony 'Tony' Manjaro prior to his death?" Van Cleef asked.

"Detective, don't ask rhetorical questions. I suppose you have my phone records to know that I placed a call recently to Tony Manjaro. Is that what straw you are grabbing at?"

"No straws, Gordon," Van Cleef said.

"So, I did indeed place a call to my 'ex-client' to encourage him to cooperate with you after your last visit. There was no discussion of any sort of dogfighting, admission of guilt, confession – and there certainly was no obstruction of justice, EVER…! in my thirty-some years of working with the LAPD."

"Did you know Sheila Evans met and was involved with Manjaro in rehab?" Van Cleef asked.

"That was none of my business," Goldstone said.

"Was it your client's business? Her husband, Jordan?"

"If Sheila was carrying on with someone, that was her husband's business, not mine."

Van Cleef played another angle and said, "Yeah, I guess the Plotkins were all about secrets, and his wife probably did not know that her husband was carrying on with his office manager and got her pregnant."

Goldstone did not seem surprised nor did he care. He continued to pack his files up for trial and was getting angrier by the minute. "What went on outside of their marriage was no business of mine," Goldstone said.

"We both know Dr. Plotkin had financial trouble and was in over his head," Overstreet said. "Everything he owned was leased or overdue. You handled quite a few of his malpractice lawsuits, so you know—"

"Lawsuits and settlements are par for the course with plastic surgeons and the medical field industry. What other straws do you have to grasp? I'm going to be late for court," Goldstone said, glancing at his watch and the detectives impatiently.

Van Cleef and Overstreet let some silence gather between them. Goldstone's eyes darted back and forth between the two of them. He said, "Go ahead and subpoena my cell phone records, detectives. I am guilty of making a call to my ex, and now dead, client. It proves nothing, and this whole show of nonsense was a waste of our time."

Overstreet stood up and said, "No need to subpoena, Gordon. Manjaro left his cell phone in the dead gangbangers back seat of the Chevy Chevelle the night he was murdered and the gangbangers were murdered. Your eleven-minute call was logged on his cell phone."

Van Cleef interjected, "Eleven minutes on the phone? That sounds like a meaningful conversation— You were talking sports, right?"

"It's a conversation you were not privy to," Goldstone said. "And unless you tapped our call, which I'm sure you didn't, I guess you will have to deduce that our "sports conversation" was all on the up and up. Good day, gentlemen."

Goldstone was fuming, his face twisted and red. He did not say another word.

The receptionist cracked a fake smile, told the detectives to "have a nice day" on the way out, and then held the door open for them to make sure they left.

50

"**YOU EVER SEE A FLICK** called *White Dog?*"

"No, never heard of it," Overstreet said, walking, watching the working girls go by.

"You should check it out sometime or read the original book by Romain Gary," Van Cleef said. They had walked over to and entered the nearby Starbucks in Century City on the corner of Avenue of the Stars and Constellation. Overstreet held the door open for Van Cleef after watching his partner get frustrated using a cane. Van Cleef smiled and continued his story as he entered the crowded coffee shop.

"Where was I?" Van Cleef said, remembering where he left off. "So, the white dog in the film had been raised by a racist, and he was trained to kill black people, but this dog's new owner played by Kristy McNichol—"

"Never heard of her," Overstreet said, looking over his shoulder at a curvaceous, model-type poured into her dress waiting for the Barista to pour her Latte.

"She was one of those actresses that retired early and fell off the map ages ago," Van Cleef said. "She was famous for after school specials and TV back in the '70s, '80s, and into the '90s— Anyway, she finds this dog—"

"Where did she find him?" Overstreet asked.

"In the road. She hit him with her car up on Mullholland."

"She ran the dog over with her car because it was going to attack her like Cujo or something?"

"No, no, nothing like that. It was an accident. The dog was in the middle of the road."

"Does the dog die?"

"No. You wouldn't have much of a movie if the White Dog dies at the beginning of the movie. Early on in the movie the girl and the white dog bond and form an attachment to each other. The dog is lost. Anyway, she takes it in, gives it a home, but starts noticing violent quirks in the dog's personality. Over-protective. Guard dog behavior."

"So, what does she do, hook the dog up with a rich Hollywood therapist?"

"It's not a comedy, Dennis. Which is sort of the whole point of the movie. The White Dog appears to make progress. He is reconditioned to a point by his trainer played by Paul Winfield."

"Who's Paul Winfield?"

"He's done a bunch of films... look him up on IMDB sometime. At any rate, he tries to reverse and recondition the dog's racist and violent behavior."

"He succeed?" Overstreet asked, already checking Paul Winfield out on IMDB on his iPhone.

"Not really. See that's the problem. Sorta like the problem we face. He seems to solve the racist issue, but he can't change the unpredictable violent streak in the dog."

"You know I'm never gonna see this flick, right?"

"I figured, that's why I'm taking the time to tell you about it."

"I thought you were taking the time to tell me about it

because the story had a purpose."

"Yes, the point or purpose of the movie is relevant to our canine homicide. The whole corrupt world of dogfighting and the stigma that pit bulls have is because of the negative conditioning these criminals have on the dog. They program them to kill. They weren't born bad, just like people aren't."

"So, let me guess, the dog gets rehabilitated in this flick at the end?"

"Well, since you're never going to bother to see it and I haven't sold you on seeing it, you won't mind me spoiling the ending then."

"So, I figured it out. They rehabilitate the dog and roll credits," Overstreet said. "God, I hate Hollywood. That's why I stick to sports."

"The dog dies in the end."

"Really?"

"Really."

"Shit, now I want to see it and you spoiled the ending for me."

Van Cleef finished his coffee and asked, "So what do you have for me regarding the dead man's shoes?'

"That Tad 'Cooler' dude?"

"How many dead man's shoes are you working on?"

"Okay," Overstreet said. He pulled out his gaudy silver notebook. Van Cleef snatched it out of his hands.

"Hey man, what are you doing?" Overstreet asked.

"Where the hell did you get this thing, anyway? It's been bugging the shit out of me."

"The 99 Cents Store on Pico. Why?"

"It looks like it."

Van Cleef read the quote out loud off the cover… "*Life is what happens when you're busy making other plans?*" Really Dennis? You can't be interviewing suspects or witnesses with that thing. Get rid of it and buy something that looks more professional. It's an embarrassment."

Van Cleef handed the gaudy silver notebook back to Overstreet and said again, "So tell me what you have."

"Okay, so I spent the afternoon with the store manager and employees of the REI, and the manager pulled all the receipts and POS data, and it looks like our man, Tad, used a stolen credit card to purchase those shoes."

"Did you verify that it was indeed stolen?"

Overstreet gave him a look, like you're kidding me, right?

He dramatically opened his notebook from his vest pocket and announced, "The stolen credit card belongs to Ken Jones, a resident of San Pedro. The employee that sold him the shoes failed to ask for ID, 'cause our boy Tad charmed and chatted him up or BS'ed him about climbing Mount Eiger like Eastwood in order to distract him."

Van Cleef looked stunned for a moment and was dead silent.

"That name mean something to you?"

"Used to."

Van Cleef asked Overstreet to give him the address and email him his report from his REI retailer interviews. He threw his coffee in the trash and told Overstreet he would meet him back at the office. Van Cleef left in a hurry and confused the hell out of Overstreet, who watched the curvaceous woman leave Starbucks with her Latte.

51

WHEN CAROL JONES ANSWERED her door, Detective Van Cleef was the last person she expected to see, but she was thrilled to see him. She grabbed her remote control off the coffee table and turned off the TV. Van Cleef guessed he caught her watching *Ellen* reruns or one of those popular daytime TV programs. He waited in the doorway of her Culver City condo.

"Well, come on in, Leo," Carol said, inviting him in. "Don't just stand in the doorway. Make yourself at home. Can I get you something to drink?"

Van Cleef entered the condo admiring the Southwest interior design and Georgia O'Keeffe paintings.

"Water is fine, if you don't mind," he said.

Van Cleef took a seat on the couch. He thought Carol looked great for her age. Mid-sixties. Hip-looking. Still wearing her hair like it was the 1970s, and she had the hip lingo to go with it. She was an attractive light-skinned Black woman that bore a slight resemblance to actress Diahann Carroll. She came back into the room from her kitchen with two Arrowhead bottles of water. She passed one to Van Cleef and then sat uncomfortably close to him.

"Man, I haven't seen you since Ed's funer—"

"Yeah, tough time," Van Cleef said.

"You were one of the few people he really liked," Carol said. "Man, I mean, he really thought you were cool in his book, and Ed didn't think too many people were cool, except maybe Clint, his idol."

"Man's got to know his limitations," Van Cleef said, imitating Eastwood from *Magnum Force.*

Carol slapped her leg and belted out an infectious laugh as if it were the funniest thing she ever heard, pointing and laughing saying, "That's it…" "That was Ed…"

They both stopped laughing after a few minutes and the mood turned serious. "So, what brings you to my neck of the woods," she asked, raising an eyebrow.

"Ken Jones," Van Cleef said, matter-of-fact.

The friendly visit turned sour and Carol's whole demeanor changed when Van Cleef asked about her eldest and estranged son, Ken Jones.

"I haven't spoken to him in years, Leo," she said, getting up from the couch and swiping her remote off the coffee table. She switched the TV back on and adjusted the volume lower.

"What about your ex, Ed Boots?"

"'What about Ed, what?"

"When was the last time you saw Ed before he died?"

"Are you asking if I had seen him or was seeing him?" Carol asked in a defensive tone.

"When was the last time you had *seen* him out at his place in Pismo, prior to his death?"

Carol had to stop and think about that. She said, "Off and on, I suppose."

Van Cleef knew she was telling the truth, stood up, and looked out the window. There were some people on her street walking dogs. People were always walking dogs all hours of the day in any given neighborhood in L.A.

"I don't recall Ken at Ed's funeral," Van Cleef said. His back to Carol, still gazing out the window.

"You recall right. Ken wasn't close with Ed at all, in fact they had a— well, I'll be polite and just call it a strained relationship."

"Not seeing eye-to-eye," Van Cleef said, turning toward her.

"Well, first off... for the record, Ken and I don't see eye-to-eye about a lot of things, let's just say," Carol said. "Oh, he'll resurface every now and then... come around asking for money in the past. But I can tell you, the few times I did talk to Ken and ask if he spoke with his stepdad, he'd grumble about it and make some lame excuse about the dog won't let him anywhere near him. He was afraid of dogs. Scared to death of them, but I think he was really more afraid of Ed. Anyway, I tried to get him to set aside his differences."

"Did you, or would Ken, for any reason, have a key to Ed Boots's place?"

"Yes, I did. Ken..? *No way, Jose.* Ed changed his locks the last time Ken set foot in his house and ranted about it."

"And how long ago was that?"

"Too long ago to remember. Over a year ago."

Carol joined Van Cleef at the window, grabbed him by the arm, and changed the subject. She said, "The neighborhood is changing. It started changing years ago. Ed wanted me to move out to Pismo... said it was safer out there. Well, I liked it here in Culver City where I grew up — Wanted to be near the entertainment industry."

"Tell me about it," Van Cleef said with a smile. "My wife is like you, she loves Los Angeles, and I lost the coin toss on that one. But I have to agree, the whole city is changing and not for the better."

"Is any place safe anymore? Now that Ed left me his

house in Pismo, I'm not sure what I'm going to do— can't imagine living there when he died there like that. I'm checking with a Realtor. I'll probably end up just selling it. It's kind of just sitting there for now, just as it was, until I can sort everything out in my life and decide what I wanna do."

Van Cleef asked, "Did Ed ever mention anything to you about the actress, Sheila Evans, that was recently murdered out in Malbu?"

"That happened after Ed died," Carol said, confused.

"I mean before he died."

"Oh," she said, thinking. "I don't recall anything— I thought that was an accident? A pit bull attack?"

"Yes, what you may not know is her death is being investigated as a canine homicide by our department."

"But the news said—"

Van Cleef said, smiling, "Carol, you really need to stop relying on the news for what's really going on in the world."

Carol's mind was racing as she tried to digest what Van Cleef was saying. She said, "Look Leo, I get that Ed and you were close— one of the few friends he had. I get that Ken and Ed were at odds, even enemies. I get that Ken hated Ed's dog… I get that Ed's dog turned on him, and you hear about that happening all the time. But what I don't get is that you seem to be implying that Ken is somehow mixed up in Ed's death."

Carol left the room momentarily to pour some coffee. She didn't offer Van Cleef a cup.

"Was Ken cut out of Ed's will, or was that ever a heated issue?"

She poked her head around the corner of the kitchen and said, "Are you serious?"

"I have to ask."

"Ken wasn't expecting a payout, if that's what you're asking. He's got nothing… I think Ed was trusting me to divvy some out to him once he proved he could 'man up' and act responsibly. That's strictly my opinion and nothing was ever said."

"Fair enough. Any drug or gambling issues you were aware of?"

"None that I was aware of."

"Did Ed ever mention anything to you about Ken's activities or associations?"

"Oh, he had an uncanny knack for falling in with the wrong crowd."

"Bad company."

"Bad?" she looked at Van Cleef incredulously. "Ed was right about him, I'll give him that. He kept telling me, he'd say 'Carol, that kid is gonna do some hard time if he doesn't clean his act up… mark my words…' that's what he used to say. Just like that… 'mark my words.' So what's he done now?"

Van Cleef didn't want to say too much, since this was a heated subject. He simply said, "I just want to ask him some questions."

Carol surprised Van Cleef when she let out a huge belly laugh and said, "Leo, you gotta do better than that. I was married to Ed and he wasn't my first love interest with law enforcement, so you wanna shoot straight or play charades here, man? What's Ken wanted for?"

Van Cleef withheld a smirk thinking this was a rarity; usually he's the one asking the hard questions, not the other way around. She was putting him on the hook.

"Murder," Van Cleef said, point-blank.

"Murder?"

"Possibly several murders."

Carol started massaging her throat and pacing the floor. She switched off the TV and tossed the remote on the coffee table and left the room again.

"I can't buy that, Leo," she said, shouting from the

kitchen, banging and clanging dishes and pots, obviously upset. "My son is no angel or apple of my eye, but he ain't no murderer."

"I'm sorry I'm upsetting you Carol," Van Cleef said, as if that would ease the tension. "I just need to speak with him."

"Like I said, I haven't spoken to him," she said reentering the room again, staring at the street outside. She turned back around and snapped back at Van Cleef. "Just need to speak with him about murder? Who do think he killed?"

"Ed, possibly."

She collapsed on the couch, shaking her head. "Ed was killed by his dog. I'm afraid I don't understand... how—" she said.

"I don't expect what I'm saying or suggesting might make any sense, but it is possible that Ed's murder was staged."

"But his dog—"

"I know."

"But the detectives and animal control said—"

"I know that too. I know what they said and how it appeared—"

Van Cleef stood up from the couch. He never touched his water.

"But his dog—" Carol said, having a hard time completing sentences.

"Is there anything else you can tell me about their relationship?" Van Cleef asked.

"The dog?"

"No, Ken and Ed."

Carol started fanning herself with a magazine from the coffee table. She took a deep breath and said, "Look Leo, they hated each other. Ed kicked him out again when he moved back in with me. Tossed all of his belongings on the front lawn. Police showed up. Ken pretty much disappeared after that. Wouldn't take my calls. Wouldn't listen. Couldn't reach him. I guess in some ways, thinking about it— I just don't like to think about it—"

The room fell silent for what seemed like ten minutes. Van Cleef could almost read her mind as she relived her relationship with Boots within the span of that moment.

Van Cleef waited and then said, "Go on, say it."

"Ken was the main reason Ed and I didn't work out, I just don't like to blame him… I guess… I mean we were on and off so many times— still seen each other off and on, you know."

"Did Ed and Ken ever get into any physical altercations?"

"Oh, Ken wanted to and kept egging him on, but Ed, God bless him, he never took the bait… he just, he just…"

"Kicked him out."

"Yes, when he turned 17, he dropped out of school and couldn't hold down a job, so Ed was hard on him in that way… I want you to know Detective Van Cleef, Ed never laid a finger on me. He was actually a pretty decent man when all was said and done."

"Yep," Van Cleef said, repeating her words with a long sigh. "When all was said and done."

He hugged her goodbye and promised not to be such a stranger. But a stranger he would remain in her life. He always felt an uncomfortable attraction and flirtation from Carol and avoided getting too close to her out of respect for Ed and his own wife, Claudia.

Van Cleef recalled a past conversation with Ed about his "deadbeat" stepson. He once made the wisecrack to Van Cleef that he inherited a monster.

Was Ed Boots's joke once again a reality?

318 • MICHAEL P. NAUGHTON

52

THE SAN BERNARDINO DEPUTY coroner investigator confirmed the John Doe in the morgue as Hamid Nazamini, Arif's brother that had delivered Kali to Tony 'Killer' Manjaro and ultimately wound up with a bullet in his back. The San Bernardino police found Hamid's body on the side of the road in a bad area. San Bernardino typically picks up the Most Dangerous City award every year, or at least makes the Top 10, and has a history of being one of the highest crime counties in California. It was a good place to dump a body and Manjaro obviously knew it. They found canine hair fibers (Kali's) on Hamid's clothing. The victim also had a distinctive blue Detroit Lions jersey with a bullet hole now in the back. He was stripped of his wallet and any identification, and his white van was found with all the parts stripped off. The Coroner Division would normally cremate an unidentified person or victim after weeks where there was no way to reach a relative, but this homicide victim struck the Sheriff as someone that was passing through the county, met with the killer, and then was murdered. The Sheriff made sure that his department took the extra time to document their findings. He ran the VIN number on the vehicle and it was traced back to Michigan. In this case, his instincts were right when Homicide Special detectives contacted him, making the connection with his brother Arif.

Van Cleef now had the breeders, the murder weapon (Kali), and the victims – all dead. There was just one person left at the root of it that he needed to pin it on.

Van Cleef placed a call to Lisa Comstock and asked for her cooperation in identifying Anthony Manjaro. He needed to get some additional statements from her regarding the Plotkins and her employment. She agreed to meet the next morning downtown at the PAB and apologized for sounding so choked-up on the phone. She was just so happy that Van Cleef and the LAPD solved these murders.

53

DETECTIVES LEO VAN CLEEF, Dennis Overstreet, and Van Cleef's recovering flu-free partner, Jose Espinoza, sat in the interview room for several moments just staring at the stoic Ken Jones who was tricked into thinking he was answering some general questions about his stolen credit card. Jones was a big guy in stature, built like a linebacker. He had a tough face and demeanor to match, a rugged outdoorsman type. His features were strong and complexion was light-skinned black, and it was hard to tell whether he was mixed with some Latino or other ethnicity. Van Cleef could still remember a younger Ken Jones from photographs he had seen over the years. Jones did not remember Van Cleef, or that he was a friend of Ed Boots.

The three detectives crowding Ken Jones out in a small interview room did not intimidate him in the slightest. His hands didn't tremble or twitch at all on top of the table. Jones played it cool. He believed he could still win, even against the brightest in Homicide Special.

"The name Tad Keller mean anything to you?" Van Cleef asked.

"Not a thing," Jones said, leaning back.

"He used your credit card to purchase some rock climbing shoes."

"Again, no connection," Jones said. "I lost my wallet and reported it stolen and some creep used it. Don't know him."

"You wear a size 15 shoe?"

"Last time I checked," Jones said. "Look, I came down here to talk to you about my stolen card, not my shoes."

"So, this creep steals your credit card and buys an extra pair of shoes in your size with your 'stolen card'?

Jones hesitated for a moment trying to read the situation. He was a quick study and realized this wasn't about his stolen credit card. He shrugged his shoulders and said, "I've purchased two different shoe sizes before. Maybe the creep was unsure which fit better, or maybe he was going to sell the other pair or some shit like that."

Van Cleef was slightly amused that Jones was thinking on his feet.

"Sure," Van Cleef said. "But why not purchase the next size up, like say a 10— 15 would be a little too big, especially for a guy that typically wears a size 9. And especially using them for such a thrill-seeking sport as rock climbing where a loose-fitting shoe could cost you your life... am I right, fellas?" Van Cleef asked his fellow detectives for a second and third opinion.

Overstreet said with a slight grin, "Dead right. Nah man, I think I read the sign, 'Falling rocks ahead."

"Is he supposed to be your comedian sidekick like in those stupid Hollywood cop flicks?" Jones said, unamused at Overstreet's quip.

"I'm more than his sidekick comedian, Ken, I'm your recent Facebook friend. Set up a fake profile and everything to see what you've been up to, and I got a chance to see wall photos you posted of your rockclimbing skills, bragging rights, and recent trips climbing mountains like Sandstone Peak, Mt. Baldy, Mount San Gorgonio. Ain't no mountain high enough for you, brother."

"Don't call me brother," Jones warned Overstreet. "I don't have any brothers, especially one as ugly as you."

Van Cleef pulled up a chair and sat directly across from Ken Jones and said, "Okay, so let's cut the small talk and the get-to-know each other BS. We know more about you than you're going to tell us, and you obviously have greater talents and skills than climbing mountains. So, let me tell you what slippery slope you're on without a lifeline as far as we have it figured out. It wasn't a big thing… sometimes the most minuscule and minute detail can connect the dots, Ken, in these murder investigations." Van Cleef stood up from the table and decided to pace and talk, cane in hand, to deliver the goods. He continued and said, "You knew Tad Keller, don't deny it. This interview will go a lot faster for all of us who want to call it a night. Detective Overstreet has a statement from the REI clerk that sold Tad the two pairs of shoes the day that you falsely reported your wallet stolen."

Overstreet placed the statement in front of Ken Jones, which Ken did not even care to glance at.

Van Cleef continued, "The clerk remembered Tad because they had a friendly conversation about Hollywood flicks— which I'm a big fan of— but of all things, Tad mentioned *The Eiger Sanction* with Clint Eastwood, which the clerk thought was completely random and odd."

"What, is Clint Eastwood gonna question me next or something. What's your point?" Jones said, looking over his shoulder at the door as if Clint were going to show up in "Dirty Harry" character.

"Well, Tad was not a film buff like me," Van Cleef said. "Not like me at all, I can assure you. And being a younger, local stoner dude with no real interest in anything except trouble and recreational rock climbing and surfing, I found it odd that he picked that particular film, *The Eiger Sanction*, out of thin air to reference. I mean, maybe Stallone's

Cliffhanger or *Touching the Void*, or *Into Thin Air*. Now, those would fit Tad's profile and references better."

"Maybe he saw it recently on cable or something. Did you ever stop to think of that?" Jones asked in a sarcastic tone.

"No, I checked all that out, Ken," Van Cleef said. "Not on any local cable channel, Netflix, or anywhere else. In fact, Tad doesn't have cable, or a Netflix subscription, or anything like that. Hell, I don't even know if he watched his 13 inch TV that was caked with dust in his apartment, which made it even more puzzling for me. He used his TV about as much as his surf board... Hardly ever."

"Avalanche ahead," Overstreet said, almost cuing Van Cleef to drop the hammer on Ken Jones, which Van Cleef was about to do. Van Cleef sat back down.

"Your stepfather was a big fan of *The Eiger Sanction*, Ken—" Van Cleef said.

"I don't have a stepfather" Jones interrupted defensively.

"Correction," Van Cleef said. "You did have a stepfather, but you murdered him canine-homicide style, and you plotted the Sheila Evans murder out in Malibu with your buddies to throw me off the scent of your trail. But it was ultimately the dead man's shoes— not just stolen credit card... that would come out later— that Tad Keller had with him in the backseat of his car the day of the murder and later locked in his trunk when he committed suicide in Blood Alley. He failed his polygraph and was way over his head, so he knew he was looking at some hard time as an accomplice to murder. The Celebrity Swat at Mel Gibson's house was a nice diversion too." Van Cleef paused a moment. He leaned his back against the wall and said, "That day I chased you from your stepfather's house I thought I was chasing Manjaro, but it was you. You got away and lost me in the crowd on Pismo Beach, but later that day, I returned to your stepfather's house in search of what you were rummaging for and got the footwear impressions in the sand. Also a confirmed size 15— I knew the person I was chasing had a key to Ed Boots's place aside from having big feet. This was no mid-day robbery. But when I went back to his house after I lost you that day… there it was, big as life: *The Eiger Sanction,* movie poster… the only poster Ed Boots had in his house. He was a big Eastwood fan, that's how I knew him." Van Cleef glanced at the floor, recollecting. "We used to talk about Eastwood films all the time— he was the one that started calling me Lee Van Cleef and doing the whistle thing— Anyway, we talked about *The Eiger Sanction* because I gave him a copy of my book, which he never returned, and I distinctly remember our conversation about the late Hollywood actor Jack Cassidy who perished in a bizarre fire. He was one of the detectives at the time who came out to investigate. Jack Cassidy, a gifted actor, co-starred with Eastwood in *The Eiger Sanction.*

"Jesus, your story is boring the shit out of me and I'd like to speak to my attorney now," Jones said, rolling his eyes and letting out a long sigh.

Van Cleef nodded to Overstreet. Overstreet stepped out of the interview room for a moment.

"Your attorney will be here soon enough," Espinoza said.

"I guess I got off on a tangent," Van Cleef said. "My point is, is that your stepfather was a smart man, damn good detective, and completely misjudged."

"My stepfather was an asshole," Jones shouted out.

"No Ken, I knew him."

"Not like I knew him."

"But, you never really knew him. You weren't around much after the divorce."

"He was never around for me."

"Funny thing, though… You started coming around right before he was murdered. When he found out that you were running with the wrong crowd. He was concerned about you. He had his eye on Manjaro, who ended up turning his estranged stepson onto bloodsports and the sick world of dogfighting. That's when your stepfather got involved in your life again."

"Gee, I thought it was because he loved me."

"Oh, he tried to love you and get you on the straight and narrow, according to your mother."

"He used to beat her."

"You see him do it?"

"I heard about it."

"You heard wrong."

"Come off it," Jones said. "Your own department retired him because he was a bigoted, racist pig."

"Is that why he married your mother... a black woman?"

"He was fucked up, what else can I say?"

"No, you're fucked up, that's what I say," Van Cleef said, sitting down, lowering his voice. "This was about protecting your own ass and covering up a murder. Your stepfather would have turned you over to the Feds if he knew you were involved in dogfighting. He was a dog lover. He followed you the night he was murdered. Followed you out to Lancaster, which was how he wound up dead later and you staged the dog attack back at his residence in Pismo. Now, you mind telling me how your stepfather's blood and DNA wound up in the Lancaster pit?"

Overstreet returned with an item in a cardboard box. He handed it to Van Cleef, who placed it on the table between the two of them.

"Isn't it a little late to be exchanging gifts, Detective?" Jones said, staring at the box with disinterest.

"This gift is something special, it keeps on giving. Go ahead and open it," Van Cleef said.

Jones played along and flipped open the cardboard box. He was as apathetic about the contents as a kid who gets socks on Christmas. He then closed the lid, pushed the box away from him and sat back, smiling.

"That's what you went back for that day," Van Cleef said, opening the box and pulling out the E-Collar shock collar. He threw it on the table and said, "And the sad part is that your stepfather was the one that must have given you the idea, because he used it once on Figaro to keep him quiet and train him. You see, he was friends with the guys down at our LAPD K9 unit who suggested it. There was even a photo your stepfather had on his refrigerator that showed Figaro wearing this strange kind of collar."

Van Cleef pulled a photocopy of the photo from Boots's residence and threw it on the table. Ken looked at it and said, "He loved that stupid dog more than me."

"That poor dog was shot because of what you did."

Van Cleef changed the subject and asked, "You ever do any line work out in Lancaster?"

"Line work?" Jones asked, mocking Van Cleef.

"Yeah, you know, your day gig, 'Line Man for the County' kinda thing," Van Cleef said. "Installing VOIP, HDTV, IP, internet, etcetera, etcetera, etcetera."

"Don't ask me stupid questions," Jones said. "So, you checked my background and work history, big-fucking-deal. I go where I'm needed."

"Says here you're an Independent Contractor for Starlit Satellite LLC," Van Cleef said, reading a report Overstreet passed to him.

"Yeah, been working with them a while," Jones said. "They subcontract with the big cable companies. I pay my taxes."

"I'm not interested in your taxes, Ken," Van Cleef said. "You did an install on a farmhouse a couple of weeks ago out in Lancaster."

"So, what, I do a lot of installs. I go where I'm needed."

"No one lives there and no one was moving in, and Starlit Satellite didn't send you there, so my question to you is:

what were you doing at an abandoned place that was later used for dogfighting?"

Ken Jones pushed back from the table. He didn't answer.

Overstreet said to Van Cleef, "Sounds to me like some Pay-per-view sneaky shit was goin' on there if you ask me — No UFC, more like UFD, as in dog."

"No one asked you," Jones said to Overstreet.

"We've got a witness that positively identified you, Ken," Van Cleef said. "A drugstore owner that sold you some unusual items for a cable installer."

"Like what?"

"Oh, items like Gorilla Glue, Vaseline, hydrogen peroxide, sponges, gauze, dish gloves—"

Ken Jones laughed and said, "What can I say, I get cut up in my line of work. Hazards of the job."

"Speaking of cut up," Van Cleef said. "You also managed to cut yourself on a neighbor's fence in Pismo the day I chased you down to the beach. We got a match on your blood type which was AB negative, a rare type, and that blood also matches the DNA on your reported stolen credit card."

"Then there's the pit," Overstreet said.

Van Cleef said, "Then there's the pit as my partner said. Your blood and traces of your stepfather's blood were both found in the dogfighting pit that was uncovered out in Lancaster several weeks ago. This is a strange coincidence, wouldn't you say?"

Ken Jones wouldn't say. He kept his mouth shut and knew the detectives had him by the throat.

"Your stepfather was tailing you, Ken, and when you found out, you and Manjaro fed him to the dogs, and then you tried to cover it up by staging a domestic dog attack at his home. But that wasn't enough, you had to take it a step further and murder a celebrity out in Malibu because your boy Manjaro blabbed to Sheila in rehab about a certain cop's stepson that was fond of bloodsports. You stepped in shit with Tad Keller, your inept lookout. See, he couldn't lie his way out of a paper bag and a dead man's shoes wound up walking all over you. Manjaro is dead, Ken," Van Cleef said expressionless. "Tad Keller is dead. We have you on two murder charges. So, we know how you were involved and with who, the only question is why?"

He laughed, sat back, and said, "Yeah, good luck with that."

"Manjaro and Keller we can't tie you to," Van Cleef said. "I'm referring to your stepfather, Ed Boots, and Sheila Evans... now those I can pin on you."

"You think you knew my stepdad?"

"I knew him better than you, I'd bet."

"You only knew the mask he wore around here."

"Mask?"

"Ed Boots was a racist, a bigot and all-around asshole. He talked bad about everyone, you included. Don't play psychologist or try to psychoanalyze me— some fucking father figure, you don't have a clue what he was about," Ken said with no remorse as if he had done the world a favor.

"What about Sheila Evans, you think she deserved what she got?"

"What she 'got' was in the way," Ken snapped back. "Her dumb luck. Her career was in the shitter anyway, and she's probably more famous now."

No remorse. Van Cleef let some time pass between them and then broke the silence.

"I have to admit," Van Cleef said, steepling his hands, fingertip to fingertip. "The vanishing dog, celebrity swat diversion... it was quite an elaborate machination. You even had Manjaro switch out your stepfather's dog with a vicious pit bull used for dogfighting, so the dog that actually killed him was not his own dog, but one of Manjaro's killer canines. That's how your stepfather's blood ended up back in the pit when the killer dog tracked it in. Then you switched them again before the police got there. Unfortunately, it was Figaro, your stepfather's dog that was shot."

"I don't give a shit. Your department fired my stepdad because he was a racist cop and there's no place for pigs like that anymore in this world."

"He tried his best to love you, Ken."

"Best? He was never around and when he was, he was just a real asshole. An all-American asshole. Real patriot piece of shit. Thought he was John Wayne or something silly like that. I hated him. You should have heard the way he talked about blacks, Hispanics, Asians… anyone that wasn't like him. He was abusive to my mom, but she was too afraid to get him fired. Afraid he would kill her."

"So, you thought you would rid the world of one less racist by taking care of him and his dog, was that your plan?"

"Fuck him and his dog," Jones said, pounding his fist on the table. "He showed more respect to that fucking dog than he did to his own family or other people. Especially people of color. Ed Boots was everything that is wrong with the world today."

"And that was for you to decide?"

"No one at this department, including you, knew him," Ken said, grinning with a defiant smile. "Yeah, I see where you're going with all this. I'm done talking with you. My attorney will have a field day with you assholes."

"No, I don't think so, Ken. We got two murders that you're responsible for. You thought that you could send us down some blind alley when you hired Manjaro to kill Sheila Evans. Make it look like some random wild dog killed a celebrity out in Malibu. But it was the vanishing act that did you in, and there were too many loose ends. That day I chased you down in Pismo beach, I couldn't figure out what the hell you were after, then it finally clicked… the shock collar. That was how the Pakistani Bully Kutta that killed Sheila Evans stopped killing on command. Manjaro later killed the dog and disposed of it up in Malibu Canyon. Two hikers later found the dead dog with Manjaro's bullet in it. Your partner in crime, Manjaro, spent some time trying to clean up his act at a celebrity rehab facility called "The Cove," which is where he met and got involved with Sheila Evans, the wife of Dr. Plotkin, and then Dr. Plotkin was later murdered and it was made to look like a suicide. Some body count, if you're doing the math."

Van Cleef set down another photo on the table in front of Ken Jones showing evidence of shoeprints.

"The day we had our foot race, I thought I was chasing Manjaro, but as it turned out, I was only chasing his shoes. You wore these in a calculated attempt to frame Manjaro, since you knew our investigation was focused on him and since he also wore a size 15 shoe. Those were Manjaro's boxing shoes and it was impossible for him to be wearing them on that day, since we tracked his whereabouts and he was a long distance from Pismo. Those footprints in that photo are from your feet wearing Manjaro's boxing shoes. So, as it turns out, we were chasing two giant hounds, the PBK and you, my friend. We're up to five dead bodies for the record. Manjaro blabbed in rehab to Sheila about a racist cop's stepson that he knew was into dogfighting. That would be you. Your hatred for your stepfather has got nothing to do with bigotry or racism, it's got everything to do with your money. Your stepfather found out his estranged stepson was involved in dogfighting. He was about to blow the whistle on you, but that's when your dogfighting partner in crime, Manjaro, found a killer pit bull to silence your stepfather. The sad part is… his innocent pit bull took the fall and was shot for your stepfather's death. This was all a very clever and convenient accident, but once again things weren't adding up. Namely, his real dog Figaro was harmless, and that's what caused his current neighbor lady, that you didn't count on, to come forward and vouch for the dog. You switched 'em out and when Ed Boots came home that evening, he found a vicious dog-fighting dog that spent time in the ring inside his home and *that* dog was the dog that killed him. That was the first canine homicide and the homicide you didn't count on me solving. Only we knew it wasn't a pit bull..." He quoted to himself the Sherlock Holmes line again, "*They were the footprints of a gigantic hound.*"

Ken Jones flashed him an odd look and defensively asked Van Cleef what he just said.

Van Cleef did not answer. There was no need to.

Van Cleef felt Ken was like talking to a wall. He sat there unremorseful. Eyes squinting, lips compressed, imagining the murder of his stepfather. His forehead was furrowed and he did not look at Van Cleef again.

Van Cleef had to control his anger and maintain his cool.

The interview was over and his case was solved.

Overstreet poked his head in the room and said, "Lisa Comstock is waiting in the next room."

"She sign her rights waiver?" Van Cleef asked.

Overstreet flashed the signed waiver and a big smile.

They left Ken Jones alone in the room and watched Lisa Comstock on video in the adjacent interview room. Lisa was looking through a folder that Overstreet intentionally left on the table in front of her.

"You made it look like you forget the folder, nice job," Van Cleef said, patting him on the back.

54

LISA COMSTOCK SAT BORED out of her mind when Van Cleef entered the room, still adjusting to walking with a cane and an armload of files.

"Boy am I glad to see you, Detective," Lisa said, shifting in her seat. "What happened to your leg?"

"Slip and fall, I'll live," Van Cleef said, smiling and pulling out a chair across from her.

"I fell in heels once at a red carpet event," Lisa said. "It was so embarrassing... I mean, I didn't have to use a cane or anything like that... not that your cane is embarrassing—"

"No offense taken," Van Cleef said. "I have some additional questions for you."

"I hope your questions are more sensible," Lisa said. "That other detective was asking a lot of strange and stupid questions."

"Strange in what way?" Van Cleef asked.

"You know how you guys do," Lisa said. "Anyway, I came down here to identify and cooperate with the police, so here I am... I'd like to wrap this thing up, whatever the thing is, and get going. I've got another job interview in the morning."

Van Cleef placed a photo of Ken Jones and a photo of Tony Manjaro in front of her on the table.

"Sure, we'll get you on your way soon enough," Van Cleef said. "Do you recognize these two individuals, Lisa?"

She studied the photographs and pushed Manjaro's photo back across the table to him. "Yeah, him. This guy's been in our office before."

"That's Anthony Tony "Killer" Manjaro, the once-famous heavyweight boxer."

"Yeah, Dr. Plotkin probably fixed his nose or something," Lisa said with a half-smile on her face.

"No, I think it was more than that," Van Cleef said.

Lisa stared back at Van Cleef with a dumbstruck look on her face and said, "Now you're starting to sound like that other creepy detective."

"My creepy partner and I know quite a bit about you, Lisa. We both know that you haven't been on the level with us from the get-go, so why don't you tell me more about the guy in the other photo. Take a closer look."

Van Cleef pushed the Ken Jones photo across the table.

Lisa denied knowing Ken Jones and pushed the photo back across the table. Van Cleef stood up, rubbed his neck, and said, "I'd like to go home like you, Lisa, but only one of us is going home tonight, so I'll tell you how you know Ken Jones and then I can get home to bed. Sound like a plan?"

Lisa didn't say another word. She gazed down in her lap and listened.

"Ken Jones is your boyfriend, Lisa. Aka, Justin Young. Our detectives had one helluva time tracking him down since he is so adventurous... You were right, he is like Rambo and is quite a moving target. We caught up with him. He's next door and going to do some hard time for the murder of his stepfather and Sheila Evans. You, on the other hand, are going to be joining him for the death of your employer and lover, Dr. Jordan Plotkin. The way we see it, is that Dr. Plotkin was not going to divorce his wife over your pregnancy and asked you to abort it, and when push came to shove… well, you pulled the trigger."

Lisa glanced up at Van Cleef momentarily and said, "That's not true."

"I wish it weren't, Lisa," Van Cleef said. "But you were the only person the night Dr. Plotkin was shot that got in and out of the parking garage with no suspicion. You belonged there, and no one questioned you. From there you walked back to the Beverly Hills hotel and made it look like you were having a celebration when I showed up. It was all a nice facade, but I didn't buy it and it didn't work. I knew you shot Jordan Plotkin and made it look like it was a suicide. You scratched the side of his Jag and our crime analyst was able to match your scrubs and hair fibers to the crime scene. The scratch was caused by the zipper on your fanny pack that you were wearing. We also found several Virginia Slims Ultra Light 120's cigarette butts nearby. You dumped the booties in the alley and detectives recovered them in a dumpster on Canon Drive with traces of Dr. Plotkin's blood. That was a big mistake, Lisa."

Van Cleef produced a photo of the disposable booties, or shoe covers, like surgeons wear before a procedure.

Lisa did not say another word. There was a long silence between her and Van Cleef. He observed her holding back the tears, but was unsure who they were for. She finally broke the silence, looked up from the photos, and said, "I didn't kill Sheila Plotkin, Detective Van Cleef. I really tried to like her… I did— I didn't know they were going to kill her… kill her that way– I didn't think—"

Van Cleef reached for his cane, got up, and hobbled out of the room with his head down, leaving that incomplete sentence hang in the air. That was the trouble with suspects and murders, and how they typically wound up here talking to him. They just didn't think, or thought they were smart enough to think they could get away with it.

Van Cleef left the interview room and thought about his German shepherd, Bogart, again and he smiled this time.

He could use a good night's sleep, and maybe taste that reward of Islay Malt and finally spend some time with Claudia. Espinoza tapped him on the back.

"You okay, boss?" Espinoza asked.

"Yeah, don't worry about me," Van Cleef said. "It's great to have you back. Overstreet still here?"

"He's in with Lieutenant Carruthers. You'd better get the story straight, or that guy will steal your thunder and tell him he single-handedly solved this case."

Van Cleef patted him on the back as they walked back to their Homicide Special office. He said, "Do I look worried?"

55

VAN CLEEF WAS PACKING UP when Lieutenant, Mike Carruthers, informed him he had a special guest that wanted to speak with him before he left for the evening.

"Mike, I can't meet anyone now, I'm wrapping up —" Van Cleef said, thinking about his wife. "If I miss one more event with my wife, she'll feed me to the dogs."

Mike Carruthers stood with his arms folded, blocking the doorway.

"It'll just take a minute, I promise," Carruthers said.

"What?" Van Cleef asked, pausing, and then curiously asked, "Who is it? Can it wait?"

Lieutenant Carruthers shook his head. He informed him that his special guest was waiting for him in the interview room. First room on the right. He left Van Cleef's office whistling the theme from *The Good, the Bad and the Ugly* as he walked down the hall.

Van Cleef sighed and packed up his briefcase and paperwork. He locked his desk drawer and made his way down the hallway to the interview room. He struggled to open the door and fumbled with his cane.

His jaw and his cane dropped when he entered the room. It was no stranger or suspect staring back up at him.

It was Serpico and his black Lab.

The guy he called Serpico. His Number 1 suspect in his neighborhood who was not picking up his dog's business.

Serpico, sitting there at the table with a Grande Starbucks coffee. Just sitting there with his obedient black dog staring back at him in his grimy poncho and unkempt beard.

"Scuz me, do I know you?" Van Cleef asked.

"No," Serpico said. "But I'm sure you recognize me and my friend here. You didn't have the cane, of course."

"Never mind the cane... I recognize you, all right, but who the hell are you and why are you here?" Van Cleef said, careful not to take a seat, unsure what this guy was up to. He watched his hands closely. There was no threat of a firearm, besides he would've never gotten it past security.

"You've been watching me for some time," Serpico said, expressionless.

"Yes, I have. I'm glad you noticed. I notice you don't read signs that clearly state to pick up after your dog. You're the joker leaving your dog's shit on my lawn. Look, if you're here to file some kind of complaint against me or some-thing, take a hike—"

Serpico cracked a smile, reached under his grimy poncho and passed Van Cleef his business card. Van Cleef studied the card. He looked over his shoulder expecting his squad room to be busting in any minute and let him know he had been "punked" or pranked. This could not be happening.

"You've got to be kidding me," Van Cleef said, his face flush with embarrassment.

Van Cleef examined the business card again.

"Let me see your badge," he said, still in disbelief.

Serpico grinned once again, reached under his poncho and tossed his police badge across the table. Van Cleef picked it up and authenticated the badge with his discerning eye.

"You gotta be shitting me," Van Cleef said. "Did Carruthers or Tanaka put you up to this? It was Ron Tanaka, wasn't it? Why are you dressed like Serpico?"

"I don't know who that is," Serpico said, lying, knowing exactly who that was, having studied and seen the Pacino film no less than twenty times in his life.

"What are you hanging around my house for?" Van Cleef asked.

Serpico kept cool, leaned back in his chair, and explained, "You know those scavengers that have been digging in your recycle bins over the past months?"

"What about them?"

"I've been working undercover. Assigned to your neighborhood to keep an eye on them."

Van Cleef imagined the homeless people digging in his trash, however, the long hours on the canine homicides was at the forefront of his mind, and he still couldn't process that this imitation version of Serpico was a real detective by the name of Dale McCafferty.

"What's the deal with the scavengers in my recycle bin?" Van Cleef asked. He pulled out a chair across from him, intrigued.

"They aren't after anyone's recyclables," Serpico said.

Van Cleef propped his left leg on one of the chairs and leaned into their conversation. He asked, "Oh, and what are they after?"

"Identity theft. Big ring of them. They work the neighborhood in a crew. They act like they're fishing around for plastic bottles, but they manage to fish out some other personal items along the way. We just busted four of them in West L.A. and wanted to let you know that one of them was trying to piece together one of your credit cards."

"Impossible, I shred everything that I toss out."

"Sure," Serpico said. "But they like puzzles and they

manage to find scraps and put the pieces back together."

"No kidding?"

"No kidding, anyway you won't be seeing any of them in your neighborhood anytime soon, and you won't be seeing me anymore either." Serpico got up and gently pushed the chair under the table. He grabbed his coffee off the interview table and said, "By the way, I wasn't the one leaving dog crap on your lawn."

Van Cleef looked embarrassed and asked, "Well then who the hell was it?"

"The blonde chick with the Chihuahua."

Van Cleef was dumbstruck. He clammed up.

"I'm a witness if you need one," Serpico said.

Van Cleef was blown away. How was he going to confess to his wife, Claudia, that he was wrong about who was leaving the dog shit on his lawn. She would never let him live it down.

Van Cleef asked, "Was it your idea to dress up in the Serpico getup?

"Yeah, I'm a big fan of Pacino and the movie. Liked his undercover style."

Van Cleef thought about the classic film and Al Pacino's great acting.

"By the way," Serpico said on his way out. "Great job on the dogfighting bust. I hope we get the chance to work together sometime."

The door closed between them. Van Cleef stood slack-jawed. He glanced up at the ceiling to see if there was a video camera, and still felt he was being pranked.

No cameras.

He studied the undercover cop, Dale McCafferty's, card once again before placing it in his wallet and shaking his head. He settled with himself that it was better to be wrong about a pile of dung than arresting the wrong suspect. He turned the light off and left for the night.

56

VAN CLEEF AND HIS WIFE TOOK Bacall, their Doberman, up to The Los Angeles Pet Memorial Park in Calabasas. She had been feeling neglected since they had both been working overtime. The loss of Bogart, their German shepherd, was still troubling Bacall too. The sun was beginning to rise over the nearby horse stable in the background, and the early morning hour allowed them some breathing space before the noise and congestion of the city stressed them out.

They pulled off of Parkway Calabasas and onto Old Scandia Ln, then drove through the gates of the serene pet cemetery and circled around to the back.

They located Bogart's plot and headstone in the "Garden of Sunshine" section tucked away on a hill.

Van Cleef got out of their car and listened for a moment to the birds and watched the squirrels chase each other.

"God, I sure do miss him," Claudia said, as they walked.

"Me too," Van Cleef said. "He's been on my mind this entire case."

"She hasn't been right either since—" Claudia said, watching Bacall, their Doberman, walk slowly alongside them.

"I know, I noticed."

"I guess another one will choose us when we're ready."

"That's what they say."

Bacall stopped dead in her tracks and her body stiffened. She started pulling hard on the leash.

A large, beefy white dog was charging head-on in the Van Cleef's direction.

"It's off the leash!" Claudia said, letting out a shriek.

Van Cleef stood in front of his family and brandished his cane. He patted his shoulder holster ready to draw his .38 Special. He was ready for another canine attack.

It was a pit bull. Unleashed. No owner anywhere around.

Here it comes. Here we go again.

Van Cleef had not recovered from the warehouse dog attack and found himself experiencing PTSD. This could not be happening. Not this soon.

His Doberman stood rigid ready to attack, quivering, barking, and showing her teeth in attack mode.

Van Cleef could see someone chasing behind the unleashed pit, desperately trying to catch him.

They heard the name, "Murphy," called out frantically.

The owner was now more visible. Yelling. Commanding, "Murphy get back here."

The pit bull did not listen.

It was then that something strange and unexpected happened that only other dogs can sometimes sense.

The white pit bull was friendly and playful and just wanted to interact with Bacall. He was also a little skittish, but knew that Bacall was harmless. They sniffed each other out and decided not to fight.

The young dog owner eventually caught up to his dog and said to his dog, "Murphy, I told you to stay."

He then said to Van Cleef, catching his breath, "Hey, sorry, man... He's friendly. He won't bite."

Claudia and Van Cleef exchanged glances and exhaled. This guy had no clue as to what they had been through. Van Cleef said, "I'm sure he is... I can see that he is..." He watched the two dogs playing with each other, sniffing each other out and said, "You should really keep him on a leash... not only for your safety but his safety as well... It's the law and I happen to be a detective, and this is not a dog park."

The clueless owner did not believe him. It was L.A. after- all and bullshit ran deep. He took offense and leashed Murphy the pit bull by the collar and pulled him away from Bacall in the opposite direction from where they came from. He said over his shoulder, "Hey man, I said I was sorry."

The pit bull occasionally looked over his shoulder, scowling at Van Cleef.

Claudia watched them walk away. She said, "Do you think he'll listen?"

"About the leash?"

"Yes."

"No."

"Do you think he believed you were a real detective?"

"I doubt it," Van Cleef said. "I also know he isn't here visiting or paying respect to his beloved pet. He's a tourist."

"How could you tell?"

"The camera around his neck."

Bacall came out of her shell now and seemed reinvigorated by the encounter. Van Cleef observed this change in her and his thoughts drifted back to Bogart and their long walks together.

Van Cleef walked over to a nearby headstone and noted the dates. He did the same for several other surrounding graves and did some quick mental calculations.

"I think Bogie here is one of the oldest dogs," Van Cleef said. "Having lived 18 years. 3 months. 3 days."

"It still never seems like enough time, does it?" Claudia said.

"Never."

Claudia placed the beautiful silk flower arrangement she made for Bogart in the cup provided by the cemetery, while Van Cleef waited near the bottom of the hill with his cane.

Bacall sat still, respectfully, for several moments by Claudia's side. She somehow knew this was where her friend was laid to rest. They walked back down the hill and joined Van Cleef.

"You know. I've seen more pit bull attacks trend on Google news this past month," Claudia said as they walked back to their car. She was hoping to get her husband to open up about the canine homicide case, which Van Cleef never discussed.

He did not say a word about the case, but he looked around the peaceful cemetery one last time and got into the car. He tossed his cane in back with Bacall.

They drove slowly through the winding road at the cemetery. They heard the peaceful sounds of wind chimes and birds. Van Cleef watched the dumb tourist still taking photos of gravesites and headstones, his pit bull still running off the leash nearby. He was right about him. No leash.

"I need a vacation from this place," he said.

Bacall looked out the back window of their car as they pulled out of the cemetery gates.

DEDICATED TO THE MEMORY OF ZUKO
(1998-2016)